ANDRULA

Titles available in this series

Yannis
Anna
Giovanni
Joseph
Christabelle
Saffron
Manolis
Cathy
Nicola
Vasi
Alecos
John
Tassos
Ronnie
Maria
Sofia
Babbis
Stelios
Kyriakos
Monika
Emmanuel
Theo
Phaedra
Evgeniy
Ludmila
Pietro
Eirini
Andrula

Greek Translations

Anna

published by Livanis 2011

ANDRULA

Beryl Darby

ISBN 978-1-9997176-8-1

Printed and bound in the UK by
Print2Demand
1 Newlands Road, Westoning,
Bedfordshire MK45 5LD

First published in the UK in 2023 by

JACH Publishing
92 Upper North Street, Brighton, East Sussex, England BN1 3FJ

website: www.beryldarbybooks.com

Author's Note

Andrula and the house at Schisma
are entirely figments of my imagination.

I would like to thank all my loyal readers who have supported me so well over the years. Unfortunately it took me a considerable amount of time to write this last book as my eye sight was deteriorating and I was not able to work at my usual speed at the computer.

I was then told by my typesetter/publisher that he was retiring and I had to work hard to complete the manuscript by a certain date. This meant I was unable to write as many pages as I had planned originally.

I hope I will be able to write another book during 2023 when my sight has finally been corrected and I will be able to see better. I feel very lost without my fictional family.

July 2016
Week Four

Marianne received an irate telephone call from Helena.

'Mother has just called me to say she is in London and travelling to Crete tomorrow. I thought she was with Andrew in New York. What has made her decide to visit you again? She's supposed to be looking for somewhere to live here so we can buy the house from her. If she delays and messes around for much longer we'll refuse her offer. She needs to make a decision and stick with it. We've already had to turn down one buyer for our house. It's all most inconvenient for us. Had I known she was planning to return to Elounda I would have travelled up to New York and stopped her,' said Helena petulantly.

'That is exactly why Mamma didn't tell you her plans. She has not seen any property that she feels would be suitable for her and is considering converting the house so she lives on the ground floor. The upstairs rooms could be made into a self contained apartment and she could rent it out for some additional income.'

'She doesn't want unknown people living above her. They could make her life a nightmare'

'I agree. I hope to talk her out of that idea whilst she's here. The house is too large for her to manage now. It would be far more sensible for her to move somewhere smaller but I think she is loath to leave somewhere that has so many memories for her.'

'Sentimental rubbish,' snapped Helena.

7

'To you maybe, but not to her. She needs to find somewhere where she feels she will be happy and in the location that she knows. She can keep in touch with the real estate companies whilst she's here and can ask for details to be emailed to her.'

'She wouldn't know where to start,' declared Helena scathingly.

'Either Giovanni or I could help and it isn't difficult. I'm sure she would very soon know how to look up real estate and access the details of any properties that they were advertising.'

'You just encourage her to be irresponsible.'

'She is not being irresponsible,' Marianne sighed. 'She had no idea how difficult it would be to find somewhere else where she would be happy to live. You have a nice enough house at present so you do not have to move.'

'She said we could buy the house. How much longer are we supposed to hang around?'

'You just have to be patient with her. When the time does come I'm sure you'll have no problem finding a buyer and property prices could have increased dramatically. You could regret having sold earlier.'

'I still think she is acting irresponsibly. She is too old to be making such a long journey alone.'

'Andrew has made all the arrangements for her and we will meet her at the airport when she arrives. Angelo and Francesca left yesterday so I only have to get the room ready for her.'

'How is she going to spend her time? There's nothing to do in Elounda. At least in New York she had plenty of places to visit.'

'She found New York somewhat lonely as Andreas had to spend time with his publisher and was only around during the evenings. She always manages to find more than enough to occupy herself when she is here and there are always people around so she doesn't feel lonely. Stop worrying unnecessarily, Helena. You know we'll look after her.'

'If she had allowed us to move in with her as we wanted I would have looked after her.'

'I'm sure you would, but that was not what Mamma wanted. You would have insisted on accompanying her wherever she went and been continually checking that she was alright. She isn't senile and wants to retain her independence.'

'I begin to think that she is senile and needs to be looked after,' remarked Helena dourly.

'If I come to the same conclusion I'll let you know and between us we'll arrange for her to have professional care. If a carer needed to live in permanently the upstairs rooms could easily be made suitable. Maybe Mamma is more organised and forward thinking than we give her credit for. Now, I really must go as I have email bookings that I need to deal with. I'm sure Mamma will phone you when she is here.'

Marianne closed her phone before her sister could object and continue their conversation. She was tempted to switch her mobile off, but she was sure if she did her mother would try to contact her and be concerned when she received no answer.

Giovanni and Marianne were at Heraklion airport to meet Elena when she arrived, looking happy and relaxed. She hugged both of them and allowed Giovanni to take her case.

'I always feel that I have come home when I step off the plane here. I think it is the smell of the herbs. So much more pleasant than the smell of diesel fumes.'

'How was your journey? No problems?' asked Marianne.

'None at all. Andrew had arranged for me to have assistance at the airports to save me having to walk and he booked my luggage through so I didn't have to wait around to collect that. I was a bit concerned that it might be sent somewhere else, but as you can see it is safely here.'

'Had that happened I am sure we could have gone into the village and bought everything that you needed until it finally caught up with you,' Marianne assured her mother. 'Now would you like to stop for some refreshments on the way home? There are plenty of tavernas just outside the town.'

'I could do with a decent sandwich. I looked at the selection of food that was on offer. The prices were extortionate and when I saw it arriving for other people it looked most unappetising. I was glad I had avoided it.'

'When we stop you must phone Helena and let her know you are safely here. She is not at all pleased with you.'

Elena laughed. 'I gathered that when I spoke to her in London before I boarded the plane. I suppose she has phoned you?'

Marianne nodded. 'She thinks you are far too old to travel anywhere unescorted.'

'Well, I would not want Helena with me. She would have wanted to spend time in London going around the shops looking for the latest fashions, not to mention the visit to the hairdresser and beauty parlour. Sitting on the plane alone gave me time to think about Andreas's future plans.'

Marianne raised her eyebrows to Giovanni. 'Let's wait until we are in a taverna and then you can tell us.'

Elena chose a tuna sandwich whilst Marianne and Giovanni treated themselves to a baklava with their coffee.

'I'll have a baklava another day. I'm not sure if it would mix well with tuna. Now, whilst I was on the plane I thought about a suggestion that Andreas had made. Andreas has said that he plans to leave his village house to the girls. I thought about it and decided that whilst I was here I would look for a small house that I could buy so that the girls could inherit one each.'

Marianne looked at her mother dubiously. Was Helena correct saying that her mother was becoming senile? 'That seems like an unwarranted expense.'

'No it makes sense. Andreas has no one to leave his house to and it would be unfair to expect the girls to share it between them. They could have very differing ideas regarding renting or selling. I would look on it as an investment for the girls. When one of them marries they will need a house of their own. One of them will inherit Andreas's house in Pano and the other could have whatever I had decided to buy. That way they would have one each. Of course, once inherited, I would have to ask you to be responsible for the property until they became of age. I want to spend some time here looking around in Plaka and Elounda and see if there is anywhere suitable available.'

Marianne was taken aback by her mother's reasoning. 'That's a lovely thought, Mamma. Are you serious?'

'Property prices are bound to rise in this area and they could always sell and buy somewhere else.'

'You wouldn't plan to live there yourself?'

Elena shook her head. 'I would modernise it if necessary and let it out during the season. I certainly wouldn't plan to live there. I really enjoyed helping Andreas and then putting on that performance, but without something like that going on I don't know what I'd do with myself during the winter. I made a lot of friends that year and I must make sure I call on all of them. I can always take a taxi wherever I wish to visit. I love being with all of you, but I don't want to be a burden.'

'You're certainly not a burden,' Marianne assured her. 'You have rather taken my breath away. You only have to ask and one of us can drive you to Elounda, Plaka or anywhere else you wish to visit.'

'It can't always be convenient for you to do that at a time when I want to go or collect me when I want to return home. You are all too busy to spend your time running around after me.'

'You don't have to worry about that. There are enough of us to act as a chauffeur for you.'

'I feel it's taking advantage of you expecting one of you to drive me around. I always enjoy taking my time wandering around and watching the visitors and locals going about their business whilst I have a coffee. There is no reason why I should not use the bus or a taxi to travel about.'

'I'll certainly take you up to see Evi and Maria whilst you're here. I'm sure they would like to see you, but one of us would certainly have to collect you. There's no way you would be able to arrange a taxi to go up to them.'

Elena smiled. 'Well, now you know my plans I suppose I should call Helena and assure her that I am safely here. Please do not tell her my plans or she will be over here on the next plane and insisting that I return home.'

Marianne could hear Helena scolding her mother loudly, whilst Elena lifted the phone away from her ear. 'I'm sure we will have to move the car shortly,' she interrupted her daughter. 'We've only stopped for a snack and my battery is getting low. I'll speak to you again tomorrow.' Before Helena could continue Elena closed the call and switched her mobile phone off.

'Duty done.' she said triumphantly. 'How I can have twin daughters who are so different I do not know.'

Marianne smiled. It had been a puzzle to her why she and Helena should have such different outlooks on life and what was important to them. Whilst her mother had been talking a thought had occurred to her and she would discuss it with Giovanni when they arrived home. It could be a perfect solution, but she would not want to mention it to her mother until she knew it was possible.

Having greeted everyone Elena agreed to go to her room and unpack. 'I may even have a little nap before our evening meal. If I don't appear please come and get me.'

Once having assured her mother that she only had to ask for anything that she wanted Marianne turned to Giovanni.

'Whilst Mamma was talking about buying a cottage in one of the villages I thought about Vasilis and Cathy's apartment. It would probably be more expensive than a cottage in one of the villages, but it would not need any modernisation or decoration. Even if she wanted to stay there for a week or two she would not have any hills to climb and be close to the shops. She could even catch the bus along to Plaka or into Aghios Nikolaos.'

'Do you think she is serious? I wouldn't want to let Vasilis think it was definite and then your mother change her mind.'

'You don't have to say anything about my mother at this stage. You just have to ask Vasilis what he plans to do with the apartment when he and Cathy move into the new house. He may already have plans for it or have promised to rent it to a friend.'

Giovanni nodded. Vasilis was a business man and he would not leave a valuable apartment sitting empty. 'I'll call him and see what he has to say.'

'Why don't you visit him? It's more personal that way. You can tell him my mother is here and we will be inviting him and Cathy over for a meal next week.'

'Now I know where John gets his devious mind from. I'll drive in tomorrow on my way to Aghios Nikolaos and if he's at home we can have a chat.'

Cathy opened the door to Giovanni and a pleased smile crossed her face. 'Lovely to see you. We rarely have visitors during the season, everyone is too busy. Come in. Would you like coffee or a glass of wine?'

'Coffee would be best, thanks. I'm driving and you do have a policeman living next door. It would be rather embarrassing if he arrested me.'

'I'm sure you wouldn't be arrested after one glass of wine. Have a seat and I'll bring the coffee through.'

'Would you like some help?' asked Giovanni as Cathy walked into her kitchen with the aid of her stick.

'I'm organised, thank you. I have a small trolley here and I place anything I want on it and push it through to the lounge. It certainly saves making numerous trips with one thing at a time.'

'Is Vasilis around?'

'He's down at the house as far as I know. Did you want him for anything in particular? I'll call him and tell him that you're here and would like to speak to him.'

'If he's busy I can easily drive down there and see him.'

'I doubt he'll be there much longer, he just likes to go down each day and check that all is being completed as he wants.'

Giovanni heard Cathy speaking briefly to Vasilis. 'He said he should be back here within fifteen minutes,' said Cathy as she wheeled the small trolley through from the kitchen laden with plates, mugs, glasses, a sugar bowl, jug of coffee and another of water along with a large sponge cake and serviettes.

'Draw up one of the little tables and help yourself to coffee whilst I cut the sponge. Take two or three serviettes as you don't want sugar all down your shirt.' Cathy cut a large slice of sponge that she placed on a plate and handed to Giovanni.

'Aren't you joining me?' he asked.

'I'm saving my slice for this afternoon. I still keep to my English tradition of a cup of tea and a slice of cake or some biscuits at about three thirty.'

'I came to visit you as well as Vasilis. My mother-in-law arrived yesterday and Marianne would like to invite you and Vasilis up for a meal.'

'I would really enjoy that. I cook most evenings for us as I find if we go to a taverna at the moment there are so many tourists there being noisy that it is not pleasant. We invite Panayiotis in occasionally or order a take away. Our socialising is very limited during the season even though Vasilis no longer has to worry about the hotel in Heraklion.'

'That must be a relief.'

'It certainly is. Now the new management is installed Vasilis only has to visit rarely. Dimitra sends a copy of the accounts through to him, but only once has he found a problem.'

Giovanni raised his eyebrows. Dimitra had been instrumental in conspiring with Alecos to falsify bank drafts to try to stop Vasilis from buying the Imperia. Alecos had then planned to buy the property himself and sell it on to Vasilis at an inflated price.

'Dimitra had entered the same invoice twice by mistake. It

meant the bank statement did not agree with the hotel accounts. Dimitra was mortified and continually apologised and promised to be more careful in the future.'

'Easy mistake to make when you have a number of invoices from the same supplier.'

Cathy nodded. 'I certainly would not want to be responsible for the accounts. Another slice of sponge?'

'No, thank you.' Giovanni wiped his lips free of sugar. 'That was delicious, but I find it very easy to put weight on now. When that happens Marianne puts me on a diet for a week and I have to watch everyone else enjoying the food that she has forbidden me.'

Cathy laughed. 'I'll have to threaten Vasilis with that. At least it might stop him from always having a second helping.'

'That is a compliment to you as a good cook.'

Vasilis entered and helped himself to coffee and a large slice of sponge cake. 'So what brings you here Giovanni?'

'I came to invite you and Cathy to come for a meal one evening as Marianne's mother has arrived.'

'Thank you. We will be delighted, but you hardly needed me here to agree to having a meal.'

'Well, as I was passing by I said I would ask you your plans for this apartment when you move into your new house.'

'We won't be moving for a while yet. I want everything completed before we move in. There's still some tiling needed at the back. We don't want to be surrounded by all the dust and noise that will create. When that has been finished we will have some of Uncle Yannis's pots delivered. There's no point in moving these from here unless Cathy has a particular favourite as the plants will probably have died off by then.'

'You'll need to speak to John about those. Uncle Yannis is still sitting outside every day and people come and look, occasionally he sells one. John keeps records of his stock up to date and has photos that he can bring and show you. The dimensions are there and you can then decide what size you want.'

'At present I'm thinking of about four or maybe six of the very large ones and then some smaller ones to place in between.'

Giovanni nodded. Marianne would be very pleased to see more pots leaving the house. 'I'll ask John to call on you. Delivery of the big ones will have to be arranged as they need at least two people to handle them. Will they be able to use the lift to take them up and then through the house to the rear garden?'

'That will be no problem. Once everything is finished to my satisfaction the house will have to be thoroughly cleaned. Cathy can't be expected to do that.'

'Won't you employ a cleaner?'

'For the big clean through I will certainly ask a couple of professional cleaners, the ones that do that regularly for when the villas have a change of guests. I thought I might ask Blerim to come once a week to clean the windows and keep the exterior clear of rubbish. Cathy insists that she can manage to do everything inside herself. If she finds it is too much for her I can always find someone to come in and help. They'll be only too pleased to have some work during the winter months.'

'Do you have a moving date in mind?' persisted Giovanni.

'When I am satisfied that the house is ready. I am expecting all to be completed within another month. Then at the end of the season Saffron will close down the gift shop and they will have time to organise whatever they want to bring down here from the big house and begin the alterations they propose.'

Giovanni nodded. Vasilis's plans were practical. 'So you're not planning to rent the apartment out?'

Vasilis shook his head. 'I've arranged for Vasi and Saffron to live here. It will be far more convenient for them during the season. What's your interest?'

'Elena was talking about Andreas's house and wishing he had bought somewhere in the village.She has indicated that she would like buy a cottage in one of the villages herself but that would probably mean spending a good deal on modernising and decoration. This apartment would have been ideal as all the alterations have been done. It could work out cheaper in the long run, but I understand that it isn't available and she will have to look elsewhere.'

'What does she want a cottage for? Is she planning to move over here to live?'

'She said she would let it out during the season and eventually one of the girls would inherit it. Uncle Andrea has said he plans to leave his property to one of the girls and Grandma Elena has said that if she does the same it will be fair.'

'What about Yiannis?'

'He will inherit the business and the house. He won't be short changed. Depending on his choice of career he can either keep everything running or sell it on. Now we should make a date for you to come over and then I ought to drive to Aghios Nikolaos. I need to go to the cash and carry.'

Cathy looked at Vasilis after Giovanni left. 'Is it really going to be that long before we move?'

'Why? Are you unhappy living here now?'

'Not at all. Shouldn't you speak to Vasi and ask for a definite arrangement? It's possible they will have changed their minds. In that case you could have an immediate sale to Elena.'

Vasilis sighed. 'I'm sure everything is fine, but I also know you will be worrying over it so I'll go down to the hotel and ask him now.'

Cathy smiled. 'I know I worry unnecessarily, but I still cannot get used to the Greek idea that paper contracts are not always issued. So much is done by word of mouth and honour.'

'That was fine in the old days when few people could read or write and you were only dealing with your immediate neighbours. Nowadays you need a piece of paper, although most people keep their word.'

Vasilis sat with his son in the office at the hotel. 'What brings you here, Pappa? Has Cathy thrown you out and you want a room for the night?'

Vasilis smiled. 'Cathy and I may have had the occasional disagreement but never anything serious enough for one of us to leave home. No, I had a visit from Giovanni this morning. Marianne's mother is visiting. She mentioned to Giovanni that she is planning to look for a cottage in one of the villages. Giovanni thought I might be willing to sell the apartment to her. Cathy is a bit worried as we have no written agreement.'

Vasi frowned. 'I thought we had agreed that Saffie and I would move into the apartment and then your original house on the hill would be converted into a self catering establishment.'

Vasilis nodded. 'That arrangement still stands, but Cathy wanted me to check with you. If you had decided to stay up at the big house I would tell Giovanni that his mother in law could buy the apartment.'

'We're planning to move down at the end of the season. I can't expect Saffron to cope with moving whilst the shop is still open and she'll need a few days to pack up the stock. I thought we might be able to bring down some items each day once you had left. Mr Palamakis is meeting with us when we have looked around and decided on the work that may be needed. It will probably only be decorating. We'll just move the furniture that is staying up there into an empty room whilst the boys do the work so the sooner anything we want is out of the way the better.'

Vasilis nodded. 'That sounds practical. I'll tell Cathy that the apartment is definitely not being sold and you plan to begin moving in as soon as we have left. If Elena wanted to stay down in Elounda for a few days whilst she's looking around I could probably let her have a room at the hotel at a cheap rate.'

'I can mention it to Giovanni and I'm sure he would pay you the going price, with the usual discount you give to certain guests.'

'I'm not having Marianne's awful sister here even if Giovanni paid me treble the usual rate,' said Vasi firmly.

Vasilis shook his head. 'As far as I am aware she is not planning to come over here at the moment. If she does you will just have to say you are fully booked up and she will have to stay elsewhere.'

'What more needs to be done at the house?'

'Some tiling at the back and I want to have some of Yannis's large pots that Cathy can plant up. I thought we could have a grassed area with an olive tree in the centre. Mr Palamakis has said he can manage it when his grandsons have completed the work they are doing on Ronnie's house up at Kastelli.'

'When will that be?'

'Goodness knows. Ronnie has only been able to afford to do a certain amount each year since the fire. That's why I didn't want to get Cathy's hopes up by giving her a definite moving in date.'

Having driven to Elounda to leave Skele with Dimitris for the night John decided to call on Vasilis and Cathy as he returned through Elounda.

'I hope this isn't an inconvenient time. Just as I was leaving to take Skele to Dimitris Dad told me that you want some of Uncle Yannis's pots. I haven't got the details with me. I only stopped on the spur of the moment. I can drop the photos and details in to you tomorrow when I take Skele back to Dimitris. You can take your time deciding what you would like and then we can arrange a time for me to come and take your order.'

'Of course it isn't inconvenient. Come on in and have a drink You're welcome to stay and eat with us.'

'Thank you, Cathy, but no. Mum would still insist that I ate the meal she had saved for me. I'll not actually stay very long. I just wanted to tell you about the pots and also to ask a favour.'

Vasilis raised his eyebrows. 'Of me or of Cathy?'

'Well, both of you, really. I had a letter from Pietro and he is arranging to have his father's remains returned to Italy. He will have to come over and sign all the official papers, of course, and I wondered if you would be willing for him to call on you at your new house? He would love to see the floor tiles that his firm supplied.'

'We won't be moving in for a few weeks yet. I want everything completed. I don't want to listen to the sound of building work each day. There is still some attention needed round at the back. Tile cutting is a horrible noise and the dust swirls around like a sand storm. When is Pietro wanting to come over?'

'He hasn't mentioned a date to visit your house so I'm sure one that is convenient for you could be suggested to him.'

'I'm longing to show off the house to everyone. I thought we could hold a party and invite all our friends.' Cathy looked at Vasilis for confirmation of her idea.

Vasilis shook his head. 'I think it would be better to have friends visit in small groups. If people want to look around too many at one time will be difficult to deal with and I don't want you to become too tired. Uncle Yannis and Marisa would be able to use the lift and come with your parents. You and Nicola could come with Saffron, Vasi, Bryony and Marcus. I'm sure your Mum would be willing to look after your children for the evening.'

'What about Ronnie and Kyriakos? They ought to be included, and Panayiotis,' added Cathy. 'We mustn't forget Monika and her mother, and Theo would probably like to come.'

'I'm sure Mr Palamakis would like to see it when it is completely finished. Would you object to asking him and his grandsons and I'm sure Vasi would appreciate Yiorgo and Barbara being invited.'

Vasilis sighed. 'At this rate the whole village will be coming. We'll sit down and make a list and then decide how to divide people up into relevant groups. I'm sure we can arrange for Pietro to join one of them.'

'Remember he only speaks Italian. It would be no good putting him with Ronnie and Kyriakos. They would only be able to nod and smile at each other.'

'Leave it with me,' advised Vasilis. 'Let me know when Pietro plans to come over and I'm sure he can be invited. It may mean that you or your father make a second visit.'

'I'm sure neither of us will object to that and my American grandmother will still be here I expect. I can drop the information about the pots in to you on my way to return Skele tomorrow evening if that's convenient with you. You can let me know when you've had a chance to look at them and made a decision about which ones you want and how many.'

'That would be fine if it fits in with your plans. We have nothing planned for tomorrow.'

'Have you done any more metal detecting?' asked Cathy.

'I've not had much time, but I have found a few bits and pieces on the hill whilst I've been walking Skele. The girls think it's a wonderful game to hide things in the garden or on the beach and see if I can find them. I have to pretend that they are so well hidden that I have difficulty in discovering them.' John rose and drained his glass. 'Thank you for the drink. I'll be off now and leave you in peace. I'll let you know as soon as I hear anything definite from Pietro.'

August 2016
Week One

John helped Uncle Yannis to take a selection of pots down to the display area. 'I believe I will have an order for you.'

Uncle Yannis raised his eyebrows. 'Where from? A museum or a shop?'

'Neither. Vasilis and Cathy want some pots to put in the garden of their new house. I'm going to drop in the photos and details to them as I go to collect Skele.'

'How many?'

'At least four, maybe six, of the large pithoi and some other smaller ones.'

Uncle Yannis pursed his lips. 'No doubt Vasilis will expect a discount again as he's buying a quantity. I gave him a discount of five percent on those he bought previously.'

'I would think ten per cent would be reasonable.'

'Ten per cent! I need to make a profit.'

'You will still make money. They only cost you about half the price you are asking for them now. You're no longer at the shop so you have no overheads. Whatever price you sell them for is better than having them sitting here. You definitely want to get rid of the pithoi. Tourists are hardly likely to buy those and pay to have them shipped home.'

Uncle Yannis gave a deep sigh. 'I suppose so, but it is wicked to put them outside and use them as planters.'

'Once some of their friends have seen them they may want some themselves and you cannot dictate to purchasers how they use them. If they were left empty they would only become full of leaves and weed.'

'Not if they were kept inside.'

'Not everyone has a room large enough to display a pithoi. I'm off to collect Skele now and when Vasilis and Cathy have looked at the photos and decided exactly what they want they are going to contact me.'

'I may have sold them if they take too long making up their minds.'

John shook his head knowing it was most unlikely. 'We'll just have to take a chance on that happening.'

John phoned Nicola from up on the hill where he was walking Skele and using his metal detector at the same time. She sounded puzzled when she answered him.

'What's wrong?'

'Nothing, but I need you to come up here in the car and collect me.'

'Are you hurt?'

'No, I'm fine.'

'Is it Skele?'

'He's fine also.'

'What is the problem then?' asked Nicola. 'If your scooter is out of petrol it isn't that far to walk back.'

'Nothing like that. You'll see when you get here.'

'Have you finally found the crock of gold that you've been looking for?'

'I wish,' John laughed. 'Just come as soon as you can.'

'I'll have to ask Bryony if she can take the girls to summer school. They love going there once a week to meet up with their friends. I hope your Mum will be willing to cope with Yiannis for a while.'

'There are plenty of people around to help. See you soon, Nick.'

It was over half an hour when Nicola finally drew up close to where John and Skele were sitting on the hill.

'That was more difficult than I had expected. Everyone appeared to have something else urgent that they needed to do today. Marcus and Bryony's car is in the garage for an M.O.T. and they were going to use your Mum's car to go to Aghios Nikolaos for Marcus to have his check up for Bell's. They agreed to use our car to take the girls to school on their way to Aghios Nikolaos to save having to move the child safety seats around. Your Dad is on an airport run and Uncle Yannis and Grandma Marisa are having an argument about sitting down at the stall with the pots. Your Mum agreed to have Yiannis provided Grandma Elena is with her to help and I am not gone too long. She says she will want her car later as Marcus and Bryony were taking it to the garage for an oil change when they collected theirs. Why did you want me to come up here?'

'Look.' John pointed to the cardboard box that was behind him. 'I can't carry these back on my bike.'

Nicola looked inside at the six small squirming puppies. 'Oh, John, have they been abandoned?'

'I imagine so. Why else would someone put them up here on the hill in a box? I'm not sure if they should have left their mother yet. Help me get the box into the car and I'll put my detector in the boot. We'll drive back to the house and I can collect my scooter later.'

'What are we going to do with them?' asked Nicola. 'Your father won't want them at the house. He only tolerates Skele so he certainly won't want puppies around.'

'We'll sort that out later. I'll sit in the back with Skele and hold the box and we can drop them off at the taverna. You look after the taverna for a short while whilst I go back and collect my scooter. They would probably appreciate some warm milk. Goodness knows when they were last fed.'

Having deposited the box of puppies in the back room of

the taverna with Skele John hurried back up the hill. He arrived where he had left his scooter feeling hot and breathless and then his heart sank. Sniffing around the area where the box had been was a female. Her teats were dark and enlarged where she had obviously been feeding offspring recently. John pulled his mobile phone from his pocket.

'Nick, I need you up here again and can you bring some string and a beach towel with you.'

'What now, John? I'm serving at the moment and I need to get back to relieve your Mum of Yiannis.'

'The pups' mother has arrived. I need to catch her and bring her down to the taverna.'

John heard Nicola give a sigh. 'Give me a few minutes. I'll put a sign on the door saying open again in thirty minutes and look around for some string. Is she friendly?'

'I've not tried to get that close to her. I don't want to frighten her away. Bring some of Skele's treats with you. If she starts to run away I want to throw the beach towel over her and then make a halter of string round her neck.'

'I'll be with you as soon as possible.' Nicola turned back to her customers. 'I'm sorry about that. My husband needs my help to catch a stray dog up on the hill.'

'Better to shoot it,' remarked the man. 'There are more than enough of them around.'

Nicola looked at him incredulously. 'Can't possibly do that. She has puppies and they need to be fed.'

'Drown 'em. How much do I owe you?'

'Seventeen Euros and thirty five cents.'

'It would be cheaper than that in the village.'

Nicola could contain herself no longer. 'In that case I suggest you shop there in future.'

'I'm going to complain about your attitude to the owner of this establishment.'

'Be my guest. When the owner, who happens to be my

husband, returns from catching the dog you can complain all you like about me. Now, excuse me. I need to lock the door and go and help him.'

Nicola opened the door and indicated that the customer should leave. She closed it firmly after him and locked it before taping a notice on the side window to say the taverna and shop would reopen in half an hour and picking up a beach towel. She checked on the puppies who had tipped up the bowls of milk in their eagerness to have some sustenance. She rummaged in the drawer where useful items were kept until she saw the ball of string. It did not look very sturdy and she hoped it would be strong enough for John to control the dog.

Skele looked at her curiously and then down at the wriggling puppies. He seemed to realise there was a problem but he had no idea how no deal with it.

'Be good, Skele, and look after them whilst I'm gone.' Nicola gave him one of his treats from her pocket, opened the rear door of the taverna and locked it behind her. Once she had driven John back to the taverna she must phone Marianne and say she was on her way home.

John was sitting on the hill talking gently to the dog who was keeping a wary distance from him, but still sniffing around in the area where the box had been. Nicola drew up a short distance away and closed the car door quietly. Without a word she approached John and laid the beach towel down beside him and handed him the ball of string and the treats. John nodded and began to measure off a length of the string, doubled it and then cut it off with his penknife. He made a noose at one end with a slip knot that he could adjust once it was around the dog's neck and stop it from tightening further if the dog tried to pull away from him. Satisfied he held out a treat.

'Get ready to grab her, Nick,' and Nicola nodded. 'There's a good girl. Come on. This is for you.'

Patiently John held out the treat and continued to talk to the dog until she came close enough to take the bone shaped biscuit from his outstretched hand. The moment she did so he grabbed the loose fur at her neck.

'Help me, Nick.'

Nicola placed the towel over the dog and held her firmly whilst John slipped the noose over her head and tied it safely so that the noose would not get tighter. The dog bucked and kicked out, trying to get free. John picked her up, still wrapped in the towel and carried her to the car.

'I'll sit in the back with her and see if I can calm her down a bit.'

By the time Nicola had driven back to the taverna the dog was no longer struggling to get free but shivering and shaking with nerves.

'You poor girl,' said John. 'I think someone has treated you badly. You're safe now and we'll make sure you are well looked after in future. We'll take her in the back way and she can be reunited with her pups. When she's seen to them she could probably do with a good feed herself.'

'Sausages?' asked Nicola. 'Skele will be jealous.'

'I'm sure we can spare one for him.'

'What are we going to do with them?' asked Nicola as she opened the door and John deposited the dog on the floor.

'We'll have to take them to one of the animal sanctuaries. There's no way we could care for eight dogs! Hopefully they will be found good homes.'

'Whoever abandoned those pups should be prosecuted.'

'I agree,' said John. 'They could have taken them to one of the sanctuaries and said they had found them abandoned. Look.'

The bitch had laid down on the floor and the pups were busy suckling from her as she lapped up some of the spilt milk. Skele sat there watching them, still unsure what was expected of him.

'Can you cope now, John? I really ought to phone your Mum and say I am on my way back to relieve her of Yiannis.'

'No problem. I can collect my bike later.'

'Just don't find any more abandoned animals. By the way, a

man may come in and complain about me. He said the dog should be shot and the puppies drowned. When I told him how much he owed me for his shopping he said it was cheaper in the village and I told him to go there in future.'

John grinned. 'Good for you. I'll have to ask you to come back up here to collect this little lot later. We can't leave them up here for the night. I'll start phoning the local dog rescue centres and ask them if they can have them for a few days even if they can't keep them indefinitely.'

'Everywhere will need a good clean later,' observed Nicola, looking at the puddles and small deposits that had been left by the puppies.

'I'll come up and do that when we've found a rescue centre. I'll call you later when I've found somewhere to take them. I'd like you to come with me as I'm not sure how Mamma Dog will behave during a car journey. You can drive and I'll sit in the back with her and the pups. Oh, no, Dad's arriving.'

Giovanni walked into the taverna and general store and sniffed. 'What's that I can smell? Have you had your dog in here, John?'

'It's not what you think, Dad. I found some abandoned puppies when I was walking Skele. I couldn't leave them there so I had to bring them here. I went back up for my scooter and the mother had turned up so I brought her back as well.'

'You've got a dog and puppies here? Get rid of them.'

'I can't just throw them out. I'm going to phone round and find a rescue centre that will take them.'

'Where are they now?'

'In the back room.'

Giovanni opened the door leading to the back room and closed it again swiftly. 'It's disgusting in there. If Health and Safety decide to pay us a surprise visit we'll be closed down.'

'I know they have made a mess but I will make sure it is all cleared up later,' promised John. 'By tomorrow you'll never know they have been there.'

Giovanni turned to Nicola. 'I supposed you encouraged him. When I saw the car I thought Marianne was here. I called in to see if she had a problem.'

'She agreed to look after Yiannis whilst I came up. Bryony and Marcus dropped the girls into school on their way to the hospital. John couldn't carry a box of puppies back and I had to help him catch the mother.'

'So now her car will smell disgustingly of dog!'

'I can take it to the garage for the oil change and collect the girls from school on the way back. Once we've managed to get rid of the pups I'll clean the car out for her.'

'So I should think. I'll be coming up here tomorrow to check on the state of the back room so make sure you do a thorough cleaning job.'

'I will, Dad. Nick ought to get back now to take Yiannis off Mum's hands.'

John pulled a face as his father walked out of the taverna. 'I'll have a look on the computer and see where the nearest rescue centres are and then start phoning them. As soon as I find one that agrees to have them I'll call Bryony and Marcus and see if one of them is willing to come up here and relieve me. Once that has been arranged you ask Mum if she can look after Yiannis again and keep an eye on the girls whilst we deal with the problem.'

Nicola nodded. Most rescue centres would take one dog that had been abandoned but to take six puppies and their mother was asking a lot of them.

'I'd better call at the bank on my way and get some money so we can make a donation to them. Let me know the arrangements as soon as you can.'

John phoned Nicola. 'Has Dad calmed down? I've tried about a dozen shelters and as soon as I mentioned the puppies they refused. I've finally found one but it's on the other side of Aghios Nikolaos on the road to Ierapetra. It will take us at least two hours to get there and back, but I've had an idea. I'll phone Dimitris I'll ask him if he will come with me. I'll have to drop Skele off with him anyway and that would mean you could go back home and deal with the children.'

'How am I going to get home if you have the car?'

'Borrow Dimitris's bike. He won't mind and I'll bring him up to collect it from the house. Marcus has said he'll come up to the taverna. I'll phone Dimitris now and I should be on my way in about twenty minutes.'

Nicola hoped Dimitris would agree to John's plan so she would not have to spend the time driving to Ierapetra when she should be supervising the girls and putting Yiannis to bed. Once they had been satisfactorily dealt with she would ask Marianne and Bryony to listen out for them whilst she returned to the taverna and started to clean the back room. She did not relish the thought.

Skele having been deposited at Dimitris's house and Nicola ridden away on the scooter John asked Dimitris to sit in the back with the dog.

'Wouldn't it be better if you sat with her?' asked Dimitris. 'She doesn't know me at all.'

'She hasn't been any problem so far. I'll drive faster than you as I know the road. I've put the pups in a clean box from the taverna and we'll need to have the windows open all the way back. Nick has promised to clean Mum's car whilst I go up and clean the back room at the taverna.'

'I'll come up and help you,' offered Dimitris. 'You'll be up there all night otherwise.'

John smiled at his friend. 'I would really appreciate that and I'll pay you for your time.'

'You weren't tempted to keep them?'

John grinned. 'The girls came out and looked at them and suggested that they had two each and Yiannis had the other two. I think Dad would have finally had a fit if I'd dared to mention such a thing. He tolerates Skele because he's so well behaved, but can you imagine what it would be like to have six untrained puppies around? They would be a full time job.'

The drive took longer than John had envisioned as he missed the turn off to the rescue centre, had to ask directions and then drive back to a rough cart track that led to a small house that had a wire fence running around the perimeter of the land. John drew up at the gate and hooted. Immediately a cacophony of barking began and a woman came out of the house looking most annoyed.

'Why did you make that racket? You've started them all off now.'

'I'm sorry,' apologised John. 'I didn't know how else to attract your attention.'

'You have a mobile phone. The dogs don't like to be disturbed once I've fed them and bedded them down for the night. What kind of dogs have you brought?'

'I have no idea. I found them in a box on the hill when I was out walking my dog. Later the mother turned up so I've looked after them all of today, but I can't keep them.'

'You're sure they were abandoned and not just left there whilst the owner went about his business? I don't want to be accused of harbouring stolen dogs.'

'You wouldn't leave them up on a deserted hillside in a box if they belonged to you. They're too young to have been taken from their mother so I imagine the owner was hoping they would die of starvation and exposure.'

'Wicked. How long do you expect me to look after them?'

John looked nonplussed. 'I can't take them back with me. I'm hoping you will be able to find good homes for them when they are older.'

'You realise how expensive it is to care for puppies and nursing mother? Once they are weaned they will need to go to the vet, be wormed and have their injections. The mother will also need to be checked out by the vet. No one would consider taking a dog that did not have a full health certificate from the vet.'

John nodded. 'I know. I've brought a donation with me. I hope it will be sufficient for their immediate expenses.' John pressed the bundle of notes into the woman's hand.

Her expression softened. 'Get them out and let me have a look at them.'

Whilst Dimitris held the bitch John removed the box from the car. The woman pulled on a pair of disposable vinyl gloves, picked up each pup and examined it carefully, checking its eyes, ears and nose and running her hands down the length of its back before tipping it upside down and looking at the sex.

'There are four bitches and two dogs. They appear to be healthy but if it turns out that they have some infectious disease I will have them humanely destroyed.' She stripped off her gloves and turned them inside out into a ball ready for disposal.

'I understand. You would have no option. All I would ask is that you let me know if such a thing has to be.'

'You'd better bring them in and take them to a spare compound away from the others. Follow me.'

John picked up the box and Dimitris followed him leading the mother by the string that John had placed around her neck earlier.

'She could be hungry,' said John. 'I gave her some sausages during the day and a can of dog food before we drove down here.'

'Sausages!' The woman's eyebrows rose in horror.

'I had nothing else. I was at my father's taverna and general store at the time. We don't stock dog food.'

'Where's that?'

'Past Aghios Nikolaos towards Plaka.'

'So why have you driven all the way down here?'

'None of the other rescue centres would take them.'

The woman sighed. 'I'm just a fool. I end up with more dogs than I can find homes for. I can never turn one away.'

'I'll make enquiries around my area and see if anyone would

like a dog. If they are interested I'll ask them to contact you.'

The woman unlocked a wire gate. 'Put them in there.'

John set the box down and lifted the puppies out gently. 'There you are, little ones. You're safe now.' He gave each one a swift pat on the back.

'You're sure you want to get rid of them? You seem quite fond of them.'

John shook his head. 'They have to go. Can I release the mother now? I have to get back to the taverna and clean the back room thoroughly. My father is worried that if Health and Safety decided to visit they would close us down.'

John removed the string collar and the bitch immediately began to sniff her pups, then laid down and allowed them to start to suckle.

'Be a good girl,' said John and was rewarded by her wagging her tail.

Relieved that the dogs were now being safely looked after John opened all the windows of the car. 'I can't smell dog in here, but I don't want Dad complaining. We'll throw the box into the first rubbish bin we pass.'

Dimitris sniffed. 'I can't smell dog, but then I've been in here with them. We need someone with a fresh nose.'

By the time they arrived at the taverna Nicola had virtually finished the cleaning. 'It wasn't too bad. The worst smell was the milk where it was on the floor and had soured. I've washed the floor twice with disinfectant and had the windows open the whole time. I'll wash it once more and then spray some air freshener around before we leave.'

'You've worked really hard, Nick.'

'Couldn't have done it if Dimitris had not lent me his scooter and gone to the centre with you. What was it like there?'

'I didn't really have a chance to look around, but the woman seemed pleasant and caring enough. I gave her the money and she seemed pleased that I had thought about that for immediate expenses. We could drive down in a week or so and see how they are faring. We could take the children with us.'

'Not a good idea,' said Nicola, shaking her head. 'They would probably be expecting us to bring them back home.'

John grinned. 'Can you imagine Dad's reaction if that happened? Dimitris, I owe you money for giving up your evening and coming with me.'

John took some more notes from his pocket and gave them to Dimitris who promptly returned them.

'Keep it as my contribution to the dogs' fees. I had nothing planned for this evening except taking Skele for a last walk before bed.'

'I appreciate that, Dimitris. I certainly owe you a big favour.'

Uncle Yannis accosted John first thing in the morning. 'Have you got the order from Vasilis for the ceramics he wants?'

'Not yet. I haven't had an opportunity to give him the photos.'

'You were out late last night. I thought that was where you had gone.'

'I had something else urgent to deal with,' explained John.

'If he takes too long to make up his mind they may all be sold.'

John laughed. 'Uncle Yannis, I think that is most unlikely. I'll take them to him later today when I take Skele down to Dimitris. You'll have to be patient whilst he decides exactly what he wants.'

'Have you got rid of those animals?' asked Giovanni as he helped himself to some coffee and a croissant.

John nodded. 'Yes. They've gone to a rescue centre down towards Ierapetra. Nick did a fantastic job whilst Dimitris and I were taking them there. By the time we returned she had cleaned the back room and you would never know they had been in there.'

'I'll be the judge of that. I'm going to call in on my way to collect a family from the apartments. If there is any smell of dog in there I'll phone you and you'll need to do some more cleaning.'

'We made sure Mum's car didn't smell of dogs also,' John reassured his father.

Marianne smiled. 'I have checked it and there is no smell at all in there.'

'Just make sure you don't find any more abandoned pups.'

'I can't afford to. I had to give the woman at the rescue centre quite a large donation to persuade her to accept them.'

'Should have left them where they were and let someone else find them.'

August 2016
Weeks Two and Three

Ronnie saw John parking his scooter just as she was leaving the post office with the parcel that Luke had sent her from Australia.

John raised his eyebrows. 'Something interesting?'

'Maybe. You remember Luke, the man from Australia, who asked me to paint some pictures of Spinalonga for his mother?'

John nodded. 'I understand she was very pleased with them. Has she asked you to do some more?'

Ronnie shook her head. 'Sadly she has died. Apparently she decided to write her life story saying how she ended up in Australia and lived on a ranch. Luke asked if I would be interested to read it and I agreed. I was expecting him to email the pages to me, but it appears he has sent them to me instead.'

'Looks like a lot of reading. I hope it isn't all in Greek.'

Ronnie looked at him in horror. 'I hadn't thought of that. Once she had made her home in Australia she no longer spoke Greek so I hope she wrote in Australian English.'

'When people get old they often revert to their mother tongue.' John grinned. 'Let me know how you get on.' With a wave of his hand he rode off in the direction of Aghios Nikolaos.

Ronnie shifted the large parcel more comfortably in her arms and waited for a gap in the traffic so she could cross the road and be in the shade. She walked carefully down the uneven steps to the waterfront area and sat in the shaded snack bar that overlooked the sea.

Having ordered a frappe she looked across to Spinalonga that was shimmering in the heat and no doubt crowded with tourists by this time. She was tempted to open the parcel and begin to read whatever the old lady had written, but resisted the urge. It would make the parcel more difficult to carry once she had unpacked it as it was likely to be loose sheets that could blow away in the wind.

Ronnie did wonder how reliable the old lady's memory was. The paintings she had completed were mostly from her imagination and how she pictured the area to be almost a hundred years earlier; but Luke had said his mother had declared them accurate portrayals of the area and been delighted. She hoped that these memoirs would not have to be translated from Greek although she knew John and Nicola would be interested and willing to do the task.

Finishing her frappe she picked up her parcel and walked along the waterfront to the centre of the town where she could take a taxi back to the self catering apartments she and Kyriakos rented from Giovanni. She would have no opportunity to open the package and start to read that afternoon as she and Kyriakos always spent the afternoon together before he went to open the taverna. Once he had left she needed to complete some paintings ready to take to Saffron the following morning. Provided Kyriakos did not ask her to go up to the taverna to help she would have an opportunity that evening to start to read them. She would have to curb her impatience until then.

'Will you need me up at the taverna this evening?' asked Ronnie.

Kyriakos shook his head. 'I don't think so, unless we have a sudden influx of patrons or a large party arriving. Why? Do you have other plans?'

'Just the finishing touches to some of the paintings and delivering them to Saffron. Then I plan to finally open this parcel from Luke and see exactly what he has sent to me. If you do need me you can always phone me and I can come up.'

Ronnie finished the paintings after Kyriakos left to open the taverna and carried them carefully down to Saffron's shop.

'Are you well stocked at the moment?' she asked.

'Can never tell. Some days I may sell one and other days I can be asked for six or more. Today I have been selling boxes. Tomorrow it could be scarves or ear rings that people want. There's only one certainty; if I don't have it in stock that will be the item that everyone wants.'

Ronnie smiled. 'Kyriakos says that about the menu. If he's not been able to purchase marinated anchovies everyone wants them. At least if you have items in stock they do not go bad and have to be thrown away.'

'That is definitely an advantage. I would hate to be in catering. I'd have no idea of the quantities I would need to keep people happy and satisfied.'

Ronnie frowned. 'The trouble is that these days so many people have the mobile phones they can take photos on that they are not so interested in buying a painting. From the requests you have given me the tourists appear to want my paintings of the church or the square on Spinalonga rather than the view of the island.'

'That's probably because they didn't think to take one when they were over there or there were so many visitors they were unable to have an unrestricted view.'

Ronnie nodded. 'I think I'll do one or two that have the parishioners entering the church and the priest standing outside to welcome them. If they're not popular I don't have to do any more.'

'Why don't you do the same down in the square? People in their doorways, or a couple talking whilst waiting to fill their water jugs? Provided you don't show any of the really bad disfigurements that some of the villagers suffered; just bandaged arms or legs, possibly someone on crutches.'

'That's a really good idea, Saffron. I could work on a number of variations. People won't be able to get those photos on their mobiles. I could even show some of them rebuilding the houses or receiving their pension from Manolis. If those prove popular I can work on more during the winter.'

'I think Vasi and I will be calling on your expertise for interior design once Mr Palamakis has finished the alterations to the big house.'

'I'd be delighted. What are you planning?'

'Making the current rooms smaller so that we can add two or maybe three more.'

Ronnie looked at Saffron curiously. 'Why would you want more rooms?'

'We're planning to let it out as a self catering establishment for holiday makers.'

'That won't be much fun if you're living there as well.'

'We won't be. As soon as Vasilis and Cathy have moved to their new house we are going to take over their apartment in Elounda. It will be so much more convenient for both of us. We won't have the time to move until the end of the season, of course, but I'm already trying to sort out what I need and what can be left behind.'

Ronnie left Saffron's shop, her head buzzing with ideas and longing to start on some new paintings of Spinalonga; then she remembered the parcel from Luke that she was desperately wanting to open. She decided she would open the parcel first and make a start on the new paintings the next morning.

She cut the sellotape carefully, finally revealing two pieces of card with hand written pages between them. To her relief the writing was not Greek. She placed them in a neat pile beside her and took up the first page.

'Uncle Yannis, I've heard back from Vasilis. He says he will want eight pithoi and seven urns.'

Yannis nodded. 'They are packed and could go immediately.'

'Not quite so fast. The tiling at the back of their house isn't completed yet and he also says he wants to have a look at them.'

'Whatever for? They're all in perfect condition, no cracks or chips.'

'I think he wants to check the size and designs so they all go well together.'

'He's seen the photos.'

'Not the same as actually seeing them,' explained John patiently. 'He and Cathy are coming to dinner on Thursday so we can have them out on display for him then.'

'That means unpacking them and packing them up again,' grumbled Yannis.

'I'm sure Marcus will help me so it will be no trouble to you.'

'Make sure you don't damage them.'

Vasilis looked at the pithoi. 'They aren't all the same design or colour.'

'Does that matter?'

'I'd rather they matched.'

'How are you planning to display them? asked John.

'Four up each side of the garden area and two at the top with the urns in between them.'

'That's no problem, then. There are six here that have the rope design and they are grey. The two cream coloured ones have rosettes. They could go at the top.' John hoped that Vasilis would not be fussy about the different design around the necks.

'I suppose so,' agreed Vasilis. 'What about the urns?'

'Same problem. Four of them are terracotta with no decoration and the other two are black. You could put the black ones up by the cream ones and the terracottas between the grey pithoi.'

'I'll see what Cathy thinks.' Vasilis went back to the patio where Cathy was with the rest of the family and helped her to walk back into the room where the pots were displayed.

'What do you think Cathy?'

Cathy nodded. 'I don't think it matters that they are not all the same colour. We don't have to decide on their order at this moment. The two cream ones could either go at the back as John suggested or be the first ones on each side.'

'I'll ask Marcus to come and help me move them so you can have a better idea of how they will look. When we deliver them we need to be able to place them in situ. They're far too heavy to move around unless necessary.'

'Suppose one gets broken? Would we be able to replace it?' asked Vasilis.

'You could order another from the suppliers that Uncle Yannis used in the past. No idea what it would cost to have it made and delivered. Provided you don't go banging them with a hammer there's no reason why they should get damaged. I'll call Marcus.'

Vasilis nodded. Provided Cathy was happy to have two cream pots he really did not mind that they did not match the others. He was planning to have artificial grass on the area between the tiles rather than having it planted naturally and had given up the idea of having an olive tree in the centre. Instead he would have two large umbrellas and garden furniture so they could sit out there during the summer.

'It's a shame it will be too late for me to think about planting them up. I can spend the winter months looking at the catalogues and making a list of the plants I think will be suitable. I'm thinking of red and white in the grey ones and maybe shades of blue in the cream ones. The terracotta urns would probably look best with just greenery in them, and either yellow or red in the black urns. I'll ask Ronnie. She has such a good eye for colour, although plants don't really clash if you put red and orange ones in together. They just seem to blend in.'

Uncle Yannis watched dubiously as between them, Marcus and John turned the pithoi onto their sides and whilst Marcus held them safely John rolled them a small distance away from each other.

Vasilis nodded approval. 'Now if you put the urns in between them we can have a good idea of the overall effect.'

'Perfect,' declared Cathy. 'I can't wait for them to be delivered.'

'You'll have to let me know when the tiling is completed. We'll pack them up securely and ask Mr Palamakis to bring his flatbed truck around. We can easily make a wooden ramp so they can be placed on a trolley and pushed on and off. We'll need to be able to use the lift to take them up to the garden area. I don't think we would be able to man handle them up all your steps. You two go back and enjoy the gathering whilst Marcus and I pack these away for the time being. You don't need to watch us, Uncle Yannis, we'll be as careful with them as if they were new born babies.'

'Would you like me to pay you now?' asked Vasilis of Yannis.

'I'm always willing to take money. You can pay Mr Palamakis separately when he delivers.'

Vasilis frowned. 'When you delivered the pots to the apartment in Elounda you did not charge.'

'That delivery was for small urns that could be handled by one person and taken to you by car. I suggest you contact Mr Palamakis and ask him to give you a quote.' Yannis smiled smugly. 'I have your bill ready.'

Vasilis shrugged. He had no choice. He would have to speak to Mr Palamakis and arrange for his grandsons to deliver the pithoi.

'I will be so pleased to see all those large pots gone,' said Marianne. 'I can't possibly move them to clean properly. I hope Vasilis will think they need some more after Cathy has planted them up. I long for the day when the last pot goes out of the house.'

'I can't imagine how Uncle Yannis will feel if that does happen,' remarked Nicola. 'He'll be desperately unhappy. Of course, he could decide to order some more.' Nicola grinned wickedly.

'Don't you dare suggest such a thing to him - ever. If a consignment arrived here I would say it was a mistake and send it back.'

'I'm sure Uncle Yannis would be watching out for it and accept it before you had the chance to turn it away.' Nicola laughed. 'Don't worry, Marianne. I'm on your side. This is your home, not a storage depot.'

'Quite true, and make sure John doesn't think he can bring any stray animals back here to live.'

'They could have a compound of their own outside.'

'Can you imagine what Giovanni would say if it was even suggested? And who would be responsible for feeding and keeping them clean, not to mention giving them exercise? We're all far too busy during the season and even some of the winter months to take on any more work.'

'Seriously, though, we could do with a rescue centre that takes dogs and is nearer than Ierapetra. Some of the stray dogs are shot by the farmers, like that horrible man suggested, and other people put down poison for them. That's not only a terrible death but people's pets can also pick the poison up. I know John watches Skele carefully when he takes him up on the hill.'

'Well if you can find someone who is willing to take on the task and has a piece of land they can use I'll support you, but I wouldn't contemplate such a thing here.'

Nicola nodded. 'I'll keep a look out for anywhere that might be suitable.'

'You'd do better to spend your time looking for a small cottage that my mother could buy.'

'Is Grandma Elena planning to stay here permanently?'

Marianne shook her head. 'No, but she says she would like to buy a little cottage of her own.'

Nicola raised her eyebrows. 'Does Aunt Helena know her plans?'

'No, and at the moment she is not to be told anything about it.' Marianne lifted the cheese pies out of the oven. 'Can you take these through for me, please.'

Much as she would have liked to sit and continue to read Eirini's memoirs Ronnie kept to her usual routine of going into the square at Plaka each morning and painting. She had photographs of the church and main square on Spinalonga and decided that she would work at home from those when she started to add people as Saffron had suggested. She wanted to experiment with her latest idea of showing the leprosy sufferers being taken to the island by boat. She would need to get the perspective right. If she tried to paint them close to the island the detail would be lost and they could be any group of modern visitors; if she painted them too close to the shore they could be going anywhere.

She sat and squinted at the island and then realised that she needed only to paint the jetty where they had been landed and some of Spinalonga in the background. Now full of enthusiasm she took a sheet of paper and attached it to her easel. She drew a rough outline of the island, mostly showing the jetty, the Venetian walls and entrance arch.

Manolis had used his fishing boat to transport the people over so it only needed one or two occupants and whatever possessions they were able to take with them. She thought of her great grandmother arriving there after she had been taken to Doctor Stavros and could imagine her distress and panic as she was placed in the boat not knowing what fate awaited her.

Swiftly she added Manolis standing in the prow, a woman in the stern, her head bowed and her hand resting on the sack that contained her belongings. She looked at it critically and felt tears misting up her glasses. It had suddenly become very personal.

'Is that how they were taken over?' asked a man who had stopped to look at her work.

Ronnie nodded and swallowed the lump in her throat. 'That was how the Cretan people were taken there. When the other sufferers were sent from mainland Greece they arrived in a hospital ship.'

'Good idea to put them all together in one place. Saved contaminating the rest of the population.'

Ronnie did not answer him. He obviously had no sympathy for the unfortunate sufferers. She placed the sketch she had been working on to one side and took a fresh sheet of paper.

'What are you doing with the picture of the boat? I'm interested in old boats and I'd like to buy it. I looked in the shop at the top of the hill but the lady up there only had prints of modern fishing boats or wooden models meant for children.'

'This one is not for sale. It is a preliminary sketch.' There was no way Ronnie was going to sell that particular picture to the man. 'I can paint you a picture of the boat separately if you wish.'

'How long will that take? We've come by coach so we only have a couple of hours. Waste of time. Apart from having a meal I can't see that there's much else to do here.'

'Most people go over to Spinalonga. There's sufficient time to visit the island and have a meal.'

The man shook his head. 'Not interested in going over there and gawping at ruins. I'd rather spend my time in the marina at Aghios Nikolaos.'

'The picture will be ready by the time you need to catch the coach back. If I'm not here then I will have left it with the lady at the shop. Tell me your name and I'll make sure she saves it for you. It will be the same price as the others that she sells.'

From the pocket in his shirt the man took a business card and handed it to Ronnie who only glanced at it briefly. 'I'll put your card with it so Saffron will know it is for you.'

He stood and watched Ronnie make a start on the picture of the fishing boat and then wandered away. Ronnie was reluctant to spend her time painting just a boat, but a sale was a sale and should not be refused. The man had unsettled her. Did visitors to Spinalonga not appreciate the sad history of the island and just view it as a tourist attraction the same as they did Knossos and the other ancient archaeological sites? Maybe she was too sensitive due to her own family history.

August 2016
Week Four

Yannis watched anxiously as the boxes containing the pithoi were man-handled onto the wooden ramp John had made and pushed up onto the back of the flatbed truck. He hoped that when they were unloaded and taken up to Vasilis's garden they would not have been damaged in transit. He was sure if such a thing happened Vasilis would hold him responsible and demand some of his money back or a replacement ordered.

He was quite surprised at the amount of extra space he found he had in his bedroom. He would have to offer to store some of the other pottery vessels that at present were distributed throughout other rooms in the house. At least he would know they were safe with him and would not be accidentally bumped and damaged when Marianne, Bryony or Nicola cleaned. Marisa understood how precious they were to him but no one else seemed to care.

'I'm going to follow down in the car and supervise the unloading and unpacking.' John assured him. 'Marcus is going to be up at the taverna and if any of the pots have to be moved around one of the Palamakis boys can help me.'

'Be careful with them,' Yannis admonished him.

'Of course. The reason I am going down is to make sure that they do not get chipped or cracked. We know that they are all perfect, so if one of the Palamakis boys does any damage he will be responsible for paying for a new pot.'

'Pithoi,' muttered Yannis. He did wish that John would call them by their correct names.

John did not return until late in the afternoon.

'All unpacked, all safe, and they look extremely good where Vasilis has placed them. Their furniture is arriving on Monday and Vasilis has already started to move their picture and ornaments. Cathy can decide where she wants them placed later. Vasi was good, he phoned and said we were welcome to go along to the hotel for a snack lunch.'

'So you won't want a meal this evening?' Marianne raised her eyebrows.

'Of course I will. It was only a snack to keep us going. I'll phone Marcus and tell him I'm on my way to collect Skele, so he can close up and come home.'

'Is it interesting?' asked Kyriakos, nodding towards the pile of foolscap papers that sat on the table as he pulled on his white shirt and tucked the tails into his black trousers ready to go up to the taverna.

'So far most of it is about her life as a child and growing up in Fourni. I'm enjoying reading about her daily life. She was obviously very well educated, unlike the other village girls, as her father was the school teacher. She describes the area as it was then and how she fell in love with a local man. It's somewhat sad. She was sent to Elounda to live with her relatives there when she became pregnant. I wish I could remember more that her son had told me about the subsequent events. I was so involved with my house in Kastelli at the time that I didn't retain the information. I regret that now.'

'So what happened when she arrived in Elounda?'

'I hope to find out later this afternoon when I have time to read some more.'

Kyriakos bent and kissed her. 'You'll have to let me know

what happens. Now, I must go. Our local travel agent has made a booking for eight people this evening. I want everything to be perfect so they take a good report back to her.'

'Of course all will be perfect. It always is. Let me know if there is anything that you need before I come up this evening and help or if you just want me to socialise with them.'

'You mean you hope to sell them some paintings.'

'It never hurts to let visitors know I am an artist,' smiled Ronnie. 'I'll bring a few with me and place them around. Someone is sure to ask about them.'

Vasilis looked around the lounge of his new house. 'What do you think, Cathy?'

'It looks a little bare. It is so much larger than our apartment that the ornaments and pictures we brought with us are somewhat lost.'

Vasilis nodded. 'We could get some more furniture.'

Cathy shook her head. 'No, there's enough furniture. If we try to add more it will look crowded. It's decorative items we need. We could add some shelves in the alcove by the fireplace and place ornaments there.'

'Why don't I speak to Vasi and we could drive up to our original house and you can have a look around and see if there are items there that you would be happy to have here,' suggested Vasilis.

'I wouldn't want to take anything that Vasi particularly wanted.'

'We can always make a list and check it with him. We don't have to take anything away with us. If Mr Palamakis is going to be up there working everything will have to be packed up out of his way. I think Vasi and Saffron have already started packing everything they want to take with them to the apartment now we have finally moved out.'

'Could we make a stop at the supermarket on the way back? I need to stock up on some bits and pieces for the kitchen and get some vegetables.'

'No problem,' smiled Vasilis. 'The benefit of being retired is that we can do whatever we want most days.'

'We'll need to get some outside seating organised. Vasi will need the loungers and umbrellas that are down by the pool so we can't take those.'

'We can have a look on the internet after lunch and see what is available locally. We don't want to have to order from Athens and pay transport costs from there if that can be avoided. You'll also need to decide on the garden furniture that you want at the back.'

'We could go to a garden centre for that and I could look at plants at the same time. I know it's late in the season, but I would like to have some colour out at the back for when we start to have visitors. The pots are superb, but they will look even better if they are full of colour. I'll tell Ronnie the ideas I have and see if she thinks the colours will go together.'

'If you're planning to plant you'll need compost. If we visit the garden centre tomorrow and you find some garden furniture that you like we could arrange to have that delivered along with the compost.'

Cathy frowned. 'I'd like to speak to Ronnie about plants first, then they could be delivered at the same time.'

'Right.' Vasilis leaned back on the sofa. 'So our itinerary for today is to go up to the house and see if there are any things there that we would like to bring here, call in at the supermarket and then look on the internet for the loungers and umbrellas. That won't be too much for you in one day, will it?' asked Vasilis anxiously.

'I'm sure it won't, besides I can always have a rest when you're on the internet.'

Vasilis nodded. 'Tomorrow we could go to Plaka and meet Ronnie. We can take her out for lunch and you can discuss floral arrangements and we can go on to the garden centre afterwards.'

'We ought to phone Ronnie and see if it is convenient for her. She may have other plans or commitments.'

Vasilis looked at his watch. 'I'll phone Vasi and whilst I'm doing that you can phone Ronnie.'

Ronnie was delighted to speak to Cathy and arrange to meet for lunch the following day, although it would disrupt her own plans for painting and reading some more of Eirini's memoirs. She was being successful in adding people to some of the Spinalonga village scenes and tourists had stopped to admire and remark upon them.

'Is this how life on the island is today?' asked a woman.

Ronnie shook her head. 'No one lives on the island now. The buildings are there and when I have painted those as a background I just add some people taking part in what would have been their daily events to make the scene more interesting.'

'How do you know that is what they would have been doing?' asked her companion. 'I understood they were all sick people who lived in the hospital.'

'Only those who were unable to care for themselves were in the hospital. The others looked after themselves in their own houses, helping each other with difficult tasks.'

The woman pursed her lips. 'How would you know that? They can tell you any story they like about the island and no one can disprove anything.'

'I know that some of the stories that are told are not strictly accurate, but my information is authentic. I have friends whose relatives lived there. They visited them frequently and one of them was married over there by the priest, Father Minos. My own grandmother was born there.'

'Your grandmother?' The woman was sceptical. 'But you're American, not Greek.'

Ronnie smiled. 'It's a long story, but my grandmother was adopted by her aunt rather than being sent to an orphanage and the family emigrated to America. My great grandparents lived on Spinalonga until they died during the war.'

The woman sniffed, obviously disbelieving Ronnie. 'Well, I'll take your word for it.' She and her companion drifted away, but a man who had been listening came forward.

'I couldn't help overhearing your conversation with that lady. Is it true that your grandmother was born over there?'

'Perfectly true,' Ronnie assured him. 'I even know which house they lived in.'

'You sound quite proud of your ancestry.'

'I am. The people who were sent to Spinalonga were amazing. They managed with very little help originally to rebuild the ruined houses and make a village where they could be proud to live. Have you been over?'

'Not yet. I'm on the next boat.'

'Then enjoy the experience.' Ronnie dipped her brush into a small container of water and wiped it carefully before replacing it back in the rack with the others.

'I'll tell you when I return.'

'I'll not be here then. It becomes too hot to paint by mid-day. I'm just about to pack up now.'

'So if I wanted one of your pictures as a souvenir I wouldn't be able to buy one?'

'Go to the shop at the top of the hill and you'll find that Saffron has plenty for you to choose from. Her prices are the same as if you bought one here from me.'

'I'll do that. Thanks.'

The hooter for the boat sounded and the man hurried down the hill and took his place in the queue of people waiting to board.

Ronnie packed up her paints and collapsible easel and carried them back to the apartment. Kyriakos had just finished showering as she entered.

'A good morning?' he asked.

Ronnie nodded. 'So so. My painting went well, but I had a woman who disbelieved that the scenes where I had added figures were authentic. She reckoned it was all imagination and everyone was in hospital over there.'

'I hope you corrected her.'

'I did, but I don't think she believed me.'

'Stupid woman.'

'I had a phone call from Cathy. She and Vasilis want to meet me for lunch tomorrow and discuss the colour scheme for her garden pots. Will you be able to join us?'

'Was I invited?'

'Of course. I'm sure Vasilis would rather sit and talk to you than listen to Cathy and I chatting about flowers.'

'So what are your plans for later?'

'I'll do some more work on my paintings and then read some more of Eirini's memoirs before I join you up at the taverna. I am longing to know what happened when she was sent to Elounda.'

'Would you be able to take the table cloths into the laundry?' asked Kyriakos. 'The others should be ready to be collected along with my shirts. I thought I had three clean ones, but I only have two.'

'I can wash one through for you.'

'The others will still need to go to the laundry.'

'Well, I'll wash one and then take the others in with the table cloths and ask if I can collect them tomorrow. If that isn't possible at least you'll have a spare clean one. I'll come up to the taverna with you and bring your car back with me. That way I won't have to carry them on the bus or take a taxi. I can then drive up to the taverna later instead of walking.'

'Whilst you're in Elounda with the car could you go to the garage and fill it up with petrol?' Kyriakos handed her some notes from his wallet.

Ronnie nodded. She ought to clean through the apartment and finish her paintings if they were going to meet Vasilis and Cathy for lunch tomorrow. By the time she had visited the laundry, filled up the car with petrol and washed through a shirt she would have very little time to read any more of Eirini's memoirs.

Ronnie enjoyed her lunch with Cathy and Vasilis as she sat discussing colour schemes for the plants with Cathy whilst Vasilis and Kyriakos discussed catering and the difficulties they had both encountered in obtaining the supplies they wanted.

'Fortunately I had a superb manager when I was in Heraklion and I was able to leave most of the problems to him to solve.'

Kyriakos nodded. 'I wish I had. Apart from the cooking I have to do all of it myself.'

'Why don't you employ someone to take some of the work off your shoulders?'

'That would be ideal during the season provided I could find someone honest and reliable, but once we close for the winter I would have to let them go. Most people would like all year round work or a retainer to ensure they had the job the next year. My taverna doesn't make sufficient to hire anyone like that except for the chef and he also works as a waiter serving snacks at lunch times when my mother often goes up to help.' Kyriakos spread his hands. 'I go up in the early afternoon to start the preparation for the evening. I prepare the vegetables and leave the chef to do the hard work.'

'But you also cook, don't you?' asked Vasilis.

'Yes. When I only had three tables I was able to manage to do that myself. As I was able to expand a little I needed help, but I cannot employ as I would like. One day I may be able to spend the evening mingling with the guests and asking if they have enjoyed their food. At present it is all work, even when Ronnie comes up to help.'

'I am so pleased that I never had to work in the kitchens. I don't know how the staff survive the heat in there.'

Kyriakos shrugged. 'Somehow we manage. Thank you for a most enjoyable lunch and I look forward to visiting your new house when you are settled.'

Vasilis watched as Kyriakos walked away from their table. 'Is Kyriakos as hard pressed for finance as he says?' he asked of Ronnie.

Ronnie shook her head. 'Have you ever heard of any business man declaring that he was making a profit? He's not rich, but nor is he struggling on a day to day basis. He could do with larger premises and being a little closer to the other tavernas. He's on the outskirts so tourists often frequent the ones they see first and don't look around.'

'I'll ask Vasi to put some advertising in the hotel recommending him and giving directions to where he is situated.'

'Wouldn't that take trade away from Vasi?' asked Ronnie.

Vasilis shook his head. 'His residents do not eat at the hotel every night unless the weather is bad. They like to go out into the town and see what is being offered elsewhere, but they probably wouldn't think of coming to Plaka for the evening. It would mean a taxi ride for those who have not hired a car.'

Although Ronnie was enjoying her afternoon her mind kept drifting back to Eirini's memoirs. 'What was Elounda like when you were a boy, Vasilis?' she asked,

'I've no idea. I didn't live here then. I was up by Chania and later in Heraklion.'

'So how did you end up down here?'

'When Cathy and I were first married we lived in my hotel in Heraklion. Not an ideal situation. One day when we were out for a drive we came down here and fell in love with the area. I decided to have a house built here for Cathy and somewhere Vasi could grow up away from the town. I made a big mistake.'

'Why?' asked Ronnie. 'I thought you were happy here?'

'We are, but I should have thought about the future. I built a property that was far too large hoping we would have a family of our own to fill the rooms. It would have been more practical to build a smaller house close to the village. It was no problem whilst Cathy was able to drive and get out, but when she needed her wheelchair the hill became impossible.'

'So why didn't you stay living in the apartment in Elounda?'

Vasilis smiled. 'My big ideas again. I saw the land was for sale and the wonderful view there would be across the bay so I went ahead and built a house that would be suitable for Cathy. At least when she is unable to get out in the winter she will be able to look at the sea rather than across the road at a neighbouring house.'

'So what are you doing with the apartment now? Selling it?'

Vasilis shook his head. 'Vasi and Saffron are moving down there. It will be more convenient for both of them, particularly Saffron.'

'And the big house?'

'I have handed that over to Vasi and I believe they have plans to turn it into self catering accommodation. They are going to visit with Mr Palamakis and then decide on any necessary redecoration. I have a feeling you could be asked to help design the interior decor.'

Ronnie frowned. 'Does this mean that Mr Palamakis will be unable to work on my house at Kastelli?'

'I'm sure that between him and his grandsons they'll cope with everything.'

'Has Mr Palamakis lived here all his life?'

'As far as I know. Why?'

'Maybe he can tell me what it was like in Elounda when he was a boy.'

'Why don't you ask Uncle Yannis and Marisa. They are older than Mr Palamakis and Yannis has lived in the area all his life. What's your interest?'

Ronnie nodded. 'That's a good idea, but they lived in the Plaka area. I'm reading the memoirs of an old lady who lived in Elounda for a while before going to Australia. I'd be interested to know if her descriptions are accurate or if time has clouded her memory.'

'I'm sure there is a book that has been written about the area as it was in the eighteen and nineteen hundreds. That could answer some of your questions.'

'Really? Have I time to visit Monika before we leave here and if she hasn't a copy in stock I'll ask her to order one for me. You don't know the title, I suppose?'

Vasilis shook his head. 'I'm sure Monika will know the one I mean.'

Monika knew exactly the book that Vasilis had referred to and produced a copy. 'What exactly are you looking for?'

Ronnie explained about the memoirs that she was reading.

'This will certainly give you a good deal of background information about the area and also how it has developed over the years.'

Ronnie opened the book and scanned the chapter headings. 'This looks ideal. I know some of the older inhabitants could probably tell me about the area as it was fifty years ago, but their memories are not perfect.'

Monika smiled. 'Ask one person and the next person you ask will tell you something quite different. Very often neither of their versions are accurate. At least you can then check in the book to verify the facts.'

'May I collect it later? I'm going to the garden centre with Vasilis and Cathy now and don't want to carry it around with me.'

'I'll put it to one side with your name on it. You can collect it whenever it suits you.'

Ronnie returned to the table where Cathy sat waiting for Vasilis to bring up the car.

'Did Monika have the book you wanted?'

'I think so. She's put it to one side for me and I can collect it when I come up to Kyriakos's taverna later.'

'Do you go up every night?'

'Usually. I would be bored sitting at home in the apartment every evening. I don't understand Greek well enough to enjoy watching the Greek television programmes and there is very little of interest on in English except the news, and even that isn't really relevant to me unless they are reporting on wild fires or shootings in America.'

'You'd be welcome to come and visit us.'

'Thank you, but I could not inflict myself on you every evening.'

'Don't you paint in the evening?'

Ronnie shook her head. 'The light is not good enough. Sometimes I sit and read. At the moment I'm reading about the lady who lived in Elounda and went to Australia.'

'So that was why you were asking who would know about the area.'

Ronnie pulled a face. 'I really need someone who is about a hundred and fifty. The chances of me finding that person are non existent. I just hope that I can find some interesting information in the book I've bought from Monika, but I doubt if I'll be able to check its accuracy.'

'Is that important?'

Ronnie shrugged. 'Not really, but I do like facts to be correct. Here's Vasilis. Have you got your stick? Can you manage or would you like to hang on to me to keep your balance?'

Cathy took Ronnie's arm and they walked slowly to where Vasilis had the car waiting. He immediately helped Cathy in whilst Ronnie took a seat in the back.

Once at the garden centre Vasilis took Cathy's wheelchair from the boot and helped her to get settled in it.

'You lead the way,' said Ronnie. 'You know the colours that you have in mind. We just need to check that they are suitable to grow together and will stay flowering for as long as possible.'

'If I buy them now I want to make sure they will grow again next year. It's hard work for nothing if they only flower in the current season and then have to be pulled up and replaced.'

Ronnie smiled to herself. It was highly unlikely that Cathy would do very much of the actual planting and if she needed new plants the following year Vasilis would buy them for her without question.

'Still interesting?' asked Kyriakos as he dressed.

'Very. She's just gone over to Spinalonga as a helper and discovered that Lucas is there.'

'You said her son told you she went to Spinalonga and that was why he asked you to go over and paint some pictures.'

Ronnie looked at Kyriakos with a triumphant smile. 'When she had arranged to go over as a helper she hoped she would be able to find Lucas's uncle. She wanted to ask him if Lucas had any relatives in Aghios Nikolaos.'

'What difference would that have made?'

'I think she would have gone running off to the town and tried to find him there. She probably had no idea how large the town was.' Ronnie gave a little giggle. 'Her aunt thought she was doing a penance for the sin of having a child out of wedlock.'

Kyriakos frowned. 'She was taking a risk going over to the island when she had a small child. Suppose she had contracted leprosy or brought the infection back with her?'

'Apparently it was considered quite safe to visit the island if you were disinfected upon arrival and before you left. I'm sure John has told me that his grandmother was married over there and other members of the family visited frequently.'

Kyriakos shrugged. 'I suppose it must have been safe or the doctor who went over all the time would have become ill.'

'So would Manolis. He was on the island every day and had a relationship with Flora. Father Minos lived there and there were the workers who installed the electricity. They would have had to go in and out of the houses to connect the supply.'

'I expect they asked for double pay claiming that they were in danger.'

'I think the villagers over there were probably in more danger of ending up being electrocuted than the workers were of becoming ill. It was very basic and rudimentary. Even now the electricity supply is not exactly up to standard everywhere here.'

Kyriakos shifted uncomfortably. He knew the electrical wiring in his taverna left a good deal to be desired.

'So did she find him?'

'She must have done.' Ronnie wrinkled her brow. 'I'm sure her son said he had a brother and Lucas was the father. I hope I'll be able to find out when I've read the next few pages.'.

'You can tell me when you come up to the taverna.'

'I'm not reading any more today,' said Ronnie firmly. 'I need to collect your shirts from the laundry and have a clean through the apartment. I didn't do the cleaning when I had planned and if I continue to read this afternoon it will still not get done. I also need to get some pictures finished.'

'I'll not complain if you haven't swept and dusted everywhere.' Kyriakos bent and kissed her. 'Come up when you're ready.'

September 2016
Week One

Giovanni drove Elena into Elounda on his way to the airport. 'Where would you like to get out today?' he asked.

'Anywhere near the church where you can stop would be fine.'

'I'll drive into the car park, then I can stop by the exit and you'll be next to the church. Don't forget to phone home when you would like someone to come and collect you.'

Elena shook her head. 'I can easily take a taxi. I don't like to be a nuisance when you are all so busy.'

'You're never a nuisance,' Giovanni assured her.

Elena watched him drive away then waited for a break in the traffic so she could cross the road to the coffee bar. There were a few cottages a short way up the hill leading from the town, but she was not sure if it was a suitable area to consider buying a property. The roads were pleasant and where the properties had been turned into self catering accommodation they looked clean and attractive, but that could mean noisy youngsters disturbed other visitors when they returned home in the early hours. There was a continual stream of traffic coming down the hill and from the Plaka road, having to negotiate the roundabout and between cars and commercial vehicles there were the coaches carrying the tourists. The side road was always busy where a one way system had been developed and once a week the market was held there, but there was a nice coffee bar and the young girl always served her with a smile.

'How are you planning to spend your day?' asked the waitress.

'I want to have a look at the area behind the main street and see if there is any property available that I could rent.' Elena was not prepared to tell the young lady that she was thinking of buying.

'That can be difficult during the season. Most of the self catering establishments are booked in advance and some people move in with relatives and let their house out to get some extra income. Where are you staying now?'

'With my relatives.'

'Can't you continue to stay there?'

'Yes, they assure me I can stay as long as I want.' Elena had her excuses ready. 'They live quite a distance from Elounda and I don't like to ask them to keep driving me in whenever I want to spend time here. They are busy as they have their own self catering apartments and a general store with a small taverna attached for their visitors. They also have young children who need to have some attention. I love the children, but sometimes I find having so many people around and so much activity that it becomes a little overwhelming.'

'I know how you feel. I love my own children dearly, but sometimes I am only too pleased to leave them with their grandmother for a short while and be able to do whatever I please.'

Whilst Elena sipped her frappe she planned where she would visit that day. She would cross over the main road to the taverna and walk along the road that ran behind the shops. On reaching the end of the road she would go to the road above and walk back along there. Once again when reaching the end she would walk up to the next road. She did not want to go any further up the hill. If she still had the energy after that she would walk back down to the main road and start to walk behind the next block of shops.

As Elena left the waitress looked after her puzzled. Why would the lady want to rent somewhere of her own to live in if she was able to stay with her family. Had there been a big argument and falling out?

Elena walked slowly along the road. All the premises behind the shops appeared to have a single door that was their back entrance. She was not impressed by that area. It would be far too busy during the day and probably noisy at night when the tourists made their way back to their hotels. On the opposite side of the road were some cottages, but they looked very drab and run down. With a sigh she continued on to the corner and walked up the short hill to the parallel road. That was more promising, the houses looked more modern but they all had two entrance doors indicating that they were apartments.

A woman was in her small front area sweeping away the dust and Elena hesitated. There would be no harm in asking if the woman knew of any cottages for sale.

The woman shook her head. 'Nothing I know about. All the apartments here are rented by local people. You need to go further up the hill or up behind the main street. You may find something available there.'

Feeling despondent Elena walked to the end of the road and then turned back down to where the shops were situated. As she turned the corner a woman was approaching, turning and looking behind to see if there was any traffic approaching. As she did so her foot slipped and she fell onto her knees and ended up sitting half on the pavement and half in the road, her bag of groceries spilled out around her. Horrified Elena bent down beside her.

'Are you hurt?' It was probably a foolish question as the woman was deathly pale and holding her knee.

'My leg. Can you help me up?'

Elena placed her hands beneath the woman's armpits and began to lift her. The woman gave a shriek of pain and Elena lowered her back to the ground.

'You are hurt. I think we should call a paramedic to check you over.'

'I'll be alright.' Beads of sweat were forming on the woman's forehead and she bent her head. 'I think I may be going to faint.'

Elena waited no longer. She pulled out her mobile phone and called the emergency number for medical help.

'I'll stay with you until they arrive.' She tipped some of her bottle of water onto a paper tissue and mopped the woman's forehead, then collected up the groceries and placed them in the woman's bag.

'I need to get home,' the woman moaned faintly.

'Is there someone at home that I could call for you?' asked Elena.

The woman shook her head and winced in pain.

'Then I'll sit here with you.' Elena looked twice at the dusty pavement but decided she had no choice but to sit down beside the woman. She could not kneel or bend down for any length of time. She took the woman's hand in her own. 'Tell me your name.'

'Irini.'

'I'm Elena.'

The woman winced with pain again and Elena hastened to reassure her. 'The paramedics are on their way. Squeeze my hand if it helps when a spasm of pain comes. My husband was a doctor and he always said that helped if a patient could grip something.'

It seemed an age before Elena saw the ambulance arrive and she waved to show them where they needed to stop.

Two men knelt down beside Irini and asked her where she was hurting. 'My knee,' she gasped.

Gently the man felt it and Irini moaned in pain.

'We'll take you back to the hospital for an X-ray. Hopefully it is just badly bruised but we need to be certain of that before we try to stand you up.' He nodded to his colleague who opened the back door of the ambulance and took out a stretcher. 'We'll give you something to make you comfortable for the journey. What about your friend? Would you like her to come with us?'

Irini nodded weakly. The pain was really taking hold now.

Elena nodded. 'Of course I'll come if you think it would help, although I don't really know the lady.'

'You climb in the back and sit down on one of the seats and we'll place her on board. The sooner she's at the hospital the more quickly they can give her something stronger to ease the pain.'

Whilst one paramedic drove the other sat in the back with Elena and monitored Irini. 'Can you tell me anything about the lady?' he asked.

'Nothing at all. I saw her fall and went to help her up. All I know is that her name is Irini.'

'When we get to the hospital they'll see if she has any identification with her and be able to notify her relatives.'

'She said there was no one at home.'

'They're probably out at work. Does she have a mobile phone? That's where most people have their contact numbers.'

'I don't know. There may be one in her pocket.'

The paramedic touched the pockets in Irini's skirt and produced a mobile. He opened it, scrolled down the list of contacts and frowned. 'There are only two numbers in here. One is listed as 'K' and the other as 'Ktav.' Do they mean anything to you?'

Elena shook her head.

'I'll try 'K' first.' The paramedic pressed the contact and waited for it to be answered.

'Hello Mamma,' said a sleepy voice.

'Good morning, sir. Can you tell me if your mother is Irini?'

'Yes. What's wrong?'

'Your mother is in the ambulance and we are taking her to Aghios Nikolaos hospital for an X-ray. She has had a fall and hurt her knee.'

'Is she alright?'

'I believe it is only her knee that is troubling her.'

'Can I speak to her?'

'Not at the moment. We have given her some sedation to help the pain so she is not really fully awake. I suggest you come to the hospital where you will be able to see her.'

'Of course. I'll be there as soon as possible.'

Hurriedly Kyriakos splashed his face with cold water and dressed. Whilst he was doing so he phoned Ronnie and apprised her of the situation.

'I'll pack up and go to the hospital with you.' As she spoke Ronnie packed her palette of paints away along with her sheets of paper and collapsed her easel. 'I'll meet you at the top of the hill.'

Ronnie had been waiting no more than a few seconds before Kyriakos drew up in his car. He looked strained and worried.

'Where did her accident happen?' she asked.

'In Elounda. Apparently a passer by saw her fall and it was her who called the ambulance.'

'Is she conscious or did she bang her head?'

'I don't know. The paramedic only mentioned her knee.'

Ronnie nodded. Once they were at the hospital Kyriakos should be able to find out more and she hoped his mother's injury was not too serious. They drove in silence until they reached the hospital.

'You go in,' said Ronnie. 'I'll find somewhere to park the car and meet you inside.'

Kyriakos did not argue, but climbed out quickly and hurried into the hospital entrance. Ronnie slid into the driving seat and began the onerous task of looking for an available parking place nearby. It took her almost twenty minutes to find a place to park legally and a further ten minutes to walk back to the hospital.

She saw Kyriakos sitting disconsolately in the waiting room and went over to him. 'What's the news?'

He gave a deep sigh. 'I have seen her and she is alright except for her knee. She's been taken down for an X-ray and we won't know any more until that has been done. I ought to phone my chef and tell him that the taverna will be closed today.'

Ronnie shook her head. 'There's no need to do that. I can go up there and once we know how your mother is you may be able to go up there later.'

Conversation between them lapsed, but Kyriakos kept looking at his watch. 'How much longer?'

Ronnie took his hand. 'You have to be patient. Once the X-ray has been developed it will have to be looked at by a doctor for the problem to be diagnosed. I'm sure they will be as quick as possible.'

'You don't have to stay with me.'

Ronnie gave Kyriakos a scathing look. 'Your mother is far more important than serving some food to people at the taverna. I'll not go until you have seen the doctor.'

Ronnie looked around at the other people who were waiting and frowned. 'I might be wrong, but that looks like Marianne's mother sitting there. I hope nothing has happened to Marianne.'

'I'm sure Giovanni would be with her.'

'He could be on an airport run. I'll go over and ask her why she's here.'

Elena looked up in surprise when Ronnie stopped in front of her and spoke in English. 'Excuse me, but you are Marianne's mother, aren't you? Is she alright?'

'Perfectly as far as I am aware. I'm just waiting for the doctor to hear about the lady I came in with. She'd had a fall.'

'Who is she?'

'I don't really know. She told me her name was Irini and I know the paramedics called her son and he should be here soon.'

Ronnie smiled. 'I think he's already here. I believe the lady to be Kyriakos's mother. Come over and tell him exactly what happened.'

It was nearly midday when the doctor finally appeared and sat down beside Kyriakos. 'I have both good and bad news about your mother. The bad news is that she has a broken knee and is being taken down to the operating theatre as we speak. Apart from a few cuts and grazes on her legs there is nothing else wrong so that is the good news.'

'Can I see her?' asked Kyriakos.

'Not at the moment. I would suggest that you come back in the early evening when she will be on a ward. She'll probably be a bit sleepy, but you will be able to see her briefly.'

Kyriakos let out a sigh of relief. 'Thank you.'

Elena leaned forward. 'I believe that is the same lady as I accompanied in the ambulance.'

'Irini Mendakis?'

'I didn't know her name, but after talking to this gentleman,' Elena indicated Kyriakos with her hand, 'I believe that to be her.'

'It was kind of you to come with her and wait to hear about her condition. I suggest you leave now and go about your day as there is nothing more you can do.'

Ronnie put her hand on Elena's arm. 'Are you going back to Yannis's house? We're just about to leave and could give you a ride.'

'I would be very grateful. I have money with me but I'm not sure if it would be sufficient for a taxi ride back to their house. I'd need to find a cash point to avoid embarrassment or wait for the bus.'

Elena walked into the kitchen at Yannis's house and made herself a cup of coffee.

'You're back earlier than I had expected,' smiled Marianne. 'There's plenty of lunch around. Tell me what you would like and I'll get it for you.'

'Some dolmades and tzatziki with some pitta bread would be quite sufficient, but only if you have them available. Don't go to any trouble. I had a lift back with Kyriakos and Ronnie.'

'That was kind of them. What were they doing in Elounda?'

'We met at the hospital.'

'Hospital? Why were you there?'

'Kyriakos's mother had a fall and I happened to see her and call the ambulance. I didn't know who she was until Ronnie recognised me in the waiting room and came over. She was concerned that something had happened to you.'

'How is Kyriakos's mother?'

'Apparently she has a broken knee and they had taken her

67

down to the operating theatre. I felt obliged to wait around until I knew. It is exhausting sitting there just waiting. I didn't even have a book with me to read.'

'I suggest you have a nap after you've eaten. When is Kyriakos able to visit her?'

'This evening apparently.'

'That means he will have to close the taverna.'

'Ronnie said she would go up to help.'

Marianne frowned. 'Arrangements will have to be made for whilst she is in hospital and also for when she returns home. I'll phone Kyriakos and see if we can help at all.'

'I doubt if he has thought that far ahead yet.'

'His mother is going to need someone with her over night whilst she is in hospital and then during both the day and night when she returns home. One of us could probably take it in turns to spend some time with her during the day.'

'I thought I would visit her tomorrow provided Kyriakos is agreeable.'

'I'm sure she would appreciate a visit from you, but you can't be expected to look after her once she is back home.'

'Ronnie will probably help.'

'It's my understanding that Ronnie and Kyriakos's mother are not friends. She disapproves of Ronnie because she is American.'

'Stupid lady. If I had told her I was American when she was lying on the ground in pain would she have refused my help? Of course not.'

'Ronnie's Greek is very limited. They find it hard to communicate.'

'I'm sure Ronnie knows enough Greek to be able to help the lady to the toilet, give her a wash and something to eat. For that she should be grateful.'

Once Elena had retired to her room Marianne explained the situation to Bryony. 'Have you any ideas how we can help?'

'I'd be willing to go in for an hour or so each day. Might be

68

better not to tell her that I also come from America or she might refuse to have anything to do with me. Have you asked Nicola?'

'Not yet. We could look after the children so we could share visiting between us. Ronnie could do the morning instead of painting and then Kyriakos could go in at lunch time before he goes up to the taverna. One of us could go in later and ensure she has something to eat and drink before going to bed. How they manage over night will have to be up to them to organise.'

'They would have to employ a nurse,' said Bryony firmly. 'If Kyriakos has been working up at the taverna he cannot be expected to sit up all night with his mother and nor can Ronnie.'

'That's expensive,' observed Marianne.

'Fifty Euros a night I believe and they would expect to be able to help themselves to food and drink whilst they were there. There are nine of us here and I'm sure we could contribute two or three Euros each to help with the cost.'

'Kyriakos is a proud man. He might not be willing to accept financial help.'

'Then get Giovanni to talk to him. It's the only practical solution other wise he might have to take out a bank loan and with the interest that will accrue he'll be paying it off for ever.'

'I suggest that he puts a collecting box at the taverna saying the money is for his mother's hospital fees. Some of his customers might put some money in there rather than leaving him a tip.'

'That's a good idea. I'll speak to Giovanni when he arrives home and see what he thinks.'

Having been told of the situation by Marianne Giovanni drove immediately up to Kyriakos's taverna.

'I've come to offer you some help,' he said.

Kyriakos gave a strained smile. 'I appreciate the help that your mother in law gave.'

'I'm talking about help when your mother returns home. She's going to need a night nurse and they don't come cheap. Marianne and I have decided that we will all contribute a few Euros to help pay the cost. You can't be expected to run the taverna and nurse your mother. The ladies have said that they will work out a rota system to call in on her during the afternoon so you must let us know when she is expected home.'

Tears filled Kyriakos's eyes and he brushed them away impatiently. 'I appreciate the thought, but I can manage the expenses.'

'Rubbish, man. How long is your mother going to need a night nurse? You don't know if it will be a for a week or a month. Accept the offer.' Giovanni took an envelope from his pocket and placed it on the table in front of Kyriakos. 'That's a start to help you initially.'

Kyriakos looked at the envelope dubiously. 'I never expected this. I am grateful and I'll consider it a loan and only use it if necessary.'

Elena phoned the hospital and asked after Irini Mendakis to be told that she was resting comfortably but visitors were not a good idea at present. 'If you wish to visit I suggest you wait until tomorrow. By then she should have recovered sufficiently from the anaesthetic to appreciate seeing someone. Her son has been in, of course, but once she had seen him she went back to sleep.'

'May I phone you tomorrow?' asked Elena, relieved in some ways that she did not have to make the journey and sit beside a bed where the patient was asleep.

'That would be a better idea.'

September 2016
Weeks Two and Three

Giovanni and Marianne drove down to Elounda, taking Yannis, Marisa and Elena with them. 'I believe we will be their first visitors since they moved in.'

'What about Bryony and Marcus? Surely they'll want to see the house.'

'Of course, but they will visit next week with John and Nicola whilst we mind the children. Vasilis is insisting that only a few people are there at any one time so that Cathy does not get overtired by showing people around. When Pietro and his wife arrive Giovanni and John will go down again so they can interpret from Italian into Greek.'

'Who else are they planning to invite?'

'Just about everyone else that they know, but some people will have to wait until the season ends and they are no longer working. You can't expect them to close their premises down for the afternoon and evening just so they can go visiting. The winter months give everyone plenty of time to socialise.'

'I'm beginning to feel quite excited. John said that he was most impressed when he delivered Yannis's pots.'

'I think that is partly why they want us to come in the afternoon; so they can show off the garden that has been made at the back before it gets dark.'

'Don't they have lights out there?'

'I expect so, but it would be better to see it in daylight first.'

Giovanni hooted as he stopped before the Villa and the gate began to swing open so he could drive his car in off the main road. Vasilis stood waiting to greet them at the entrance to the garage.

'I'll show you how to use the lift. Cathy will be waiting at the top. One at a time and then we youngsters will climb the steps.'

Giovanni and Marianne waited until Elena was settled in the lift and then followed Vasilis back to the steps. By the time they reached the entrance Cathy had the front door open and was ready to welcome them.

'Before you all get settled I want you to have a look at the view from the front patio and then we will have a drink in the garden. After that I'll give you a conducted tour inside and then we can sit down and have our meal.'

'That is amazing,' said Marisa. 'You can see all around the bay and the villages up on the hillside. I could sit here all day and look at that. From Yannis's house you can only see a part of it at any one time unless you go outside.'

'I will probably spend a considerable amount of time out here during the good weather and even when the tourists have gone home I'm sure there will be plenty to look at. Just watching the sea when it is rough will be a pleasure.'

Cathy led the way down the path to where the garden was situated. She stood to one side and hoped it would be admired.

'It's beautiful,' exclaimed Marianne. 'The pots and the flowers in them look superb.'

Yannis grunted. He had to admit that the pots with the riot of colour that was in them did look spectacular, but he still did not approve of having his precious pots used in a garden as planters.

'Sit down and tell me if you find the furniture comfortable. It was only delivered three days ago so we haven't really had a chance to try it out.'

Vasilis handed round glasses of champagne and they raised their glasses in a toast.

'To your new home,' said Giovanni. 'I hope you will both be very happy here.'

They sat outside until darkness fell and the outside lights came on illuminating the garden and then returned to the lounge.

'Now I will show you around inside. It won't take very long.'

Cathy led the way to their bedroom and ushered them inside. 'Vasilis has designed it in such a way that even when I am confined to a wheelchair I will still be able to have access to the bathroom and use the shower. Now, back to the dining room,' announced Cathy. 'You can have a quick look at the kitchen and then we can sit down and eat before we retire to the lounge.'

Giovanni looked at the floor. 'Are these the tiles that came from Pietro's factory?'

Vasilis nodded. 'I think we made a good choice. The ripples in them detract from the starkness of a single colour and they don't show the dust so much.'

'I think Pietro will be impressed when he visits.'

'I hope so,' smiled Vasilis. 'If he disapproves I certainly can't afford to have these taken up and another lot laid.'

'It doesn't matter what he says. If you're happy with them that's all that matters.'

By the time they finally said farewell it was obvious that Cathy was tired. Tactfully Vasilis stood up and gave an almighty yawn.

'I don't want to throw you good people out and it has been delightful to have your company but I'm not used to late nights nowadays. I really have to go to bed.'

Cathy smiled at him gratefully.

'We're all tired,' Marianne admitted. 'I nearly dropped off to sleep a little earlier. I am full of good food and wine and this sofa is so comfortable. If Giovanni goes down and gets the car ready can you see the others into the lift? I can wait for them at the bottom.'

Marisa took a last look out across the bay. The houses and tavernas in the villages were lit up, some of them no more than a dot of light on the hillside, and the lights of the cars could be seen moving along the main road from Plaka to Elounda. The rhythmical throb of a fishing boat's engine could be heard as the owner made his way to the fishing grounds he patronised at night; his lights showing his progress across the calm sea.

'You can't see Spinalonga,' remarked Marisa. 'Somehow I had still expected to be able to see it.'

Yannis shook his head. 'Of course not. They didn't have electric lights over there for years and even then they had house lights before we did at Plaka. When you looked out at the bay at night you might see the lights of a fishing boat but everything else was in darkness.'

'I remember,' sniffed Marisa. 'It just seems such a long time ago now,' she said wistfully.

'Is there anywhere you would like me to take you this morning?' asked Marianne of her mother. 'I'm planning to buy some flowers for Cathy and drop them in at their new house as a thank you for entertaining us last night.'

'If you're going down to their house I could take advantage of a lift and have a walk along to the salt pans and maybe across the Causeway. I'd like to see what has happened down there recently. You could drop me off first. If we both arrive Cathy may think she has to invite us in and she's probably tired this morning.'

'I could leave you at the windmills. I'll need to drive along there to be able to turn the car safely.'

Elena smiled. 'I have been planning to walk along to the canal. I want to have a look at the Basilica. I do hope they have done something about preserving the mosaic before any more of it is lost to the weather.'

'You could have a coffee at the taverna there. That would not be too far for you to walk back and I'm sure Vasi would be delighted to give you a snack as you returned. You could phone home from there and one of us could come down to collect you. I thought I would leave in about twenty minutes. Would that suit you?'

Marianne drove slowly along the seafront road, past Vasilis's house, Vasi's hotel and the self catering apartments that were lower down. Children were playing outside making use of the climbing apparatus that had been designed for them whilst adults sat around the pools or at the snack bars.

'Do you ever bring the children down here?' asked Elena and Marianne shook her head.

'They'd be welcome by the owners, but the children who are staying there are never particularly friendly. They seem to think they are the only ones who are allowed to play there, although the notice on the gate says it is open to everyone. Nicola prefers to take them up to the playground at Plaka.'

Marianne drove over the bridge of the canal and turned into the parking area by the windmills. 'Is this where you want me to leave you?'

'It's perfect. Tell Cathy how much I enjoyed our evening.'

With a wave of her hand Marianne drove away and Elena walked to where she knew the entrance to the Basilica was behind the taverna. She shook her head in despair when she looked at the mosaic. More of the tesserae had disappeared and she wondered why no one was bothering to preserve it. Another few years and there would be nothing to see except a patch of rough ground.

Thoroughly disappointed she returned to the taverna and then walked to the edge of the canal. The water was high and a couple in a canoe were carefully guiding their small craft through, being careful not to touch the rocks at the side. She watched them for a few minutes then walked back to the bridge. The remains of the original bridge, just two pillars were still there, and she shuddered at the thought of walking across the expanse of water on a piece of planking, probably leading a donkey or carrying a heavy sack of grain from the mill.

It would not take her very long to walk back to Vasi's hotel and it would be far too early to have a snack lunch. She would walk across the spit of land that bordered the salt pans and she could stop for a coffee at the taverna that she knew was over there. Then she had the choice. She could retrace her steps to the Causeway or continue up the lane from the taverna where she would eventually arrive at the main road.

Whilst she drank her coffee she decided that she was not tired and walking back along the Causeway was preferable to walking along the main road with the fast moving traffic passing her continually. It might be possible to take a short cut across the salt pans as the old retaining walls were visible above the water and she had seen people using them to cross over on previous occasions.

As she paid for her refreshment she asked the waiter how feasible such a venture would be and he looked at her doubtfully and shook his head.

'I would not recommend it, Madam. Some of the youngsters take the chance, but many of the walls are crumbling and you could lose your footing. You would end up ankle deep in the mud.'

Elena smiled. 'I'll take your advice. I certainly would not want even one foot to slip into the water. I might have to call for help and I am not sure how I would be rescued.'

'Very wise, Madam.'

'It's a shame there isn't a proper pathway that leads from here round to the paved area that leads off the Causeway.'

He nodded and walked away. Why would anyone want a path around that side of the salt pans? There was only one deserted house there and no one ever went near that.

Elena walked slowly back to where the Causeway road led her to the paved area that would take her to the other side of the salt pans and then up onto the main street. She decided it was not worth the effort that day as she would only have to retrace her steps if she did not want to walk down the main road into Elounda.

Irini Mendakis was making slow progress. She had been discharged from the hospital wearing a cumbersome and heavy brace down the length of her leg, only permitted to remove it at night when she was in bed. She was tempted to stay in bed all day but the night nursed strapped the brace to her leg each morning and insisted she rose, washed and dressed.

'What would your son think when he visited if you were still lying in bed? He would think I was not looking after you properly and ask for you to be readmitted to the hospital, You wouldn't want that to happen, would you?'

Irini shook her head. If she was back in the hospital she would just be left lying in the bed most of the day whereas now she was home she could watch the television and it was amazing how many people called in to see her and spend some time with her. She had been given a walker that allowed her to move around, albeit slowly, and told she must put no weight at all on her damaged leg.

The visits she had from Elena, Marianne, Bryony and Nicola she really appreciated. They would bring a meal with them and sit with her whilst she ate, chatting easily with her and assuring her that Kyriakos was managing well up at the taverna with the help of Ronnie.

'I do wish that girl was not an American,' she sighed.

'What difference does that make?' asked Bryony. 'Although I consider myself to be a Greek I spent most of my years in America. It was not until Hurricane Katrina struck that Marcus and I came over to live with Marianne and Giovanni.'

'That's different,' commented Irini. 'She has bad blood.'

'What do you mean? Bad blood?'

'Her grandmother was born on Spinalonga.'

'That doesn't mean she has bad blood. She was fit and healthy which was why her aunt was allowed to adopt her and take her to America with them when they went over there.'

'I suppose so.' Irini was ashamed that her husband had been declared infectious, but thankful that she and Kyriakos had remained free of the disease. She had never admitted to anyone at the time and simply said that her husband had gone away to Aghios

Nikolaos and subsequently died. It was only when Kyriakos was forced to go to the doctor to undertake a test himself due to his skin condition that she finally confessed the truth about his father to him.

'And there's another thing,' continued Bryony. 'You are happy that Elena visits you and that she took you to the hospital. Her parents were Greek and they worked on a research programme at the leprosarium in New Orleans. She was brought up in America and married an American. Marianne is also American by birth so you are being illogical in refusing to accept Ronnie.'

Irini did not answer. Maybe she should make more of an effort to get to know the girl when she visited.

John and Nicola made another visit to the animal sanctuary and had been delighted to find that all but two of the female pups and their mother had been adopted by various people. Three of them were actually going to different countries and their health had been checked and all their vaccinations and animal passports were in order.

'You won't have the remaining dogs destroyed, will you?' asked John.

'Certainly not. I just hope no more come in over the winter months. It always costs more then to ensure they have sufficient bedding.'

John realised it was a hint that the woman would like more funds and handed her some notes. 'We can't afford to do this for ever. This should help you for a while and I hope you will find some good homes for the others.'

'Not easy at this time of year, but we can always hope that a local farmer needs a new dog.' She stuffed the notes into her pocket. 'I appreciate your help. If you hear of anyone who wants a dog please send them down here to me.'

As John and Nicola walked back to the car, Nicola stopped. 'I've had an idea.'

'Tell me.'

'Vasi loves dogs. Why don't we tell him about them and ask if he would be willing to have one?'

'Actually that is a good idea and we should have thought about it before.'

'He would probably have been too busy with the hotel to considerate it during the season, but now he and Saffron are moving down to Elounda they would both have time to take a dog for a walk.'

'I thought they were going to be busy converting the big house?'

'Mr Palamakis will be doing the work. They only have to decide on the decoration when he has finished. Vasi used to have a man locally who looked after his dogs when he wasn't there, maybe he would also like a dog of his own.'

September 2016
Week 4

Giovanni collected Pietro and Gabriella from the airport. 'So what are your plans whilst you are here?' he asked.

'Well, I have to go to Aghios Nikolaos with my papers and then I will be given a permission form that allows me to take my father's ashes back to Italy. I'm not sure if I have to make an appointment or if I just turn up at the office.'

'If you give me the phone number I'll enquire for you. You don't want to spend most of a day sitting around in an office only to be told to return another day. If you have an appointment they cannot refuse to see you.'

'I'd be really grateful. I could spend the week sitting down there and leave empty handed. Once I know when I have to go there I can plan the rest of our time. Gabriella will be happy to sit on the beach whilst I'm gone. I have to find out when I can visit Vasilis and see the tiles now they are in situ and also make arrangements to visit the Colonomakis family. Apart from that I thought I could rent a car and we could drive around and see more of the area.'

'Visiting Vasilis will be no problem. He'll be happy to see you. When you visit him John and I will go with you as neither he nor Cathy speak any Italian.'

Pietro gave a sigh of relief. 'I did wonder how I would be able to talk to them.'

Giovanni grinned, imagining the scene of hand waving and gesticulation that would take place to convey the simplest message.

'The same when you visit the Colonomakis family. John will arrange the visit and accompany you. Once you know when you can visit Aghios Nikolaos it would probably be best to arrange your visit to them next. Vasilis will fit in with whatever suits you.'

Gabriella nudged her husband. 'I thought you said you would ask Giovanni to go to Aghios Nikolaos with you? If the people you have to deal with only speak Greek you will have no idea what you are being asked.'

Pietro looked embarrassed. 'You've all been so good to me I didn't like to ask for more favours.'

'Rubbish. Greek people are only too pleased to help a foreigner if they can.'

Pietro was not sure of the veracity of that statement. The Colonomakis family had been most unhelpful to his father and shot him before they knew why he was visiting them.

'Vasi does not speak Italian, but the receptionists at the hotel speak a number of languages fluently. They will be able to understand any requests that you make so don't hesitate to ask them for anything that you need. I'm sorry we couldn't ask you to stay with us, but my mother in law is here at present.'

'We were very comfortable when we stayed there before,' Pietro assured him.

Giovanni checked that Pietro had all the official papers he would need to enable the release of his father's body to be repatriated to Italy and then accompanied Pietro to Aghios Nikolaos. It seemed to take an age as they were moved from one department to another, the same questions being asked time and time again and the official papers being scrutinized. Sheets of paper were filled in with Pietro's details and requiring his signature before they were countersigned and an official stamp placed on them.

Finally they were handed to him and he was told that if he took them to the morgue he could make arrangements for the body to be released and placed on the flight he planned to take back to Italy.

Back at the car Pietro mopped his forehead. 'I found that a most unnerving experience. I kept expecting to be told that I had given them the wrong information and I would end up in jail.'

Giovanni grinned at him. 'Not at all. I expect I would have found it just as disconcerting if I did not speak the language. It was really all very straightforward, but papers were needed in every department and they would not accept photocopies.'

'I expect it would be the same in Italy, but I've never had to deal with a situation like this. It was not so complicated when I collected my grandfather's remains.'

'That was because he was a victim of the war so entitled to be returned to his country of origin. This time you had to deal with a murder victim. They needed to ensure that you were not the murderer and entitled to claim the body. Be thankful that you did not decide to press charges against the family. Can you imagine the hours you would have spent in court being cross questioned?'

Pietro shuddered. 'I will be very relieved when he is back in Italy and we can have a proper burial ceremony. Only then will I feel that the whole episode can be put behind me.'

'I'll take you to the morgue now and help you with any problems you encounter there. Then I suggest you and Gabriella have a couple of days relaxing before you arrange to meet the Colonomakis family.'

'I still feel a little unsure about the reception I might receive.'

'I'm sure you have no need to worry. They are not likely to take a gun to you and John will be with you.' Giovanni reassured the Italian.

Vasilis welcomed Pietro and Gabriella, along with Giovanni and John.

'Please explain to our guests that they are welcome, but neither

Cathy nor I speak Italian.'

'That is why Pappa and I have come with them. I'm sure Vasilis will want to show you around the rest of his house when you have admired the floor tiles. I suggest that Cathy, Gabriella and I go off on a conducted tour and later you can go around with Vasilis. It won't take long and I know Cathy will have refreshments ready for us on the outside patio afterwards.'

Cathy found it tiring as she led Gabriella and John through the rooms and had to wait for John to interpret Gabriella's comments and then her reply. Gabriella was entranced by the kitchen.

'Everywhere is magnificent, but your kitchen is out of this world. You have every possible device you could possibly need. I wish my kitchen was as well equipped.'

John laughed. 'I can see Pietro is going to have a hard time when you return and decide you want your kitchen renovated.'

Gabriella shook her head. 'After looking here I would like the whole house remodelled but I can't see that happening. Even our tiles will look old and worn after seeing these.'

'Shall we take Gabriella out to see the garden?' suggested John. 'I know you love to show it off, Cathy.'

'It is my pride and joy. The house is beautiful, but apart from a little dusting and sweeping there is little for me to do inside. In the garden I can always find something that needs to be done with the plants. Vasilis is very good. He does the watering for me if Blerim is not visiting to clean the windows or sweep around outside.'

Gabriella commented admiringly on the display of flowers in the containers. 'They look like the ones we saw when we visited your house. There is one down by the gate and some others in an area further up with a table and chairs.'

'They are part of the stock that Uncle Yannis has back at the house. He hates to see them being used as planters. My mother was just pleased that so many had been removed. There are still plenty more pots of various shapes, sizes and designs that Uncle Yannis is trying to sell. He had a shop originally and when he closed down he brought everything back to the house. Occasionally he makes a sale and I also advertise them on the internet for him.'

'Do visitors buy them to take back home with them?'

'Some of the small ones. The larger ones usually go to a museum and are displayed as replicas. Local people will buy one or two to use as planters as Cathy has. It is not exactly brisk business, but it keeps Uncle Yannis occupied and happy. It's a bit of a chore to take all the smaller ones in and out each day, but we leave the pithoi out there until the end of the season. I'm not prepared to shift those continually as it takes two of us. Shall we go back to the patio? You can sit and admire the view whilst I help Cathy to bring us refreshments.'

Gabriella looked at the pool enviously. 'That looks so inviting. I wish I had brought my costume with me.'

'You're welcome to come another day to use it, unless you can persuade John to go back and collect your costume.'

John raised his eyebrows at Gabriella and she shook her head. 'I'll not impose on you further. Do you use the pool, Cathy?'

'Every day. I enjoy swimming up and down and I also do my physio exercises in there. The water takes the weight of my body so I don't feel in the least tired when I have completed them.'

It was early afternoon by the time that Pietro and his wife left, thanking Vasilis and Cathy profusely and hoping they would be able to meet up again before they went home. Cathy was exhausted and declared that she was going to have a rest.

'They are very nice people, but I found it so frustrating having to wait for John to interpret everything.'

Vasilis placed an arm around her shoulders. 'I agree, it was difficult. We don't have to invite them again unless you want to ask Gabriella to come for a swim. I was pleased that Pietro was so impressed by the tiles now he has seen them in situ.'

'He's probably going to have a hard time when they get home as Gabriella wants her kitchen remodelled.'

Vasilis smiled and shrugged. 'He would probably do better to find a property where the kitchen has already been updated than suffer the upheaval and disruption in his current house. You go and rest for as long as you want. I'm going to check the accounts that Dimitra has sent through so I am going to be fully occupied for quite a while.'

John telephoned Pietro. 'I've arranged for you to visit the Colonomakis family tomorrow. Does that fit in with your plans?'

'Of course. Tell me the time you would like me to be ready.'

Pietro had to tell Gabriella that their plans for the following day had been changed. 'I could hardly refuse. There's no need for you to come with me so you can stay here and have the morning on the beach.'

'I thought we were going into Aghios Nikolaos,' frowned Gabriella.

'I doubt if I shall be there that long so we could go in this afternoon or have a drive around in a different direction. Aghios Nikolaos is just another town and I don't imagine it has anything very different from Elounda.'

John arrived promptly to collect Pietro and drove up the main road until they reached the walled property that belonged to the Colonomakis family. John alighted from the car and opened the wooden gate, drove through and then closed it again carefully before continuing.

'I don't think they have any animals that would stray out onto the road, but you can't be too careful.'

Pietro was feeling nervous, he clenched and unclenched his hands as they drove up the path to the house. Three women and a man were sitting outside waiting for them and he swallowed hard. These people were murderers. Was it safe to visit them?

As John parked his car the man stood up and stepped forward.

'I understand that this could be a difficult meeting, but I can assure you that we mean you no harm and only wish to explain our actions to you.'

John translated for Pietro who gave a slight smile. 'We may as well get off on an amicable footing. Please tell them that I appreciate their willingness to meet me.'

Pietro and John walked over to the empty chairs that were underneath an awning and greeted the ladies who were sitting there.

'I am Christos. This is my wife, Despina Elena, my mother in law, Adonia Evangelina and her mother, Despina Maria.' He indicated each lady with his hand. 'Can we offer you a drink? There is beer in the fridge or fruit juice if you prefer it.'

The men chose beer and Despina Elena and Adonia hurried inside to produce the bottles, glasses and a plate of biscuits. There was a strained silence, then Despina Elena began to speak.

'As a family we have to apologise for our actions. Not for shooting the soldiers during the war. My great grandparents had no way of knowing if the soldiers were friendly or if they had come to take them prisoner or kill them.' She spread her hands. 'They knew of the atrocities that were taking place in many of the villages. It was self defence on their part.'

John translated rapidly and Pietro nodded. 'Please tell them that I understand their actions. I am sure the local people would have declared their actions heroic.'

'My great grandparents never told anyone, but the disappearance of the soldiers was talked about in the community and I understand that the villagers considered who ever had killed the men were heroes. Although other soldiers were sent out to look for their bodies they were not found and no one pointed the finger at our family. Eventually the search was given up. I think the family had forgotten about the incident until your father came and wanted to know if they had any information.'

'He meant no harm. He just wanted to know what had happened to his father,' protested Pietro.

'Understandable, but my grandfather did not know that and

unfortunately he gave him no chance to explain. He thought your father could be from the Italian authorities and as such was threatening his family. I think my grandfather fired his gun to frighten him away. According to my grandmother they were both shocked when they found the man was dead. They panicked and decided they must get rid of his body which is how he ended up being buried on the patch of waste ground down by the shore. I knew nothing about the incident until the police came and informed us that a body had been found. We need to apologise to you for those actions and ask your understanding and forgiveness.'

'Why did no one come forward when his body was discovered?' asked Pietro.

'The disclosure sent my grandmother into a complete panic. She was convinced that she would be arrested and sent to jail for murder, although she had not fired the gun. It was only then that she told us of the events that had occurred. She had never spoken of it before. We assured her that we would tell no one. We tried to protect her when the policeman came and wanted to speak to her, but he was insistent and finally she had to tell him the truth. She admits that she should have confessed earlier for the sake of your mother.'

Despina Maria sat there nodding her head and fingering the cross she wore around her neck. 'I am sorry. I have suffered from guilt for many years, but she has suffered the loss of her husband and not knowing what had happened to him.'

Pietro looked at John and shrugged. 'What can I say except that I understand their actions during the war, but I cannot condone them for shooting my father who came here making an innocent enquiry. Had they allowed him the time to explain they could have declared that they had no knowledge of the incident and sent him away. I accept that they did not mean to kill him, only frighten him and were too scared of the repercussions to confess to his murder. I am only relieved that I am now able to take his remains back to Italy and give him the proper burial that he deserves. I have met with them as they requested and I think now that the matter should be forgotten.'

Pietro placed his empty glass on the table and stood up. 'Thank you for your hospitality and explaining your actions to me.' He began to walk back towards the car.

John stood and shook hands with everyone, explaining that the Italian needed some time to himself to think about the information he had been given.

'Now you've done your duty by Pietro shall we speak to Vasi and ask him if he would like a dog?' asked Nicola.

John nodded. 'We could at least ask him if he would be interested. We could call on him and Saffron this morning. If they are busy we don't have to stay.'

'I don't think they will be that busy until Mr Palamakis has finished decorating the big house. She and Vasi are hoping that it will be ready to rent out to guests by the beginning of next season so they may not want to become involved with looking after a dog.'

'That could be a bit ambitious. Vasi knows how to run a hotel but to let out self catering apartments is somewhat different. I hope he realises what he has undertaken. There will have to be someone there to let visitors in and also to check them out to ensure that they've not done any damage and then left without paying for it.'

'I'm sure Vasi will have thought of every eventuality,' answered Nicola placatingly. She was not going to become involved in Vasi and Saffron's venture.

Saffron and Vasi were sitting on the sofa looking at a programme on the internet.

'Just in time to give your opinion,' said Saffron as she opened the door to them.

Nicola raised her eyebrows? 'Really? We came to ask you for your opinion about an idea that had come to us.'

'I can offer you some coffee and biscuits,' said Saffron. 'I'm afraid I have been too lazy to do any baking and I haven't been out this morning to buy anything special.'

'That's no problem. You were not expecting us and we won't stay that long. You look as if you are busy.'

'This is what I would like your opinion about. Give me a minute and I'll be back.'

'We'll put our suggestion to Vasi and if he thinks it's practical he can discuss it with you later. We don't need an immediate decision.'

Vasi raised his eyebrows. 'This sounds intriguing. Tell me more.'

'Well,' John sat down beside him, 'You remember that we found some pups and their mother who had been abandoned and we took them down to the sanctuary the other side of Aghios.'

'I remember your father complaining that you had taken them back to the taverna,' smiled Vasi.

'By the time I returned from the shelter Nick had done a wonderful cleaning job and you would never have known they had been there. We went down the other week to check up on them and two pups and their mother are still there. We're a bit concerned that if they are not rehoused soon the woman who runs the sanctuary will say she can no longer keep them and you know what that would mean.'

Vasi nodded. 'Very sad, but the sanctuaries cannot keep dogs indefinitely even if they are young and healthy.'

'We know how fond of dogs you are, and we wondered if you would consider taking one.'

'Me? I had dogs when I lived up at the big house, but a dog is hardly suitable for an apartment.'

'Many people do have a dog that lives in their apartment. They only need to be taken out for a walk and these are not big dogs like you had before. They don't need a lot of space and need to run free all day.'

'What's this about a dog?' asked Saffron as she brought in

the tray with coffee and biscuits. 'Do you want us to look after Skele for you for a while?'

John shook his head. 'No, we are here to ask if you would contemplate actually having a dog of your own.'

'Here? In this apartment?'

'They are not big dogs.' John held his hand a distance up from the floor. 'The mother is about that high and the pups are going to be about the same size when they are grown. We rescued six, three were taken by visitors back to Europe and one was re-homed locally. That leaves two and their mother. You and Vasi discuss it when we have gone and let us know. We will understand if you refuse.'

Saffron looked at Vasi and could see the enthusiasm in his eyes. She had a feeling that whatever she said Vasi had already made up his mind.

'Now,' she said quickly. 'I would like your opinion. I have asked Ronnie to work out colour schemes for the rooms in the big house. Have you any ideas?'

'How large are these rooms going to be?' asked Nicola.

'They will be the same size as they are at present. We were sitting here thinking about the bathroom tiles. We don't want them to look like hospital bathrooms and the current tiles need to be replaced. Over the years some have become stained and the grout no longer looks clean and white.'

'Coloured tiles could work with white and chrome fitments to break up the slabs of colour, or maybe just coloured tiles in the shower cubicle and white elsewhere.'

'I've asked Ronnie for suggestions. She knows which colours go best together. I don't want to make a mistake and make the rooms look garish and cheap or full of frills and flounces like a brothel.'

Nicola laughed. 'Vasilis would have a fit if he thought you were turning the house into a brothel.'

Saffron nodded. 'That's why I want everywhere to look perfect.'

Vasi appeared deep in thought. 'John, tell me more about these dogs? Are they healthy? Are they dogs or bitches?'

'The two pups are bitches, as is their mother of course. I gave the woman at the sanctuary money to cover their food and veterinary fees. It should have been sufficient to cover all their vaccinations.'

'Have they been spayed?' asked Vasi.

'I don't know. She may have decided that operation unnecessary and too expensive in case she had to have them destroyed eventually.'

'I certainly cannot make a decision without discussing it with Saffie. If she agrees then we would want to see the dogs.'

'Of course. Think about it, talk it over together and let me know. I'll understand if you say no.'

John left Vasi and Saffron feeling hopeful. Vasi had not given an outright refusal.

October 2016

Vasilis sat and dozed gently on the sofa. He was feeling happy and content. They had entertained one afternoon and evening each week. Now they had a short respite until the end of the season and then they would have to invite the rest of their friends whose businesses would have closed by that time. Everyone who had visited his house had complimented him upon it and admired the view. He felt their comments had been genuine. Most importantly of all Cathy appeared so happy there. She used the pool each morning whilst it was still warm and occasionally again in the afternoon. She found that using her electric chair far easier along the coast road than in the village. She was able to ride in the road and not have to continually negotiate kerbs, parked vehicles and pedestrians. The traffic she encountered was patient with her and gave her time and space to pass them. Vasilis had accompanied her at first but when he realised that she was more than capable of going out alone he no longer worried when she said she was going out for a drive.

The added bonus was the lift that gave her independence and she now used it with confidence, manoeuvring herself into her electric chair upstairs at the apartment and opening the door to the garage entrance with the electric control that was attached to the arm of the chair. Even when she did not go out Cathy seemed happy to sit in the shelter of the patio or even inside in the lounge and look out across the sea. She declared that there was always something to look at, unlike when they lived up at the big house or in the apartment in Elounda.

As the weather had become cooler Vasilis had arranged for Mr Palamakis and Blerim to visit and place the large carpet squares that had been removed from the big house over the floor tiles in the lounge, hallway and their bedroom. He was not entirely happy with them, but they had been carefully secured at the edges where they met so that Cathy would not catch her foot and trip. The squares might be suitable for the big house after the renovation had taken place and then Cathy would be able to choose the design and colour of new ones for next winter.

Whilst Kyriakos had spent time with his mother and at the taverna Ronnie had worked out some colour schemes for the big house to show Saffron and sat and read through Eirini's memoirs a second time. She looked at the original lists that she had made and added more queries to them. The next time that Kyriakos went down to Elounda to visit his mother she would ask him to take her to Yannis's house so she could give the manuscript to John and Nicola. Once they had read it she would ask John if he could visit them in Kastelli and see if old Cassie had any useful information about the family.

Saffron began to clear her shelves and pack her stock away. Trade had dwindled during the last two weeks giving her plenty of time. She made copious lists and labelled the boxes carefully. At least this year she would only have to take them back to the apartment in Elounda and she hoped there would be sufficient space to store them. Vasi had promised that if it appeared to be a problem he could have them at the hotel until she planned to open up the shop again in the following season.

Ronnie sat in Saffron's shop watching her pack her remaining stock. She had offered to help, but Saffron had only asked her pass items to her. Whilst Saffron wrapped them and placed them in the boxes Ronnie was thoroughly bored.

'I feel I am rather useless to you. I had hoped we could discuss my ideas for the decoration of the big house.'

'Go ahead. I can listen and comment whilst I pack,' Saffron smiled.

'I just want you to consider my current thoughts. You may not like them and then I will have to think again.'

'Tell me and then I can either say I like your ideas or give you a definite no. I'll have to run them past Vasi; after all it is his house now.'

'Well, depending how many bedrooms you have with a bathroom en suite I thought they could be colour themed. Nothing too bright or garish. Maybe a blue room, white walls, blue drapery and bedding and pale blue tiles in the bathroom area. Then the same for a green room and yellow room.'

Saffron nodded. 'I like that idea. We have decided that four bedrooms and bathrooms are quite sufficient. Originally we had thought about having six. That could have meant that twelve people were staying there and all trying to use the kitchen at the same time.'

'How do you feel about lilac?'

'That covers the four.'

'I thought pink would be best avoided. How do you feel about flowers or leaves? If you don't like lilac one could be a Spring room with the curtains and bedding having flowers or an Autumn room with leaves on the furnishings.'

Saffron smiled. 'Those are good ideas. What about the bathroom areas?'

'You could go for white tiles and have them interspersed with either the flowers or leaves to carry on the theme from the bedroom.'

Saffron looked at Ronnie in appreciation. 'Now you know why I asked your advice. When I helped Vasi design his apartment years ago I spent hours looking on the internet for ideas. You seem able to pluck the most suitable ideas from thin air.'

'They are only ideas and can be adapted or changed however you want.'

'Leave it with me. I'm sure Vasi will approve.'

Monika listed her current stock of books on the computer and made a note of those that had sold well during the season. She would need to order more for next year, buts she could tackle that chore later. She only planned to have the shop open two mornings each week once the season ended. Local people knew how to contact her if they had a particular requirement or wanted to come in for a short while to browse and buy a book to read during the winter. She was now looking forward to visiting Vasilis and Cathy at their new house, along with her mother and Theo.

Yiorgo arranged for his boat to be placed in the dry dock so that he would be able to view the underside and do any repairs and maintenance that was necessary. He was pleased he was going to work at the 'Imperia' again during the winter months so he would have a regular income and not have to ask his grandfather for any of the building work that he hated. Vasilis had arranged for him and Barbara to visit them at his new house the following week and due to his proximity he had watched the exterior taking shape with interest. Now he was curious to see exactly what Vasilis had done inside.

Ronnie packed up her easel and paints and took them back to the self catering apartments. There were few people visiting Plaka now. She had spent time visiting Kyriakos's mother and had to admit that their relationship had improved. Mr Palamakis had visited her and assured her that the latest work he had been commissioned to do at the house was completed and now she was longing to decide what work should be done next to the main house.

'Do you want to hear more about Eirini and what happened to her?' she asked Kyriakos.

'Have you finally finished reading it?'

'I've read it through a second time to make sure I hadn't missed any relevant information.'

'Tell me whilst I get ready to visit my mother. Did she find Lucas?' asked Kyriakos as he bent to lace his shoes.

'Whilst she was helping on Spinalonga Eirini became friendly with my great grandparents. They realised the man living two doors away from them could be the Lucas from Fourni whom she had loved. When he returned home that day they asked him if he knew a girl from Fourni called Eirini and he said he had been courting her.'

'How hadn't she seen him if she was working over there?'

'Well, for a start she didn't know he was there so she wasn't looking for him and their paths had just not crossed. There were an awful lot of people living there.'

'So how did she expect to be able to find his uncle?'

Ronnie smiled. 'She just hadn't thought it through. She did not know his uncle's name and had no idea what he looked like. She seemed to think she would find him by asking for Lucas's uncle.'

'Pretty naive of her.'

'She was only about sixteen and had led rather a sheltered and unworldly life in both Fourni and Elounda. She was probably quite pleased to get away from her aunt for part of the week.'

'I'm surprised she was allowed to go over there.'

'She had the agreement of the doctor and the blessing of the priest. She had convinced them she was doing a penance to ask forgiveness for her sins so her aunt and uncle could hardly refuse her permission. She certainly knew how to be devious to get what she wanted.'

'She found Lucas had admitted himself voluntarily to the island when he realised he was infected and just told his family that he was going to Aghios Nikolaos.'

'Did they believe him?'

'Apparently. Of course having finally found Lucas they resumed their relationship and she became pregnant again. There was no way she could go and live on Spinalonga and she begged to be able to stay in Elounda so she could visit him, taking the children over with her. Her father refused to contemplate the idea.'

'I'm not surprised. She would probably have ended up having more children or becoming infected.'

'She was prepared to take that risk.'

'Ronnie, how old was she by then - about seventeen? She had no real comprehension of the consequences.'

'They could at least have let her stay in Elounda so they could see each other,' replied Ronnie mutinously.

'Suppose she or one of her children had developed leprosy? She had to put their welfare first. Sooner or later the villagers would have discovered that she was having a relationship with a man on Spinalonga. They would have shunned her and the other village children would not have been allowed to mix with hers.'

'That was a medieval attitude,' replied Ronnie scornfully.

'You have to remember that until after the war life over here was very different from the way it is today. People did not move around very much, they tended to stay in their villages, marry the girl next door and most of the inhabitants were related to each other. Formal education, particularly for girls was considered unnecessary. They would have learnt how to cook, clean and weave from their mothers and no one asked any more of them. Anyone who deviated from tradition was eyed with suspicion. Illness, particularly leprosy, was to be avoided.'

'Very ignorant and short sighted of them,' replied Ronnie.

'If you knew no better a cut that did not heal as expected made them dread having a limb amputated or being diagnosed with leprosy and sent to Spinalonga. You are looking at life as it is now and not the way it was then.'

Ronnie sighed. 'I suppose you are right. We take so much for granted nowadays. I find it difficult to believe how ignorant the people were a hundred years ago.'

'Bear in mind that life everywhere was very different before the war that ripped Europe apart and caused so much suffering. What happened when she was pregnant again?'

'That was when her parents decided to take her to Australia.'

'That was a bit drastic, wasn't it? Why didn't they just move to Heraklion or Chania?'

'I think they wanted to ensure that she could never return to the area.'

'But to take her off to Australia! That really was extreme. Surely they could have moved to another island or even mainland Greece? What must it have been like for her? Pregnant and having to go on a long sea voyage.' Kyriakos frowned. 'Weren't her parents with her?' asked Kyriakos as he buttoned his shirt.

'Oh, yes, she wasn't alone as such, but it still must have worried her. She must have suffered nightmares that the ship would sink and she might not be able to rescue Little Luke.'

'I imagine her father was also worried. After all, he was responsible for all of them. Did they have any relatives over there that they could stay with?'

'No. They seemed to have arrived knowing no one and only having a limited knowledge of the language.'

'I think her father made a very rash decision. It would be one thing for a young man to go out there to try his luck and hope to make his fortune, but to take your family there without even knowing the language seems utter foolishness to me.'

'Well,' Ronnie hesitated, 'She seems to have settled down and worked in a shop and also at a tavern to earn enough money for them to live decently. She touches briefly on the war and how it affected them. Her friend's husband was killed and she has no idea if any of her relatives in Crete are still alive. She expects that Lucas is safe enough as he is on Spinalonga.'

'Of course, she would have no way of knowing that the

Germans stopped supplies going over so that so many died from starvation,' said Kyriakos as he tucked his shirt into his trousers.

'I'm so pleased that John found out that Lucas survived and finally went to the hospital in Athens. That must have been a comfort to her when she was told. What's more she described the house where Fotini and Aristo lived. It had blue curtains. I must have found the correct house when I discovered the curtain ring. If only I had known that when Luke was here.'

'What difference would that have made? You painted a picture that the old lady said was just as she remembered the area.'

'I could have asked if I could communicate with his mother and ask her to tell me everything she could remember about them. Eirini knew my great grandparents and Luke played with my grandmother.'

'Wasn't that all in the papers and letters that John and Nicola translated for you?'

'There was a good deal of information about them, but it would have been wonderful to speak to someone who actually knew them.'

'You'll have to tell me more later.' Kyriakos looked at his watch. 'I need to go now. My mother will be anxious if I am late arriving.'

Kyriakos propped himself up comfortable on the pillows next to Ronnie when they returned from the taverna that evening. 'So tell me more about this girl going to Australia.'

'You're treating it like a bedtime story,' giggled Ronnie.

'Hearing your voice makes me relax and forget the problems of the day. I will be so glad when I no longer have to visit my mother each morning and have her complain that I am hurting her when I put that brace on her leg. The last X-ray showed that the break is healing well so she may not need that support for very much longer.'

'Well,' Ronnie tried to recall where she had left off that

morning. 'She met an Australian man out there who had been sent to Crete during the war and had to walk to Preveli to escape.'

'Did he have any news of her family?'

'Of course not. Even if he had met them he would not know they were related to Eirini. He talked to her father, but was somewhat reticent about the information he gave to her.'

'I'm not surprised. Who wants to hear about the atrocities that were committed?'

'The world generally should know so that such a thing never happens again, although I don't want to hear the grisly details.'

'And this Australian that she met who had been in Crete? What happened with him?'

'Well, by all she says she led a blameless life, bur Fred, the Australian, wanted to marry her. She gives the impression that she was not happy living with her parents so she may have seen him as a way of escaping. She agrees and foolishly becomes pregnant again.'

'So he left her.'

'Not at all. Apparently he was delighted. They were married and he carried her off to his ranch in the outback where she had quite a number of other children and lived there until Luke decided they should move to the town of Broome. There is a good deal more I can tell you about her life there, but that can wait. I want to ask John if he can find out some details about the family and where they lived in Fourni.'

'What was their name?'

'So far she hasn't mentioned anyone's name.'

'So how would you expect John to find them?' asked Kyriakos.

'I'm sure someone must know the name of the school teacher. The villagers may have known the family had gone to Australia; that would surely have been a talking point and Lucas had a brother, he may have married and his children might still live there.'

'Why do you want to know?'

Ronnie smiled. 'Curiosity, I suppose.'

'You're becoming a bad as John wanting to know everyone's family history.'

'If John and Nicola hadn't translated the old diaries that I found in my Kastelli house I would never have known about my great grandparents or my grandmother. It shouldn't be that difficult to track this family down,' said Ronnie confidently. 'When are you planning to close the taverna?'

'The end of this week. We've had so few customers during this week that it's pointless staying open and buying food. I'll be able to spend a bit more time with my mother now she is progressing. I can go down early in the morning and strap the brace on her leg and see to her needs. There will no longer be the need for a night nurse. I also have to take her to the hospital for another X-ray to ensure her bone is mending as it should. If they are pleased with her she may be able to leave that brace off.'

'Are we going up to Kastelli then?'

'No reason why we shouldn't. When I clear the freezer I'll bring everything back here and we can take it up to Kastelli with us.'

'I hope there will be a reasonable variety. I hate eating the same thing day after day.'

'We can always buy other items for you to make a meal or go to the taverna in Kastelli. We'll just have to keep an eye on the 'use by' dates.'

Ronnie looked at the calendar that hung on the wall. 'I'll check with Saffie when she's closing. I need to chat to her some more about my decorative ideas for the big house and hear what Vasi had to say about them. I'd rather meet her whilst we're still living down here than make a special journey.'

'That's no problem. I will have to come down regularly to visit my mother. You arrange a meeting with Saffie and I can fit in around that.'

Ronnie smiled at him gratefully. She had not relished the

possibility of having to take a taxi both ways. 'I also want to deliver Eirini's memoirs to John for him and Nicola to read.'

Kyriakos shrugged. He saw no urgency for the meeting with Saffron or delivering the papers to John.

'I'll also have to buy some books from Monika. I hope she'll have the same arrangement as last year when you could take them back and get another for half the price. How are you planning to spend your time?'

'I haven't thought much about it yet. It will depend how my mother progresses. I can't expect our friends to continually go in to her and take her meals. Once the taverna is closed down I can do that every day. Once she has recovered I'll have to spend some time at the taverna giving it a thorough clean and then decorating as necessary.'

'Don't forget we are due to visit Vasilis and Cathy and view their new house. I have that pencilled in as being next week. I understand that Saffie and Vasi will be there, but I don't want to spend all evening talking about colour schemes.'

Once Kyriakos had left Ronnie took a piece of plain paper and began to make a list of her queries. When she and Kyriakos returned to Kastelli they would be able to make enquiries locally about the family. She would ask John for help in tracing Eirini's father and finding the family's surname. There was also the uncle who had worked as a manager at the salt pans, there should be a record of him. It was quite likely that the Tsantakis family still lived locally; and then there was the mysterious aunt who had lived in Elounda and Eirini knew nothing about.

The fact that Luke had played with her great grandmother on Spinalonga made her feel bonded to him and she was sure he would like to have the answers to her questions and any further information she could discover. She would not mention this in the email she would send to him, telling him she had finished reading his mother's story and found it fascinating. She had to face the fact that she might not be able to find out anything and she would not want to raise his hopes.

Some parts of Eirini's life had been so sad, but she had obviously been a woman of strong character. When she had more time she would read the life story again, sure she had missed some details having read only a few pages at a time as the opportunity arose due to working at the taverna and visiting Irini. There were so many questions she would like to have answered.

November 2016
Week One

Ronnie read the book that she had purchased from Monika from cover to cover but she could not find the information she had been looking for. There were accounts of a school that had operated in Elounda and photos of the teachers. There was also mention of one in Plaka and another in Pines but nothing about a school in Kastelli. Finally giving up she asked Kyriakos to take her to the shop close to the self catering accommodation hoping she would find John there.

'Shall I wait for you?' asked Kyriakos.

Ronnie shook her head. 'Skele is sitting outside so John must be there. I don't know how long I'll be with him. If you phone me later when you have visited your mother I'll be grateful for a lift back to Kastelli. If it isn't convenient for you I can always have a taxi.'

Ronnie pushed open the door. 'John, may I come in?'

John straightened up from where he was cleaning the inside of a freezer. 'I'll be happy to take a break from this horrible job.'

'I'm hoping you may be able to help me?'

John raised his eyebrows. 'If I can. I'll be going into Aghios Nikolaos later this week if you need any paint or paper.'

'Thanks for the offer, but I'm well stocked at present and shouldn't need more until next season. You remember you found out that Lucas Tsantakis had gone to the hospital in Athens when the island was closed?'

'Yes, he died over there. I think he would have been in his seventies.'

'Would you be able to find out about Eirini's parents? They lived in Fourni and her father was the school teacher in Kastelli.'

'What was his name?'

'I'm not sure.' Ronnie wrinkled her forehead. 'I don't remember her mentioning her parents' names. I think her father was called Dimitris as I remember she said she had called her second son after him.'

'There should be records held at the Town Hall of all the teaching staff in the area. Have you an idea of the date when her father was there?'

'She was about seventeen when they went to Australia and I know she mentions her Citizenship papers as having her date of birth. I should be able to work out the years her father was a teacher. Would there also be a list anywhere of the men who worked at the salt pans?'

John laughed. 'I doubt that.'

'Surely there must be something in the accounts saying how much was paid out to the workers. I want to try to find out the name of the one of the supervisors. He and his wife were very religious and could well have played a role in the church. Eirini was sent to live with them when it was found that she was pregnant.'

'I can see what I can find out about the salt pans but if he was a member of the church you might find out more information there. Why are you interested, Ronnie?'

'I've finished reading Luke's mother's memoirs. She describes her life here before going to Australia and I'd like to find out more about the family. She mentions that her mother and sister owned some cottages in Fourni so they must have been quite well off. There could be something in the old village records about them.'

'How urgently do you want this information? I'm going to be somewhat busy until the end of the month,' frowned John.

'There's no rush. I thought Kyriakos and I could start some investigation when we return to Kastelli.'

'Old Cassie would probably be the best person to ask.'

'Of course. Why didn't I think of her?'

'She may not be able to remember that far back. I'm not sure how old she is.'

'Would you and Nicola be interested in reading the memoirs? You might think of a question that hasn't occurred to me.'

John smiled at Ronnie's enthusiasm. 'Drop them down to the house when convenient for you and I'm sure we'd both like to read them.'

Elena looked across the bay towards Spinalonga. The island was hardly visible as it was shrouded in low cloud. Not for the first time she thought how miserable the inhabitants of the island must have been on some days; often unable to see any land, suffering from the unrelenting heat in the summer and then the gales and cold that accompanied them during the winter. She hesitated, and then picked up her coat. She might well need that as she walked along the waterfront that day as she planned. Tomorrow Marianne was taking her up to visit Evi and Maria for the last time before she had to leave and fly back to New Orleans. She did not relish the thought. No doubt Helena would immediately begin to harass her about selling her house.

On her previous visit to Evi and Maria she had mentioned that she was considering buying a cottage in the village and asked them if they knew of anywhere that might be for sale. They had promised to ask around and had been delighted to think that she might become a neighbour and they could spend time together.

'Are you ready, Grandma?' called John and Elena picked up her coat and went to find him. 'Are you going to be warm enough with just a jumper? The wind is beginning to get up.'

'I have my coat with me. If the wind drops I will probably be too hot and then I'll have to carry it.'

As they drove into Elounda she saw that a number of tavernas had already closed down and the self catering establishments were already looking sad and deserted, although the village itself was bustling with people.

'Where would you like me to drop you?' asked John.

'I thought I'd have a last walk along the coast road.'

'I doubt if many of those tavernas are open.'

'That's no problem. It's a pleasant walk and I enjoy watching the sea if it gets rough. I shall probably go along as far as the salt pans. I heard that a heron was seen there the other day.'

'Wish I had known. I would have driven along and tried to take a photo.'

'If I see it I'll call you and you could come back.'

John shook his head. 'If it's there again today it is probably going to come back on a number of occasions so I will probably have an opportunity some other time. You enjoy your walk, but don't get cold. If you feel tired phone home and one of us will come to collect you.'

Elena set off along the coast road. John was quite correct when he said that most of the tavernas would be closed down. Tables and chairs had been stacked up inside and covered with a tarpaulin to protect them against the weather; the plastic windows that were rolled down when it was wet or windy to protect their customers had been taken down and tarpaulins had been fixed across the openings. Everywhere looked somewhat sad and abandoned. It must be the same every winter she realised, but when she had visited previously during those months she had been far too busy with Andreas and spending time up in the villages helping him with his research.

The low cloud that had hung over Spinalonga lifted gradually as the breeze increased and became a wind blowing off the water. Elena pulled on her coat, pleased she had thought to take it with her. The further she walked the more the wind seemed to increase until small waves began to wash onto the road. She shivered. It was not a good idea to walk across the Causeway. She would turn down at the salt pans and take the paved area to the other side and then walk up to the main road. It would be more sheltered up there. She stopped and scanned the murky water for any sign of the heron, but nothing was stirring, not even a ripple from a fish.

Once across the open expanse she stood where it was more sheltered and she looked back. A brave young couple were crossing the Causeway, trying hard to dodge the waves that were sending up spray on both sides. She wished she was as young and fit as they were so she could enjoy the experience with them.

A particularly strong gust of wind stopped her in her tracks. It would be more sensible to continue up the paved area to where it joined the main road. There were a few houses on the way and it would be more sheltered up there. She saw a turning leading off to the left which had high bushes on both sides making it sheltered from the wind. She had no sooner walked more than a hundred yards when the road ended and became no more than a cart track. She continued along it; maybe this was a usable path that would take her along the edge of the salt pans to where there was a taverna. If it was open she would stop and have a coffee before continuing up to the main road. She could at least investigate and it was not as windy due to the path being sheltered by the bushes. Occasionally there was a small patch of scrub land and the wind blew across that vigorously If the path did not lead to the taverna it might be a short cut up to the main road. The path seemed to become narrower the further she went until it was completely blocked by trees and bushes. Elena looked at it in annoyance; unless she could find a way through she would have to retrace her steps.

She peered as best she could through the greenery, pushing aside some of the overhanging bushes to see if it was possible to walk on. An unpleasant smell was coming from somewhere. There must be a sewerage plant or rubbish tip nearby. To her surprise she saw there was a small house hidden there. Her curiosity aroused she pushed back more of the bushes until she could see the building more clearly. It looked in a ruinous state and it was obvious that no one lived there. The smell seemed even stronger and she turned away, feeling quite nauseous. She would ask John later if he knew anything about it.

Vasi thought about the dogs that John had told him about. He had loved dogs ever since his grandfather had given him Monty and hated the thought that they were living in kennels. Dogs needed love and care. It was not an ideal situation now he and Saffron were living in an apartment in the town. A dog would have to be taken for a walk at least twice every day whatever the weather. Saffron would not have time to do that when she reopened the gift shop.

His working hours were more flexible, but would he have sufficient time? He could get up earlier and take the dog for a walk then, leave the hotel for a short break at midday instead of working through as usual and then take the dog out in the evening before Saffron arrived home.

He was not at all sure how she would feel about having a dog inside the apartment with them during the winter. He needed to talk to her and if she did agree then he would want to see the dogs before he decided to take one. He looked around their lounge. The space where Cathy had kept her wheelchair could accommodate a dog bed.

'Saffie, how would you feel about having a dog around?' he asked that evening.

Saffron smiled. 'Would it make any difference if I said I hated dogs or was allergic to them? You've made up your mind that you want one.'

'Only if you agree,' Vasi assured her.

'Out of season it would be no problem, but what happens when we are both back at work? I couldn't leave the shop to take it for a walk.'

'I wouldn't expect you to. That would be my responsibility. I can walk it in the early morning and evening and steal a little time away from the hotel during the day.'

'Is this apartment large enough to have a dog living here? If we were still up at the big house there was the large garden where it could run free.'

'John said they were not big dogs, not like the ones I had up there originally.'

'Don't you think you should see them before you make a decision?'

'Definitely. I wouldn't want to find that I had committed us to having a German Shepherd, but nor would I want a dachshund. I'd also want to know that the dog was healthy to start with. If there was anything physically wrong I wouldn't consider it. I could find that in about six months it had to be destroyed.'

'So why don't you phone John and arrange to go to the sanctuary with him and have a look at the dogs yourself? There is one proviso, you are not to bring them all back here!'

'Would you come with me? I wouldn't want to decide on one that did not take to you or you felt threatened by.'

Saffron smiled. 'Well, at least if I was with you I could insist that you only brought back one.'

John was pleased when Vasi phoned and asked if he would be willing to take him and Saffron down to the animal sanctuary.

'I'd like to have a look at the dogs before I make a final decision. I've discussed it with Saffron and at the moment it would be no problem to take a dog for a walk. Once the season starts I may have to find a dog walker.'

'I'm sure that would not be a problem. Many people are happy to take a dog with them when they go out walking. When do you want to go to the sanctuary?'

'Tomorrow would be fine if it suits you.'

'I'll be with you about ten. It takes a couple of hours to drive down there and I'm sure we can find a taverna somewhere to have a snack.'

With far less traffic on the road now the tourists had left it took John less than two hours to drive to the sanctuary with Vasi and Saffron. He parked outside the gates and used his mobile to phone the owner.

'Do you remember me? I brought a bitch and six pups down to you some time ago. I have some friends with me who would like to have a look at the two pups and the bitch you still have.'

'I'll let you in, but I only have the one pup left now.'

The woman led the way to the compound where the dogs were housed. Inside was the bitch with one puppy.

'A farmer came a while back and took the other pup.'

'May I handle the dog?' asked Vasi.

'Certainly.' The woman went into the compound and scooped the puppy up in her arms. 'She's getting a bit big to be carried about now,' she stated as she placed the dog on the ground and held it by the scruff of it's neck.

Vasi picked the puppy up and examined its eyes and ears, then felt it's stomach and ran his hand down its spine.

'You say she's been vaccinated?'

The woman nodded. 'I have her papers back in the office. The vet gave her a clean bill of health when he checked her over.'

Vasi looked at Saffron. 'Yes?'

'If you're happy with her.'

'I'll take her.'

A look of relief crossed the woman's face. One less dog to feed and care for during the winter months. 'Come up to the office.'

Vasi placed the dog carefully back in the compound and its mother immediately came over and sniffed at her before they laid down side by side.

Having looked at the certificates Vasi nodded. 'All seems in order. Have you a collar and lead I can put on her? That way I can keep control of her. She's not used to being in a car and I want to sit in the back and keep her close to me. I don't want her leaping into the front onto the driver and causing an accident.'

The woman produced a somewhat frayed lead and a leather collar. 'This should do until you can buy her something more appropriate.'

They retraced their steps to the compound and the woman placed the collar around the dog's neck and clipped the lead in place. 'That collar is a bit loose, I suggest you hold her by that so she cannot slip her head out.'

Vasi took a firm grip on the collar and they began to walk away. Saffron looked back. The bitch had dropped her head and flattened her ears. She gave a low whine.

Vasi hesitated. 'I can't leave her. I'll take the bitch as well.'

Saffron smiled. 'I thought it was only the English who were sentimental about animals. Are you sure, Vasi? We agreed on one dog.'

'A second will make very little difference. They can be walked together at the same time.'

Saffron shook her head. 'I was supposed to come with you to ensure that you only returned with one. Thank goodness all six pups were not still here.'

Elena packed her case sadly. Although she had no desire to spend the winter months in Elounda she was not looking forward to returning to New Orleans. Sooner or later she would be forced into making a decision about selling her house and moving elsewhere, but she had decided that she would stay there until she finally found somewhere she felt was suitable. She had told John about the ruined house she had seen on her walk from the salt pans but John said he knew nothing about it. During her final visit to Evi and Maria she had mentioned to them that she would like to buy a small cottage in their village if one became available. They were delighted to think that she would become their neighbour and she had not disclosed that she had no intention of living up in the village.

November 2016
Week Two

'I thought we could drive up to Kastelli today, meet Ronnie and take Old Cassie out for lunch and see if she can tell us anything about the Tsantakis family or Eirini,' suggested John. 'I know Ronnie had said she and Ackers would meet her and see what they could find out, but Ackers only knows what Ronnie has told him and he's been so busy with his mother that I doubt if he's remembered very much.'

'That sounds like a good idea, but I can't come with you. The children are at the dentist this afternoon for their check up. I can't ask your Mum or Bryony to take them in case Yiannis makes a fuss. Give Ronnie a call and see if it's convenient for her. You can tell me later whatever information you managed to get from Old Cassie.'

'It's not every day that you want to take me across the road for my lunch. It must mean you want something from me,' said Old Cassie as she gave a toothless grin. She picked up her stick and allowed John to help her to hobble across the road to the taverna where Ronnie was waiting.

John smiled as he poured a helping of whisky into the old lady's glass. 'You are too astute by far. We would like to ask you about some of your memories from when you were a child or young girl.'

'That was a long time ago.'

'We'll understand if you cannot remember. You were so helpful previously telling us about the tax collector who lived in Ronnie's house. It was also thanks to your sharp eyes that Babbis was prosecuted for setting fire to the property.'

Cassie shrugged and held out her glass to be refilled. 'So what do you want to know?'

John related the story of Luke asking Ronnie to paint some pictures of Spinalonga so he could take them back to his mother in Australia and that Luke had subsequently sent Ronnie a copy of his mother's memoirs. 'Do you know the Tsantakis family?'

Cassie shook he head. 'Not really. They lived somewhere over by Fourni. I did hear that one of them had been diagnosed with leprosy and sent to Spinalonga.'

'Do they still live there? We'd like to meet them and ask them some questions about the family.'

'I've no idea. My son might know. You'll have to ask him.'

'What about the Ioannakis family? I understand that Dimitris Ioannakis was the local school teacher. Did you know him?'

Cassie nodded. 'I knew who he was, but I didn't go to school, of course, only the boys. He seemed a decent, polite man. He would give us girls a smile when we were in the village and he was passing through.'

'Did you know his daughter, Eirini?'

'I knew her, but not well. We lived in Kastelli and they lived in Fourni. The villages only joined up on special occasions, like weddings or funerals.'

'Ask Cassie about the other sisters,' prompted Ronnie.

Cassie smacked her lips. 'I only know what my mother told me. She said they were the talk of both Fourni and Kastelli. According to my mother they were a bad family. I remember her telling me about them and holding them up as an example of what happens to a girl who allows a man favours before their wedding night. Their protestations of undying love means nothing once they have had their way.'

'In what way were they bad?' asked John.

'Well, it seems that there was plenty of money. There were three girls and their parents owned some cottages in Fourni.' Old Cassie rolled her eyes. 'The Turks were still over here at that time. Many of them were living on Spinalonga and would come over to the mainland for supplies. They would go up to the villages and help themselves to whatever they wanted. The oldest sister struck up a relationship with one of them. Once her father found out he forbade the association but she took no notice. She ran away to live on Spinalonga with him. Her family completely disowned her and told her she would never be welcome in their home again. My mother said she had also made a bad decision. It was rumoured that the Turk was violent towards her and would use his fists at the slightest provocation, but no one could prove that.'

'If it was true why didn't she leave him and come back over here to live?' asked Ronnie when John told her.

'There was no way she could leave him. He would have found her over here and taken her back. Her parents had made it clear they wanted nothing more to do with her. There was no love lost between the Turks and the Cretans so the locals did not want to know her.'

Ronnie frowned. 'I'm sure Eirini said she had an aunt who lived in Elounda so she must have returned.'

Cassie nodded. 'That was later when the island became a leper colony. The Turks left the island immediately, but her partner did not take her with him, only their two boys. She had no choice but return to Crete. No one here wanted to know her, but her father relented somewhat. He bought her a small house at Schisma and allowed her to live there, but she was forbidden to have any contact with either of her sisters.'

'How did her father find her?' asked John.

Cassie shrugged. 'How would I know? Maybe she swallowed her pride and asked him for help or he may have seen her wandering around begging.'

'Where is Schisma?' asked Ronnie.

'The area right at the end of Elounda where the salt pans are. We don't think of it as Schisma now, it is just an extension of Elounda,' explained John.

'Is the house still there?' asked John.

'I don't know. I haven't left my village for years.'

'Did she ever marry?'

'Of course not,' said Cassie scornfully. 'Who would want a Turk's cast off?'

'How did she manage to buy food?'

'It was before my time, but I expect she begged and stole in order to survive; or her father may have made her a small allowance. I've only told you what my mother told me. She used it as a warning not to be a loose woman and to avoid Turks.' Cassie looked at her empty glass and John hastened to refill it.

'So that explains why Eirini had no idea where she lived or why the family refused to talk about her.' Ronnie nudged John. 'Ask her about the other sisters.'

Old Cassie frowned. 'This is all hearsay from my mother. I have no idea how true it is. Apparently a man from Elounda, who was an overseer at the salt pans, was courting a girl in Fourni. That was quite a prestigious job in those days. Anyway the middle sister took a fancy to him. He was not interested but she pursued him and finally declared he had made her pregnant. Her father confronted the man and persuaded him that for the sake of his good name he should marry her. If he refused he threatened to spread the knowledge throughout the village and he could well lose his job.'

'Surely that was blackmail on the part of her father.'

'He was probably only concerned with his daughter's reputation. Fathers do not take kindly to knowing that their daughter has been deflowered.'

John smiled at the old fashioned wording. 'What was his name?' he asked.

Cassie shrugged. 'Not sure if I ever knew his name. If I did I've forgotten now. According to my mother he insisted that he could not be the father. He was an ardent church goer and fornication was forbidden to him. Finally he agreed to marry the girl. Within a few weeks of the marriage ceremony taking place she declared that she had miscarried. Everyone thought she had made the story up so she could marry the man she fancied.'

'Maybe Eirini had inherited that devious streak in her nature,' observed Ronnie.

Cassie continued. 'She had made a bad choice. She did not appreciate how very religious her husband was. He would not perform his marital duties by her and insisted that it was retribution for her lies. In the hope of making him change his mind she became as fanatically religious as he was, but there was never a child.'

John translated the information to Ronnie.

'That explains all the prayers and Bible readings that Eirini had to endure and the fact that her aunt wanted to keep Lucas. Ask Cassie about the youngest sister. She must have been the one married to the school teacher and the mother of Eirini.'

Cassie nodded. 'The other sister married the man who came to Kastelli as a school teacher. They continued to live in Fourni in one of her mother's cottages and he had to climb the hill every day. When the old man died his wife looked after her mother until she died. They seemed decent enough until their daughter got herself pregnant.'

'What happened to the cottages?'

'I don't know what arrangement the old lady had made. The sister in Elounda used to visit once a month and people said it was to collect her share of the rent, not that she had done anything to deserve it.'

'What about Lucas Tsantakis? What was he like?'

Cassie shrugged. 'I only saw him when I was working up in the fields and I had been told to keep my distance from him. It

117

was rumoured that his uncle had been sent to Spinalonga to live.'

John winked at Ronnie. 'So what happened to Lucas Tsantakis?'

'I've no idea. He disappeared and I was told that he had gone to Aghios Nikolaos to work.'

'Did you believe that?'

'Why shouldn't I?'

'Didn't people suspect that he might have left the area because he had made Eirini pregnant?'

'As he left the village at the same time when it was discovered that Eirini was pregnant the finger was pointed at him. The Tsantakis family denied it, of course, and Lucas Tsantakis was not around any more.'

'Did Eirini's father go looking for him in Aghios Nikolaos?' asked Ronnie.

'I don't know. Her father took her away somewhere to have the baby so I don't think he ever found the man. Had he found Lucas Tsantakis he would have been forced to return and marry the girl. As far as I know Eirini never returned to Fourni.'

'You don't think Lucas Tsantakis had also become ill and gone to Spinalonga?'

Cassie almost choked on her mouthful of whisky. 'Is that true? The family never mentioned it.'

'The family did not know. We only found that out from reading Eirini's life story. Her father had placed her with her aunt and uncle down in Elounda and she arranged to go over to Spinalonga as a worker. She had no idea how many people were living on the island and thought it would be quite simple to find Lucas's uncle and ask him if he had any relatives in Aghios Nikolaos.'

'What difference would that make?'

'I think she would have gone to the town looking for Lucas to tell him that he was the father of her child. Instead she found he was living on Spinalonga.'

Cassie raised her eyebrows and emptied her glass again. 'So the child was the offspring of a leper.' She crossed herself and touched the evil eye charm that was pinned to the neck of her blouse.

'The child was quite healthy and she actually had another child by Lucas Tsantakis.'

'Another! Was the girl out of her mind?'

'It was then that her father decided to take them to Australia so she could start a new life over there.'

'I remember that being the talk of the village, but no one believed it.'

'So where did the villagers think they had gone?' asked John.

'Probably Heraklion, maybe as far as Chania possibly. It was a momentous event if you moved to a new village when you married, but to go across the sea to a new country was unheard of.'

John smiled. 'Well if there are any other villagers around who happen to remember them you can tell them that the family did go to Australia.'

Cassie shook her head. 'They wouldn't believe me. They'd think I was rambling in my old age. What happened to them over there?'

'By all accounts they were able to find some work and Eirini married an Australian.'

'Weren't there any other Greek men over there that she could have married?'

'Plenty. Apparently there was quite a large Greek community where they lived. Eirini had two boys and she would leave them with her mother whilst she worked in a bar.'

Cassie sniffed. 'She was obviously no better than her aunt.'

'According to her she kept to herself for a number of years, expecting to be able to save sufficient money to return to Crete with her sons. It was only when she met a man who had been in Crete during the war that she realised that to return here would be impossible He told her of the devastation that had been caused by the invading armies. Their relationship blossomed, he married her and took her to live on his ranch where he kept cattle.'

'She saw her chance and took it,' observed Cassie.

'It appears to have been a happy marriage as she had more children and gave up any idea of returning to Crete.' John defended Eirini and a possible ulterior motive for marrying Fred.

'What happened to her boys who had been sired by a leper? Did they stay with her mother?'

'Eirini took them with her and according to Luke, her oldest son whom we met here, they thoroughly enjoyed living on the ranch. Neither he nor his brother knew about their Cretan father until she asked him to take back pictures of Spinalonga. Then she told them that their father lived there. Although she had taken Luke, the older boy, over to visit his father, he had no recollection of the event and the younger boy was born in Australia. Lucas Tsantakis had always insisted that his family were not to be told that he was living on Spinalonga.'

'So that is why you want to speak to the Tsantakis family? You want to ruin their lives by telling them the truth.'

'I don't know if there are any relatives around who would be interested. They might like to know that Lucas finally died in the hospital in Athens when the remaining inhabitants of Spinalonga were moved there after the war. We thought if we could speak to them they would have the opportunity to know the truth about Lucas's disappearance. If they are not interested we need say no more.'

Cassie's lip curled. 'How would you feel if you were told that you had leprous relatives?'

'I have,' said John, 'And I am very proud of him. He was a fine man. Ronnie's great grandmother was also born over there and she was delighted when she found out.'

Cassie sniffed. 'I don't think that would be my reaction.' She indicated the bottle of whisky with her hand. 'I think I need a stiff drink so I can forget all this rubbish about being proud of having leprous relatives.'

'So what do you think, Ronnie? Should we forget about finding the Tsantakis family?'

Ronnie shook her head. 'I think we should speak to them. They should have the opportunity to know what happened to their relatives. There may be no one alive now who is interested, but Luke in Australia is related to them and they should know about him.'

'We can but visit them and gauge their reaction. If they tell us to mind our own business and go away then that is what we'll do.'

'Have you managed to find out any more about the religious uncle who worked at the salt pans?' asked Ronnie.

'Not really. I looked at the church records and made a note of the names of the various men who had taken an active part in the church activities, not including the ordained priests, of course. I also looked at any records I could find of workers at the salt pans. There was a list of names of the overseers and I made a note of those. None of the names were mentioned in the church archives so I couldn't hazard a guess which one may have been him.'

'We should have asked Old Cassie if she knew the names of the sisters. There may be a record of a marriage in the archives.'

John shook his head. 'Records of births, marriages and deaths were not recorded in those days. It was not until after the war that a law was brought in that made it compulsory for people to have identity cards. Many of those would have been incorrect at the time as people would have hazarded a guess at when they were born. They might remember their mother telling them that it was winter time or the summer and they may have been called after a saint whose day coincided with their birth but they were unlikely to know the year. Those who were illiterate would not have known how to spell their name correctly, just how it sounded when they said it.'

'So that accounts for the variations in people's names even when they are close relatives,' mused Ronnie.

'Exactly. You cannot rely on any of the records being truly accurate.'

'Where do we go from here?'

'We can visit the Tsantakis family provided we can find them in Fourni and after that I think we are at a dead end.'

'What about the sister who went off with the Turk?'

'Even more unlikely to be able to find out anything about her.'

Ronnie shrugged. 'Well at least I can send Luke the scant information we have about his mother's family.'

'Hold off on that until we have visited the Tsantakis family. We may find something useful about Lucas. I could come up again some time next week and we could visit Fourni if that suits you.'

'I'd be grateful, John.'

John grinned at her. 'Nick and I are as interested as you. She'll love the information that Old Cassie gave us and might even think of a possible lead to find out more.'

Nicola listened to John's account of their conversation with Old Cassie. She frowned.

'It does seem as though you have met a dead end unless the Tsantakis family are willing to talk and able to come up with some new information. What about the house Cassie mentioned at Schisma?'

'Nick, you're brilliant. I'll go down and have a look. Grandma Elena mentioned that she had seen a deserted house down that way and I thought no more about it. I imagined it was probably an old storage building that the salt pan workers had used to store their tools.'

'It might well have been, but worth going to have a quick look. It will be a possible lead ticked off your list. If your Mum and Bryony will look after the children we could drive down there tomorrow.'

John shook his head. 'I'm spending tomorrow helping Dad and Marcus to secure the carpets in Uncle Yannis's and Grandma Marisa's bedrooms so they cannot trip over the edges. At least it will be easier in Uncle Yannis's room this year without so many pots around. I'm pleased I persuaded him to leave the two large pithoi outside covered in polythene to protect them against the weather. We could probably go the following day.'

November 2016
Week Three

'Where is this house?' asked Nicola as they drove along the main road out of Elounda.

'I'm not sure. I know Grandma had walked along to the salt pans and then across the pedestrian area to where the road started. The wind had come up by then and she thought it would be easier and more practical to walk back through the town than risk being blown off her feet. She saw a side road and thought it might lead back to the taverna or be a short cut up to the main road.'

'So we need to take the road that leads down to the pedestrian area and start looking from there.' Nicola looked out of the car window as John drove slowly down the road. 'It can't have been any of the houses down here. You can see them all and they look in good repair.'

'I think it will be further along. We need to park and walk around. It might be easier to find if we were on foot and it can't be that far away.'

Nicola pulled her coat closer round her as they left the car. 'Just because the sun is shining I tend to forget that it is November and can be quite cold in the shade. Do you know which side of the road the house is supposed to be?'

John shook his head. 'No, but I expect it to be on the seaward side.'

Together they walked slowly along the side road scanning the waste ground that they passed on both sides of the track.

'What do you plan to do if we find it?'

'It depends. If there is a high fence or a wall we can only look over, but if it's just protected by bushes and shrubs we should be able to find a way in to have a closer look. It's a bit smelly up here.'

'If anyone asks what excuse do we give for poking around,' asked Nicola.

John shrugged. 'We'll say that our Grandmother saw it and as she is looking for a small property to buy in the area she asked us to come down and see if it was for sale. That looks like a building through there.'

'I hope there isn't a vicious guard dog chained up behind the bushes.'

'I'm sure there isn't. He would have barked at us as we approached and he certainly will if we try to force a way through. If that happens we just retreat rapidly. Don't worry, Nick, I'll go first.'

'Skele isn't very happy.'

John looked at his dog who was cowering some distance away. 'Come here, Skele.'

Reluctantly Skele walked to John's side, his belly close to the ground and his ears down.

'There's something wrong,' said Nicola. 'He doesn't usually behave like that.'

John patted Skele's head. 'There's nothing to worry about, old boy. You stay here. We won't be long.'

Skele moved further back down the path and sat down obediently.

Cautiously John parted the bushes and then stood in the gap he had made. Nicola stood behind him and as he repeated the process she followed him until they were both standing looking at an overgrown garden with a semi derelict building.

'That doesn't look like a storage building for workmen's tools,' observed John. 'It must have been quite a decent little house at one time. Let's see if we can see anything through the windows.'

The window glass was broken and the frames sagging or lying on the ground. Much of the roof had disintegrated, hanging down dangerously. John looked through a window and stood back in surprise.

'It looks as if someone left in a hurry. There are the remains of their bed in this room. The bedding looks pretty mouldy but it's still there.'

Nicola looked through the window to the next room and wrinkled her nose. 'I see what you mean. There's a table with a plate and mug on it and a horrible smell.'

'You'd think if the occupant moved elsewhere they would have taken their belongings with them. Shall we see if we can get inside?'

Nicola shook her head. 'I don't want to. It's giving me shivers up my spine and the smell is making me feel quite sick. I'd like to go, John.'

John smiled at her temerity. 'I doubt if there's anything more to see inside anyway.'

'I don't think I ever want to come back here again. There's something evil about this place.' Nicola shivered. 'No wonder Skele behaved so strangely.'

John took his wife's hand. 'Alright, we'll go. I'm sure we've found the house Grandma said she had seen and I think it has to be the one that was given to the woman who had run off with the Turk.'

'Surely the house must belong to someone?'

'Shall we drive down to the taverna at the end of the salt pans?' suggested John. 'We could park just before the windmills and make our way across the sand spit.'

'Will we be able to walk across there at this time of year?'

'Probably, but if not we'll just have to drive back and go down from the main road.'

'I doubt if the taverna will be open.'

'There could be someone around that we could speak to.'

'I don't want to go along to that house again,' said Nicola firmly.

'I won't make you. I'd just like to know more about it and why it appeared to have been vacated so rapidly.'

'There is a horrible atmosphere surrounding it. Did you notice that when we pushed our way through the bushes there was no sign of any animal scurrying away or a bird flying off? That's not natural.'

John nodded. He had noted the absence of wildlife himself, but not mentioned the fact to Nicola.

Nicola and John walked briskly along the spit of sand that separated the salt pans from the open sea whilst Skele happily ran ahead of them. Nicola pulled her scarf closer.

'This is when I wish I had a coat like Skele.'

'Not so good when it's hot in the summer,' grinned John. 'He's loving running along in the wind.'

'I wish I was,' complained Nicola. 'I do hope there will be someone at the taverna where we can at least find some shelter and get a hot drink.'

'Are you really that cold?' asked John. 'We can turn back if you want.'

Nicola shook her head. 'We're nearly there. If we turn back now you'll only want to come again another day and it could be even colder then.'

Finally they reached the entrance to the taverna. The tables and chairs were stacked up and covered against the winter rains and everywhere looked deserted.

'I'll bang on the door,' announced John. 'There could be someone working inside.'

John knocked loudly and waited until a face appeared at a window. He smiled and waved and a short while later the door was opened and a young man looked out.

'What do you want?' he asked. 'We're closed for the season.'

'We just wondered if we could come in for a short while and get warm and maybe have a hot drink? We don't want anything to eat.'

The man shrugged. 'I suppose so. What about your dog?'

'I doubt that he's cold he's been running around and I have some water with me for him.'

The man shook his head. 'I mean what will happen to him if you come in? I can't have him inside. We have four cats.'

'I'll fasten his lead to a tree and he'll be fine out here for a while. We'll not stop long as I expect you're busy working.' John tied Skele's lead to a nearby tree and the dog looked at him reproachfully. 'Be good and stay,' said John as he patted him on the head and placed his bowl of water within reach.

The door was opened wider and John and Nicola walked inside. Tables and chairs had been pushed back against one wall and the man was obviously in the middle of washing the floor. He pulled out two chairs and indicated that they could sit there.

'What do you want to drink?' he asked.

'Hot American coffee or chocolate. Whatever you have that's convenient.'

Nicola unwound the scarf from around her neck and rubbed her hands together.

'You ought to take your coat off or you won't feel the benefit when we leave,' John advised her as he unzipped his parka.

'We don't want that man to think that we are going to stay here for hours.'

'I doubt that we will. I just want to ask him about the house, but I imagine he's too young to have any real information.'

The man appeared with two mugs of steaming hot chocolate and placed them on the table next to them.

'That smells really good,' said John appreciatively. 'We've walked across from the windmills with our dog and it was colder than we realised with the wind coming off the sea.'

The man nodded and went to return to the area where he had made their drinks. 'Could I ask you a question?' asked John.

'If it's about this room it isn't for hire outside of the season except on very special occasions. We use it occasionally in the summer months if we have an unexpected spell of bad weather.'

'You're fortunate to have the facility,' observed John, 'But that is not what I wanted to ask. My grandmother was staying with us recently and she walked around the pedestrian area by the salt pans and down a side road. She has been wandering around everywhere hoping to see a small cottage that she would be able to rent or buy. She saw one through the trees that appears to be in a bad state of repair and wondered if that was available.'

The man shook his head. 'No one would want to buy that house or even live in it if was given to them.'

'Oh, why is that?'

'It has a bad reputation.'

'Do tell me more,' said John, leaning forwards. 'I'm John and this is my wife Nicola.'

The man nodded. 'I'm Mikhalis. I don't really know any more about the house except that no one goes there. They say an evil spirit lives there.' Mikhalis crossed himself.

'Really? What gave rise to that idea?'

'You'd need to talk to my grandfather. He could tell you more.'

'Is he around?'

'Not at the moment. He only spends time here in the summer months when he is able to go out and catch the fresh fish for us to serve.'

'Where would we be able to find him?'

'Probably in one of the tavernas that are still open down on the waterfront, otherwise he's at his house. Why are you so interested?'

'We're trying to track down a family who came from this area originally. We understand that one member of the family had a cottage at Schisma and as far as we can tell the deserted house is the only one that it could be.'

'Best avoid it. Bad things happened there apparently.'

'What kind of things?'

Mikhalis shrugged. 'I don't know. Before my time. I was always told never to go there.'

'Would your grandfather know what happened?'

'Probably.'

'We'll see if we can find him and ask him to talk to us. Someone in one of the tavernas must know him.'

'Ask for Mikhalis the fisherman.'

'Thank you,' said John as he drained his cup of hot chocolate and placed some money on the table. 'We appreciated being able to come in here to warm up a bit. Come on, Nick. We'll make our way back to the car and go home.'

John untied Skele from the tree and they began to make their way back to the car.

'Are we looking for Mikhalis the fisherman today?' asked Nicola.

John shook his head. 'We've done enough for the time being. There are not many tavernas open now so he shouldn't be that difficult to track down. We can look another day when we haven't got Skele with us.'

Two days later John and Nicola drove to the square in Elounda and parked their car.

'We can walk along and check the tavernas gradually. The fish taverna is open and that could be a good place to start.'

'Hello, Christos,' said John as he pushed open the door.

Christos frowned. 'Are you here for a meal? We're a bit busy at the moment. If you can come back in about an hour I'll reserve a table for you.'

John shook his head. 'Thank you, but we're not able to stop for a meal today. I just wanted to ask if you know Mikhalis, the fisherman.'

'Of course.'

'Is he here today?'

Christos glanced around and shook his head. 'I haven't seen him. He probably went elsewhere when he saw we were busy.'

'Thanks anyway. We won't interrupt you any longer.'

'Just because he wasn't in there today doesn't mean he won't be tomorrow,' remarked Nicola. 'He may have decided to stay at home.'

'That's not very likely. Once the season has finished you know everyone likes to be out and about meeting up with their friends and neighbours. He's probably in one of the others.'

They trudged from one taverna to another until they had visited every taverna that was still open in the village, but no one admitted to seeing Mikhalis that day.

'He must be playing backgammon in someone's house. We'll have to come back another day and look for him.'

'He could even be on his boat playing cards,' observed Nicola.

'Do you know the name of his boat?' asked John.

'Of course not. You should have asked his grandson when we were there.'

It took three more visits to Elounda before they finally found Mikhalis in a taverna gazing morosely into a glass of whisky. He looked up as John and Nicola joined him at the table.

'May we sit here and talk to you.'

Mikhalis shrugged. His grandson had told him that some people were looking for him and he had avoided the village for a while. He was not sure he wanted to speak to them about Old Andrula.

'Can we refresh your glass?' asked John and indicated to the barman that a refill was required. 'At this rate I'll be charging Ronnie for whisky expenses,' muttered John to Nicola. 'I thought the older generation always drank raki.'

John waited until the fresh glass had arrived along with a beer for himself and a coffee for Nicola before he began to question the fisherman.

'We visited the taverna at the end of the salt pans and spoke to your grandson. We asked him about the deserted house further back. He said we should ask you.'

'You don't want to go near there. It's an evil place.'

'Why is that?'

The second glass of whisky seemed to have given Mikhalis the inclination to explain more.

'The witch Andrula lived there'

'A witch? Did people really think that she was a witch?'

Mikhalis nodded and crossed himself. 'She would wander around begging from the fishermen and when they refused to give her anything she would point her finger at them, mutter something in an unknown language and say she had cursed them.'

'And that was why they thought she was a witch?'

'At first they just laughed at her. Then some of the men she had cursed fell ill, had accidents or their boats were caught in a storm and damaged. Two men actually lost their lives at sea and people began to believe that she had the power to curse them.'

'Did you believe that?'

'My father said that if I saw her I should throw her a fish to avoid her curse. She would put the fish in her apron pocket and walk away without a word.'

'And you and your father were never ill or had an accident?'

Mikhalis shook his head. 'This is not suitable talk in front of a lady.' He looked pointedly at Nicola and also at his empty glass.

'I'll go over to the supermarket and get the shopping,' she said, realising that Mikhalis was not going to tell John any more whilst she was there. 'I'll meet you back at the car.'

Mikhalis watched her go out of the door and waited until his next glass of whisky arrived.. 'What you tell your wife is up to you, but I wouldn't want to upset her.'

'I appreciate that, and I'm sure Nick understands. I'll use my discretion about telling her anything you are able to tell me.'

'It was not only her muttering curses at people that made people think she was evil. Cats and dogs would disappear at regular intervals and the villagers declared she must be killing and eating them.'

John looked at the old man in revulsion. 'Would people really eat cats and dogs?'

'If you're hungry you'll eat whatever is available. The soldiers stripped the houses and fields of any food they could find. The people were slowly starving to death. Anyone found concealing food or harbouring a man of fighting age was shot. You just wanted to fill your belly. Even animal bones, once they had been sucked clean were pounded down and made into soup. During the war the people here would scour the fields for any wild life they could find that was edible. They collected herbs and the wild greens from the hills but you cannot live just on those. Maybe she used the fish I gave her to entice the cats to come close so she could catch them.'

'So what happened to her? We looked through the windows and it appeared that she had left in a hurry. The bedding was still there and dishes were sitting on the table.'

Mikhalis crossed himself again. 'When the Italians were down here during the war two of their soldiers went missing. No amount of searching ever found their bodies. When people were questioned they said that Andrula had probably spirited them away and eaten them.'

'They accused her of cannibalism?' John was horrified.

'People accused her of being the cause of any misfortune that befell them, including being invaded by the German and Italian soldiers.'

'Did they really believe that she would have eaten the men?' asked John.

'They were convinced that she was a witch and had put an evil spell on them to make them disappear. Some of the villagers told the story to the soldiers and they repeated it to their Commander. If you had any information that could be useful to the soldiers you were supposed to tell them. You have to remember that during that time the slightest misdemeanour or disobedience of the rules the invaders had imposed and you would be taken away and shot in front of your family. Withholding information about suspicious activities was classed as a criminal offence. They shot people as an example to keep the people in fear.'

'So what happened?'

'Soldiers were sent to the house. Apparently they found no sign that the men had ever been there, but she cursed them. Because of that they dragged her out and marched her, kicking and screaming obscenities, up to the Canal. They tied her to a tree and left her there whilst they went back to the village and rounded up all the inhabitants. They made them all walk up to the Canal, the old and infirm along with children. No one dared to disobey or they would probably have been shot. When they reached there a statement in Italian was read out. I have no idea what it said, but I can only assume that it declared her to be a witch and possessing evil powers. She was untied and marched up to the top of the headland where the villagers were made to stand and witness her punishment. She was bayoneted time and time again. With her dying breath she was said to curse everyone in Elounda.'

'Did you witness that?' asked John.

'I was only a boy at the time and tried to hide behind my father. I'll never forget her screams as they took their time, stabbing her again and again until she finally fell to the ground.' Mikhalis shuddered.

'So what happened next? Did they make the villagers dig a grave?'

Mikhalis shook his head. 'The soldiers threw her body over the headland into the sea. It landed on the rocks down there and as far as I know that is where it stayed.'

'It can't be there now.'

'Most unlikely. During some of our winter storms it would have been washed away. We don't fish too close to that area. We don't want to find any remains in our nets.'

'Do you believe that she was a witch?' asked John.

Mikhalis crossed himself. 'Who knows?'

'So that is why the old house is deserted and said to be evil. Did you never go and play there when you were a child?'

'I don't remember much play time when I was a boy. As soon as I was old enough I was expected to help my father on the boat. Until I was strong enough to haul in a net I used to sort the fish into the buckets. Finally my father was forbidden to take his boat out so he left the village to join the resistance. I was too busy helping my mother to gather food to have any time to play. We would certainly have avoided old Andrula's house as we had heard that she was a witch. If I did meet up with my friends we never discussed the war or anything that had happened to our relatives. You could not trust anyone, even your closest friend, not to repeat a conversation to a soldier and the next thing you would know they would be knocking down your door.'

'That must have been a terrible time,' sympathised John. 'Did your father return?'

Mikhalis shook his head. 'We never heard from him again so eventually we decided he had been killed.'

'How sad.'

'It happened to many families. Once our island had been liberated the men gradually returned but my father was not amongst them. I am sure he died an honourable death.'

'I appreciate you telling me about the house and all that happened there. I won't go into the details when I tell Nick. Now, are you having a meal here or just a drink?'

'Are you going to join me?'

'No,' smiled John. 'I was planning to pay for whatever you wanted.'

'In that case I'll have a meal and another drink. Talking is thirsty work.'

John joined Nicola in the car. 'I'm sorry you had to leave, but I'm sure Mikhalis would not have told you all that he told me had you been there. Did you get the shopping you wanted?'

'I didn't actually need anything. It was just an excuse. So, tell me what Mikhalis told you.'

'It isn't pleasant,' John warned her. 'Apparently the old lady used to curse people if they did not give her anything when she was begging. Probably by coincidence a number of them met with illness or an accident and she was blamed. Along with that a number of cats and dogs went missing and the villagers thought she was catching them for food.'

'Horrible thought.' Nicola shuddered. 'I would have to be desperate.'

'True, but as Mikhalis so rightly said, when you are starving you will eat anything. Now, this is the really interesting bit. When two Italian soldiers disappeared without a trace she was accused of spiriting them away and eating them.'

'John, that's not true,' exclaimed Nicola. 'You found the soldiers' grave in the olive grove belonging to the Colonomakis family. Their deaths were nothing to do with the old lady.'

'We know that now, but when they could not be found originally it was all too easy to accuse her of cannibalism. She was arrested and taken up to the headland by the Canal. They killed her in front of all the villagers and threw her body over onto the rocks below.'

'How awful. That sounds like the witch hunts that took place in the Middle Ages.'

'Not only were the local people very superstitious they were also in fear of the soldiers. Had one of them protested they would probably have met with the same fate.'

'So what are you going to do?' asked Nicola.

'There's nothing I can do. It happened during the war, seventy years ago. As far as we are aware the only distant relative to Andrula who is living now is Luke. I'm not sure he would want to know that she was considered a witch and I think it would be unlikely that he would want to boast about that to his friends.'

'Are you going to tell Ronnie?'

'Yes, but it will be up to her what information she passes on to Luke. I'm going to tell Panayiotis. As a policeman I think he would be interested.'

November 2016
Week Four

'Do you want to drive up to Kastelli and see Ronnie or shall we go to Fourni and see if we can find any trace of the Tsantakis family?' asked John.

'A visit to Fourni would be most sensible. Then we will have followed up every possible line of enquiry and answered most of the questions that Ronnie gave us.'

'It's a shame we couldn't find anything about the uncle who worked at the salt pans. He and his wife are really the only loose ends.'

'I think we've done tremendously well in finding out the information we do have. I'm sure Ronnie will be pleased. I'm looking forward to seeing what Mr Palamakis has managed to complete on the big house. I'm sure Ronnie will be only too pleased to show off any improvements that have been made during the summer.'

They drove up over the hill from Elounda to the start of the Lassithi Plain and then down to the village of Fourni.

'Where do we start?' asked Nicola.

'The taverna is probably the best source of information. If we don't find out anything there we can then go to the church. They should have some records of the residents, however scant they may be.'

Nicola followed John into the open area of the taverna. It looked deserted, but the door was open and led into a large room holding tables and chairs. There was a bar at one side and a kitchen area at the back.

'Anyone around?' called John and a woman appeared holding a small child in her arms.

She placed a finger to her lips. 'He's almost asleep. Give me a few minutes to settle him down and I'll be with you. Help yourself to a drink whilst you wait.'

John looked at the array of bottles on display, they all had a high alcohol content and he finally selected a bottle of beer and two glasses, sharing it between him and Nicola.

'A very trusting soul,' he observed. 'We could have walked off with anything whilst she was dealing with her child.'

'I don't think so,' smiled Nicola, and pointed to the elderly woman sitting in the corner. 'She may look as if she is asleep, but I expect she is keeping an eye on us. Are we going to ask for something to eat?'

'We'll see what she says when she returns. It's often easier to get someone talking when you've ordered a meal.'

The woman returned and sat down in a vacant chair at their table. 'Sorry about that. He's cutting another tooth and feeling thoroughly miserable.'

Nicola nodded sympathetically. 'They do suffer then. I remember the sleepless nights I had when all I could do was walk the floor and cuddle them until they finally slept.'

'I don't remember that,' said John.

'That was mostly when you were in London for your operation. I had your Mum and Bryony to help me so I could always have a sleep during the day.' She smiled brightly at the woman. 'If it's any consolation it doesn't last for ever.'

'So I'm told. Now, would you like something to eat? I can't offer you the full menu as we don't keep large stocks of food out of season. We get an occasional passer by like yourselves or a family may drop in for a meal if they are celebrating a special occasion.'

'Whatever you have that is available will be fine with us. We don't expect a banquet and we will also be expected to eat a large meal when we return to our family this evening.'

'Help yourself to another drink whilst you wait.' The woman walked off into the kitchen area and three more women appeared as if from nowhere.

John grinned. 'I think you were quite right. I don't know where they all sprang from, but I expect they were watching us whilst we thought we were alone.'

'Good job we're honest and didn't try to hide bottles under our coats. I don't want another beer, John, but you have one. I can always drive us home. I do hope they are not preparing too much for us. It will be embarrassing if we cannot eat it all.'

'We can always hide some of it in your bag and take it away with us.'

Plates of food began to arrive, mostly consisting of stuffed vine leaves, courgette strips coated in cheese, hard boiled eggs, tzatziki and freshly baked rolls.

'I'm sorry there is no meat,' apologised the woman.

'No problem at all. This looks superb. Just what we needed,' smiled John. 'When we've eaten I was wondering if we could ask you a few questions.'

The woman frowned. 'It depends. I may not know the answers.'

'We'll understand as we will be asking about the village as it was years ago.'

'Then the best person to speak to would be my grandmother.' She indicated the old lady sitting in the corner and walked away.

John and Nicola helped themselves to the food that had been placed before them, both finding that they cleared the plates easily.

'Shall I ask for coffee and then we could speak to the old lady?'

Nicola nodded. 'What are you planning to ask her?'

'I thought I would ask about the houses that were owned by Eirini's grandmother. They may no longer be there or the sister could have sold them. Then I want to ask if the Tsantakis family are still living in the area. If she can't help then I suggest we go over to the church and see if we can find out anything from the priest. If anything occurs to you interrupt me in English. I hope she is not another whisky drinker. This investigation is becoming expensive.'

John asked for coffee to be taken over to where the old lady sat and also anything that she would like. To his surprise the woman took over a small slice of baklava.

'She's only allowed this occasionally as a special treat as she is diabetic. Would you like some?'

Nicola nodded. 'I'd love some, but I wouldn't want to know we had made your grandmother ill.'

'A piece that size won't hurt her and I'll make sure she has nothing else sweet for at least twenty four hours.'

Nicola made sure she did not drink more than a few sips of her coffee as it was traditional Greek coffee and she did not want to end up with a mouthful of coffee grounds in her mouth. She found the baklava incredibly sweet and she wondered at the wisdom of allowing a diabetic lady to have even a small slice.

The old lady looked at them with tired eyes. 'I'm told you want to ask me some questions about the old days.'

'We would certainly like it if you could help us. We'll understand if you don't know or get too tired. We have been in touch with some friends and their family lived in this area before the war. He was the school teacher in Kastelli and his mother in law owned some cottages here in Fourni. I understand that when the teacher's wife and her sister inherited them she sold her property later to her sister as they were going to Australia.'

The old lady snorted. 'That was the story they put out. That woman always thought herself better than us as she had married a teacher rather than a local farmer and had some cottages. Hardly mixed with the rest of us. He was more down to earth. I think he was disappointed that he had a daughter rather than a son and he spent a good deal of his time educating her at home. She could read and write, unlike the rest of us village girls. It was her father who allowed her to join us when we were working up in the fields. He said she should know how hard we worked to make a living.'

'Quite right,' agreed John. 'Everyone was expected to work and help their family.'

'She was a foolish girl. Was taken in by the attention that one of the young men paid to her and before you knew it she was pregnant. Of course, the man disappeared and was never seen or heard from again. Once her parents found out they took her away to stay somewhere else. They were ashamed of their daughter and she never returned to the village.'

'Why was that, do you think?'

'Maybe she met another man who was willing to marry her or maybe she had got herself into trouble again. It was probably about two years after that when the woman sold her cottages to her sister and they said they were going to Australia. No one believed them, of course, and thought it was just an excuse to move away from the area.'

John smiled. 'I'm sure it seemed unbelievable at the time, but it was quite true. They did go to Australia. It is the relatives they have there who have asked us to ask about Fourni. We wondered if the cottages are still there and if so who is living in them.'

The old lady shook her head is disbelief. 'So what happened to their daughter? Did they take her with them?'

'They took her and her little boy. She married out there, became the wife of a rancher and had some more children.'

'So these are not Cretan relatives who are looking for information. What are they hoping to find out? That they have a string of cottages they own and can turn into holiday homes for tourists?'

'Not at all. The man we have been in contact with is the son of the Cretan farmer. He is not interested in owning the cottages. He would just like to know more about his family history.'

'Well I can't tell you any more. As far as I know the cottages are still there and families live in them. If you walk back up to the village square and branch off to the right you'll find them.'

'Thank you. We'll go and have a look, maybe take a photo to send to him.' John finished the last of his baklava and drank some of his water to cleanse his mouth of the sweet cloying mixture. 'I suppose you don't know if the Tsantakis family still live in this area?'

The old lady wrinkled her brow. 'One of them still lives here, but the others have moved away to the town for work.'

'Where would we be able to find her?'

'Here, of course. She's my granddaughter.'

'Really? You mean the lady who served us that delicious meal is the very person we are looking for? Then maybe she would be willing to talk to us about the family.'

'She might. You'd have to ask her and ask her for another slice of baklava at the same time.'

Nicola gave John a pleased smile. 'That could save us trekking around the village looking for relatives or having to spend time asking the priest if he had any records. Let's go back to our table and see what she has to say.'

'Your grandmother was very helpful to us and has said that you may well be able to help us further.' The lady raised her eyebrows. 'She also said she would like another piece of baklava.'

'She's not having another piece. I have to be careful to regulate her diet and also make sure she cannot help herself to unsuitable food. As people get older they seem to become more crafty.'

'That's true,' agreed John. 'Can you spare us a few minutes to answer some questions?'

'No problem as we are not exactly overwhelmed with customers today. Tomorrow would be a different story. There's a funeral taking place at the church across the road and we have been asked to provide refreshments afterwards.' The lady pulled out a chair and sat down at their table.

'Your grandmother said that you are related to the Tsantakis family and they were the next people we were going to try to find.'

The woman nodded. 'My grandmother was a Tsantakis until she married. What did you want to know?'

'For a start are there any other members of the Tsantakis family still living in the area?'

'Not now, only me. I am Despina. My sister, Adelphi, lives in Aghios Nikolaos. Her husband has a shop there and my father lives with them.'

'The old lady you called your grandmother is not a Tsantakis?'

'I married her grandson. The other ladies you have seen are my husband's aunts.'

'I understand the Tsantakis family had a farm. What happened to that?'

'My grandfather gave his farm to his remaining son before he died. One of his sons had died during the war and the other had disappeared. He struggled to make a living from it for a while and then sold the land to a man who started a timber business. We collect our wood for the winter from him. He grows a little fruit and vegetables in the season and goes around the villages with his van selling the produce to the locals.'

'Do you know any history of the Tsantakis family from before your grandfather's time? We are not just being nosy. We believe you could have a relative living in Australia,' explained John.

'I don't know anything about that. There was a rumour in the family that my great grandfather's brother had been sent to Spinalonga. No one really spoke about him.'

'I also believe that one of the men went to Aghios Nikolaos for work and never contacted his family again.'

'I had heard that story. When they never heard from him again they assumed he had died or committed a crime and was in prison somewhere. By the time my grandfather died I think the family had forgotten about him. Could he have gone to Australia and is this the relative you think we may have?'

John shook his head. 'He was not a criminal. Do you want to know what happened to him?'

Despina considered. 'You've made me curious now so I'd like to know.'

'It's quite a long story, but I need to tell you from the beginning.' John related how Luke had visited from Australia and told them about his mother having a child by Lucas Tsantakis and finding him on Spinalonga.

Despina sucked in her breath. 'So he had leprosy?'

John nodded. 'That was why he disappeared and never made any contact with his family. He did not want to have them ostracised by the villagers if they discovered his whereabouts.'

'That was both brave and sad. I'm sure his family would have liked to know and kept the knowledge to themselves. What happened to him? Did he die over there during the war?'

'No, he survived and went to the hospital in Athens along with the others after they had been tested and most of them found to be burnt out and no longer infectious.'

'Why didn't he come back here?'

'He had no idea if his family would accept him or even if there were any of them still living. He accepted going to the hospital and I understand that he was well cared for until the day he finally died.'

'That at least is a comfort.' Despina frowned. 'So is it his child who is in Australia now?'

John nodded. 'Luke is obviously an old man now. His mother did not disclose the facts about his father until he was visiting Crete with his wife. She then told him everything and later she wrote down her memoirs from when she was a girl. Luke and his wife looked after her until she died and then he sent a copy of her memoirs to our artist friend who had painted the pictures of Spinalonga. She would like to send him as much information as we can find out.'

'Well, I'm afraid I have not been of any great help to you. In fact you have told me more about the family than I knew. I'll tell my sister when I next see her. We don't really consider ourselves as part of the Tsantakis family now.'

'I appreciate your time. If you should subsequently remember anything that you think could be important please contact me.' John wrote down his phone number on a serviette and passed it to Despina.

She looked at the number briefly and John had a distinct feeling that once they had left she would throw it away.

'That was not exactly useful,' said John to Nicola once they were back in their car.

'At least we know we don't have to go around the area looking for people called Tsantakis.'

'So we have reached a dead end in our inquiries.'

'Not entirely. I want to speak to Panayiotis and tell him that the old lady was accused of murdering the Italians. There's nothing that can be done about that now, but I would like to find out if Luke actually owns the derelict property as the only descendent.'

'How will Panayiotis know that?'

'I don't expect him to know, but he might be able to tell me where I could start enquiring.'

'What about Ronnie? Should we visit her now and tell her everything we have found out?'

John nodded. 'It would be helpful if you could write out the salient points of our enquiries. If we just tell her she may forget something important or we may miss a piece of information out. I don't think we should tell her that I am asking about the owner of the cottage. I wouldn't want Luke to think he owned it unless I could prove it.'

'I don't know how you are going to do that, but there is certainly no need for her to know at present. I'll happily write everything down and you can check it to make sure I haven't forgotten anything. When you have done that we can arrange to meet Ronnie and it will be up to her the information she passes on to Luke.'

'I'll try to contact Panayiotis and see when we could visit him. It will depend upon when he's on duty, of course.'

'Try Panayiotis first. That will give me time to write everything out.'

'Are you going to tell Pietro about the story Mikhalis told you about his grandfather?'

John shook his head. 'No, as far as he and I are concerned that is over and done with. Why tell him a nasty story that has no truth in it at all?'

Panayiotis agreed to meet John and Nicola two days later when he was not on duty. He moved some piles of fishing magazines from the chairs so they were able to sit down.

'Sorry about my mess, but I never seem to get sufficient time to clear up properly. When I have finally finished reading my magazines I will put them away elsewhere. Did you know that Vasi and Saffie have two dogs now they have moved next door?'

John winked at Nicola. 'Yes, we did hear that. I hope they are no trouble to you.'

'None at all. I only found out when I happened to see Vasi taking them out for a walk. The older one is very good and docile, the younger one is a bit skittish still. Now, what did you want to see me about? You haven't found any more bodies anywhere I hope.'

'No, thank goodness, but I wanted to tell you a little more about the two Italian soldiers. We were talking to an old fisherman and he said that when they disappeared it was rumoured that a rather strange lady who lived down at Schisma had put a spell on them.'

Panayiotis chuckled. 'What was she? A witch?'

'That was what the villagers thought. Unfortunately they voiced their suspicions to the soldiers who were looking for their missing comrades and they arrested the old lady and put her to death.'

Panayiotis looked horrified. 'That was awful. She had no hand in their deaths. We know that.'

John nodded. 'Exactly, but although I wanted to tell you that, there was something else I wanted to ask. As far as Nick and I have been able to find out there are no living relatives of the old lady living on Crete. There is a man in Australia, I believe he would be her great nephew. Would he have any claim on the cottage?'

Panayiotis considered. 'I don't know. Has no one moved in and claimed it as their own?'

'People will not go near it. They say it is an evil place. Nick is refusing to go there again and our dog would not go near the boundary.'

'Very odd. There could well be someone living there unlawfully. I'll go and have a look the next time I am down that way. As regards ownership, all I can say is that you need to consult the Town Hall and see if they can find any records of the owner. The man in Australia would then need to produce paper work to say that he was a descendant. It could take a very long time before he inherited if it was proved to belong to him.'

'Thanks. That has at least told me where I need to go next. We are not going to mention it to him until we have found out some more information and the protocol.'

Panayiotis was intrigued by the history of the house at Schisma. He had to admit that he had never had occasion to investigate the area. He would allow himself time to drive down before he needed to be on duty at Aghios Nikolaos police station.

Having parked he walked along the overgrown pathway. He felt as if the bushes were pressing in on him and he shivered and told himself it was due to the time of year and lack of sunlight. He reached the area where the path ended and he could see the bushes that John had pushed aside to allow him and Nicola access. Automatically he placed his hand on his gun. He did not want to come face to face with a vagrant who might become violent when disturbed.

Panayiotis saw no one as he made his cautious progress

towards the building. He was conscious of the strange smell that seemed to have enveloped him and also the total silence. There was no sound of any animal or bird as he peered through the grimy windows, making out the mouldy bedding and dirty dishes on the table. He placed his hand on the door and it opened easily.

'Hello,' he called. 'Anyone there?'

There was total silence, but as he stood there he felt overcome with nausea from the smell that was emanating from the house. He bent over gasping for breath. He placed his hand back on the door frame and told himself to stay calm. Cautiously he stood upright, taking tentative steps back towards the bushes. As he neared the road the nausea gradually lessened and by the time he reached his car he was able to breathe normally again.

Should he call in at the hospital so he could be reassured that all was well. He looked at his watch. He was already late for his duty. It wasn't possible. He was sure he had spent no more than a few minutes at the house. He checked his mobile phone and that showed the same time as his watch. Had he passed out? If so his blood pressure must have spiked. It would be necessary to call the station and explain that he was feeling so unwell that he was going to the hospital as a safety precaution.

Three hours later Panayiotis entered the police station.

'Should you be here? What did the hospital say?'

Panayiotis shrugged. 'Must have been indigestion. They examined me, hooked me up to their machines and could find absolutely nothing wrong with me. I know I have missed some hours of my duty and I'm willing to work overtime to make it up to whoever covered for me.'

'We'll see how you go before we arrange that. If you get a repeat of the problem let me know and I'll arrange for you to be taken home.'

December 2016
Week Two

Elena phoned Marianne. 'I have some good news. Purely by chance I met a couple who had lived close to me some years ago. We had always been quite friendly and they asked if I was still living at the same address. I told them I was looking to move somewhere more convenient. They suggested that I looked at the estate where they lived and offered to drive me down there to take a look. I was impressed. They have a one storey building with a small garden around it, but the real benefit is that it has a secured entrance. The only way anyone can gain access is by calling me and asking me to release the gate.

'They were happy for me to look around their house and it would be plenty large enough for me. As luck would have it there was a similar property up for sale at the other end of the estate. The man who had lived there had needed to go into a Care Home and his family wanted to sell to help with the cost of the fees. I took his phone number and he was only too pleased to meet me and show me the house. They have cleaned it and removed all his belongings. It will need to be redecorated and the kitchen and bathroom will have to be modernised, but I placed an offer immediately and it has been accepted.'

'Well, you really have taken my breath away,' said Marianne. 'You're quite certain you are doing the right thing? You can still withdraw if you have second thoughts.'

'I am happy with my decision. If I really do not enjoy living there it should be no problem to sell on, particularly when I have made the necessary improvements.'

'Then I am very pleased for you. Send me some photos of before and after.'

'I have to decide on the fitments I want and arrange for builders and decorators as I want everything completed before I move in. I'm pencilling in a date for the New Year, but there is no urgency. I can always wait another week or so.'

'How close are you to the shops?'

'All I need are within walking distance. If that becomes too much for me I can always call a cab.'

'Have you told Helena?' asked Marianne, expecting to have a phone call later from her sister.

'Not yet. I want to have everything finalised and the work completed. If I tell her now she is bound to find something wrong with it and give me second thoughts. She has invited me to spend Christmas with them and I thought I would tell her then.'

'Have you sufficient funds until Helena and Greg have bought your house? If you need any more please let us know.'

'Thank you, Marianne, but I should be fine at present. I would ask you a big favour, though. Are you cooking a traditional Christmas dinner?'

Marianne laughed. 'I think everyone would leave home if I didn't. What do you want me to do?'

'Could you make two small Christmas cakes and deliver them to Evi and Maria? I'm sure they would appreciate that.'

'That's no problem at all. I'm not sure who'll be joining us. I think Vasilis and Cathy will want to have this Christmas in their new house. I expect Kyriakos will spend time with his mother so we could ask Ronnie to join us. He could visit later and they could stay for the evening. With so many of us around catering for one or two extra is never a problem.'

Ronnie showed John and Nicola the progress that had taken place in her house.

'At least the upstairs floor is now in and the iron work for the hand rail should be delivered and placed in situ this week. I don't know how much more will be completed this winter as I know Vasi and Saffron want Mr Palamakis to work on the conversion of the big house.' She smiled. 'At least it gives me time to save a bit more money then I can ask him to put up the dividing walls for the upstairs rooms.'

'What will you do with the house when it is finished?'

'I haven't thought that far ahead yet. Kyriakos and I are happy in the apartment at present. If his mother needed to come and live with us we might have to think about making some alterations to the ground floor and we would have to move in here to look after her. Although I am getting on better with her at present I don't relish that thought and I'm sure she would hate to live with me.'

'Let's hope that day is a long way off,' said Nicola. 'We really came up to tell you everything we have found out so far about Luke's family. I don't think we can progress any further and it is up to you what you tell Luke and if you mention Panayiotis's idea to him. I've made you some notes so that you don't forget anything relevant.'

'I really appreciate all the work you have done and I'm sure Luke will also. I wonder if he and Ingrid will come back over here if he is the owner of the Schisma house?'

'Rather a long way to come to look at a derelict house with such a bad history,' remarked John. 'I don't suggest you go down there to look at it. It certainly freaked both Nick and Skele out. He wouldn't go anywhere near the place.'

'I'm not interested in looking at it. What Luke decides will be up to him.'

Ronnie read through the notes that John and Nicola had left. She was pleased she had them as she was sure she would have forgotten something relevant and important when she emailed Luke otherwise. She would tell Luke everything, including the strange feelings that Nicola had experienced when looking at the house at Schisma and Panayiotis's idea that he could be the legal owner of the property. If he was interested she would have to ask him to search through his mother's papers and see if he could find anything that would give him a legal claim. If it did actually belong to him what would he do with it?

Vasi and Saffron drove up to the house and waited for Mr Palamakis to arrive. It was also a good excuse to take the dogs up on the hill for a long walk, rather than just along the seafront road and the Causeway.

Saffron looked around critically. 'I think the idea of white walls everywhere and then matching bedding and curtains is best. I think terracotta accessories would be better for the room that is going to be called Autumn. Orange is somewhat harsh and bright. The bathroom tiles could be white and I'm sure we could find some tiles with orange autumn leaves to make it look less austere.'

'Why should it look like a stir?' asked Vasi.

Saffron laughed at him. 'Not 'a stir' – you do that when you are cooking. Austere means blank or severe.'

Vasi nodded. There were still some English words that he was not familiar with. The bathrooms at the hotel were all decorated exactly the same with fawn tiles. They were serviceable and practical. The bedroom walls were white and the bed covers in each room were the same colour throughout and the rooms themselves were distinguished by the numbers that were on their doors.

'I'd like to look at some more tile patterns to see if we could find anything suitable for the other bathrooms, nothing too flowery and certainly not fish.'

'We can do that later today when we get home. We need to decide about the downstairs area.'

'Apart from a fresh coat of paint on the walls there really is nothing that needs to be done. I'll check all the kitchen appliances to make sure they are in good working order. One or two may need to be replaced. I'll have to look at the china and cutlery as well. We cannot say this is a luxury villa if nothing matches when it's put on the dining table.'

Again Vasi nodded. He would leave all those decisions to Saffron.

'And there are towels. They need to be the correct colour for each bathroom and plenty of them. We'll also need some that people can take down to the pool with them.' Saffron frowned. 'We'll have to think about ornaments and pictures and see if there are suitable items stored here. We don't want everywhere looking bare and unfriendly.'

'Why don't you make a list and we can work through it gradually? There's plenty of time before the start of the season.'

Saffron shook her head. 'If we want to be able to start having visitors at Easter it is only four months away. We don't want to order something in January and find there is a two or three month delay. Better to know now and change our ideas to suit whatever else is available. We also have to think about marketing. We need to have a web site that shows how attractive the house is. Obviously we cannot put photos on until it is completed, but we can make a start on the wording that we want to use to attract people.'

'What about children?'

'We'll not make any rules about those until we see how much interest we receive from prospective customers. We may have to accept children to cover our costs.'

'There is one strict proviso,' said Vasi. 'Under no circumstances is Marianne's sister to be allowed to stay here.'

'That's easy. If she did want to stay here we'd simply tell her that we are fully booked or say we were having work done on the drains and there was no running water. We'll collect the dogs from the garden and when we get home I'll start to look on the internet and make lists.'

It took Ronnie some considerable time to compose an email to Luke including all the relevant information that John and Nicola had found out. She had included the story of the old lady being accused of witch craft and her ultimate fate. She also mentioned that the house at Schisma was derelict and John and Nicola both said that an unpleasant smell seemed to emanate from it. They had advised her not to go down there. Despite being curious she would abide by their instructions even if Kyriakos offered to accompany her.

'I trust Nicola and John. They said that even their dog was unhappy about being there. After they spoke to Panayiotis he went there to have a look and had a bad experience that sent him to the hospital thinking he had a blood pressure problem.'

'What did the hospital say?'

'They could find nothing wrong with him, but apparently he had opened the door to the cottage when he began to feel ill and the nasty smell he had noticed earlier became much stronger. I'm not superstitious in the same way as the Greek people are, but I still do not walk under a ladder and I throw salt over my shoulder if I spill it. Suppose the old lady really was a witch and she was able to put some sort of spell on people so they became ill?'

Kyriakos shook his head. 'I do not believe in witches and casting spells. I think it more likely that there is something growing there that smells bad or a dead animal and that is why John's dog would not go near.'

'Nicola would not have picked up on that unless the smell was so strong that you could smell it from quite a distance away. The area is best avoided.'

'It could be the rancid smell of the salt pans or where people have been dumping their household rubbish,' suggested Kyriakos.

'Their dog is used to that smell as they walk him down by the salt pans and the Causeway frequently. I know, it could be due to a number of things, but I'm not prepared to go down there to find out. Please, Kyriakos, promise me you'll not go down there.'

Kyriakos smiled. 'I promise.' For all his talk about not being superstitious he was not prepared to take a chance and visit the area. Even if it was household rubbish that was smelling badly he could catch a nasty germ from it and the fact that it had also affected Panayiotis was worrying.

Luke opened the long email he received from Ronnie and read it through with interest. He must show it to Ingrid and see what she thought. He did not consider himself a superstitious man but he would still touch wood and knock three times on occasions to ward off any malignant spirits that were in the area. He found it intriguing to think that he could be distantly related to a woman who was considered to be a witch and wished his mother was still there. She had always wanted to know about the mysterious aunt that no one would have anything to do with.

He was not sure if he wanted to find he was the owner of a 'haunted' house, but the land could be valuable and he had his sons to consider. Although the ranch was as profitable as ever and Luke knew that he should have more than enough assets to pass on to his boys eventually one never knew what the future might hold and a little more would not come amiss.

Luke opened the bureau drawer and removed the old cash box that held his mother's papers. He laid them out separately on the table. His immigration papers were there, in the name of Lucas Tsantakis, along with his mother's, showing her date of birth and the date they had entered Australia. He also had his grandparents' papers showing the same date of entry and their dates of birth. Along with those was his brother Dimitris's birth certificate with his death certificate clipped to the back. He looked at it as tears misted his eyes. He and Dimitris had been close, despite going their separate ways in later life.

There was his mother's marriage certificate from when she married Fred, along with his birth and death certificate and Fred's parents' marriage certificate. The birth certificates for all his half brothers and sisters were in a separate envelope and clipped to all of them, except George and Maggie's, was a death certificate showing when and how they had died. His and Dimitris's adoption papers were there showing when Fred had legally adopted them and their surname changed.

Luke collected most of them together and placed them back in the cash box. The only ones that were relevant to him at present were those showing the details of his mother and grandparents. There was nowhere he could look for further information in Australia and wished he had asked his mother for details of her grandparents and the aunt and uncle she had lived with in Elounda.

He read through the email from Ronnie a second time and as he did so a thought struck him. John and Nicola had talked to the old woman in Kastelli who had known Eirini vaguely and also her parents; they had also talked to the one person in Fourni who was a descendant of the Tsantakis family, but they had not approached the church in either village to see if there were any records of the families. Would John and Nicola be prepared to visit the areas again and see if there were any more details that could be gleaned from the church?

The more Luke thought about it the more he felt that he must ask them. If they found nothing it was most unlikely that he would be able to prove that he was entitled to the property at Schisma that they mentioned. He opened up his computer and began to compose a letter of reply back to Ronnie and also his request to John.

Ronnie had expected a conventional thank you for the information she had sent Luke which he would ask to be passed on to John and Nicola. He went to great lengths to explain how grateful he was to them so far and delighted to know that the old lady to whom he believed himself related was not responsible for the deaths of the soldiers. He then continued that he had been unable to find out any more information about the family from his mother's papers but he would like to ask John and Nicola to visit the churches at both Fourni and Kastelli now he knew the names of his grandparents and see if there were any records of the families held there. He had decided that he would like to inherit the cottage at Schisma if it could be proved that he was the owner.

Ronnie replied that she had forwarded a copy of Luke's email to John and asked if he would reply directly to Luke. She could certainly not commit John and Nicola to investigating the man's ancestry any further.

John read the email and called Nicola to read it also.

'I feel quite stupid. Why did we never visit the churches and ask if they had any old records?'

'We thought that after talking to Despina in Fourni we had reached a dead end,' said Nicola placatingly. 'Had Despina not been able to help us we were planning to go to the church, remember.'

'I blame myself for not going to the church afterwards. It's possible that there are baptismal records for Eirini's mother and her sisters. We might even be able to find out the name of the sister in Elounda.'

Nicola nodded. 'I suppose that's possible.'

'I'll reply to Luke and ask him to send me all the details he has from the immigration papers. That would at least give us a name for Eirini's mother and possibly her date of birth.'

'It could have helped if he had sent that information to us a long while back.'

'You can't blame him,' protested John. 'He did not know that Ronnie was going to become curious and ask us to find out about the family. He only sent his mother's memoirs as he thought she might be interested.'

'You don't think we offended him by trying to dig into his mother's past?'

John shook his head. 'If he was offended he would not have asked if we could find out any further information. He actually sounds as if he wants to be the owner of the house at Schisma.'

Nicola shuddered. 'I can't think why, but then he hasn't been down there and felt the evil that seems to surround it. I'm not prepared to go down there again even if he begs me or offers me a fortune.'

'Actually I don't think we will be able to do much more until after Christmas. We could try the churches, but they are probably busy arranging their Christmas services and won't want us around. I'll explain to Luke that we will visit the churches as soon as the New Year festivities are over and I'm sure he will understand. Let me know if you come up with any other ideas that could help.'

January 2017
Week Two

Vasilis and Cathy had celebrated Christmas in their new house with Vasi and Saffron. Saffron had helped Cathy with the cooking which Cathy had appreciated.

'I can manage perfectly well provided I do not have to stand too long at the hob or have to keep moving around. Having you here to help me fetch and carry made a tremendous difference.'

'I'm pleased you found me helpful. It's always difficult to have two women in the kitchen.'

'Vasilis wants to throw a New Year party, but I have said that would be better once the New Year had been celebrated by everyone else. It would be something for people to look forward to.'

'Will you be cooking again?' asked Saffron.

Cathy shook her head. 'It will just be drinks and nibbles. I can cope with that.'

Ronnie had agreed, somewhat reluctantly, to go to Kyriakos's mother and cook a traditional Christmas dinner for her.

'It would be difficult to bring her up to us even now she no longer has to wear that brace the whole time and by the time we had driven down everything would be spoiled. I'll help and I'll also make sure my mother keeps out of the kitchen and does not come to interfere with whatever you are doing.'

'Provided that is a promise, Kyriakos. I do not want you

disappearing off to have a drink with friends. I'm sure your mother would be convinced I was doing everything wrong. We'd probably end up coming to blows. If you would prefer to spend the time just you and her together I will understand.'

'My mother has to realise that you are part of our family and accept you. I think she was impressed that you made the effort to go down and look after her and keep her company some of the time. For all her scathing remarks about Americans when she realised that Marianne's mother and her other relatives were Greek Americans that raised your status in her eyes.'

'I do admit that she became easier to be with after a while. I wish I could speak Greek properly so that we could talk.'

'I can help you whilst the taverna is closed. We can spend part of each day speaking only in Greek. You'll soon pick it up then.'

Ronnie looked at Kyriakos dubiously. There had always seemed to be someone around who could speak English well enough to help her if she had a problem.

Evi and Maria were delighted when Marianne had arrived with a Christmas cake, along with tins of biscuits, crystallized orange slices and a box of chocolates for each of them.

'What are you doing for Christmas,' Evi had asked and seemed disappointed when Marianne said they would just be having a large lunch that day with the family.

'Is your mother coming over?'

Marianne shook her head. 'Not at the moment. She will spend Christmas with my sister and her husband in New Orleans. She has just sold her house in New Orleans and is planning to move to an apartment as soon as some building work has been carried out.'

'Does that mean she will not be moving over here to live in our village?' asked Maria eagerly.

'I'm not sure if she will want to live up here. She finds the hill rather too much for her and it depends upon a suitable property becoming available.'

'You can always use your car to collect her and bring her back.'

'That would be fine out of season, but we all become very busy once the tourists start arriving.'

'Or if it snows,' remarked Evi dolefully. 'I heard the weather forecast the other day and they say that snow is likely at any time now.'

'Well, if you are snowed in for a few days you will both have plenty to eat.' Marianne indicated the gifts that sat on the table. 'Of course my granddaughters are hoping that it will snow. Their father has promised to take them up on the hill to sledge and play snow balls.'

'I hate the snow,' remarked Evi. 'Always have; nasty cold wet stuff. Goes right through you, far worse than rain and makes everywhere slippery.'

'You hate the sun also when you say it gets too hot to go out,' countered Maria.

'At least you can stay inside then and keep cool.'

'So if it snows you stay inside and keep warm.'

Evi sniffed and glared at her friend. Marianne sensed the beginning of an argument between them.

'I really must go. I left Bryony and Nicola looking after the children along with Marisa and Uncle Yannis. They're probably being run ragged by them all by now. I'll come up and visit you again in the New Year.'

'Don't forget to tell your mother that we are looking forward to having her as a neighbour.'

Marianne nodded. Obviously Maria had forgotten that she had told her that her mother did not intend to live in the village.

John looked out of the window. 'It's trying to snow,' he announced to Nicola.

'Proper snow or just that sleety stuff that we usually have down here?'

'Just sleet at the moment, but I expect there's snow up on Lassithi.'

'I'm so glad we do not live up there. I'd hate to be snowed in for days at a time.'

'I imagine you get used to it if you've always lived up there. We get used to a rough sea down here.'

'At least we don't usually have to go out on the sea if the weather is bad. If you live up in the hills and have animals you still have to go out to feed them.'

'I thought I could take the girls a short distance up the hill and see if there's enough snow for them to build a snowman and I could take some photos.'

Nicola shook her head. 'That's fine by me, but don't let them get too cold. I'd far rather stay here and keep Yiannis amused. I might even let him play with his cars in the kitchen for a while if no one is around.'

'There's one thing for sure,' continued John, 'If the snow does lay the road up to Kastelli and down to Fourni will be impassable. We'll have to delay our visit to the churches up there.'

'I'm sure Luke will understand. I don't think he is expecting any results that quickly and we are going to Vasilis and Cathy tomorrow for late New Year drinks and nibbles. I've arranged for Lena to come in and look after the children so we are able to spend a reasonable amount of time there without having to rush back home.'

Vasi received a telephone call from Mr Palamakis. 'My men are stopping work early on the house today. It's snowing quite hard up there apparently and they don't want to find they are unable to get home later.'

'I understand. I just hope this spell of bad weather will not last too long.'

Vasi relayed the message back to Saffron. 'We could drive up as far as possible and take the dogs for a walk. If we find the roads are reasonable we can tell Mr Palamakis.'

'We don't want to get stuck up there either,' said Saffron.

'The house is only half way up the hill and we were always able to drive up and down even when the people on Lassithi were snowed in for a few days. We can always put some duvets in the car, take a flask with us and something to eat. It isn't that far to walk back if we can't drive safely.'

Saffron shook her head. 'There's no need for us to go up there. The dogs need a walk so we could drive along to the salt pans and walk over to the Causeway. That way we wouldn't need to take duvets, flasks and food with us and should be able to return easily to the car and drive home.'

Vasi was forced to agree that was a better idea than driving up the hill to the house and risking getting stuck. 'Put some warm clothes on and we'll go before it gets dark.'

Saffron placed an extra jumper on, wound a woollen scarf around her neck and zipped up her winter parka. She took a second pair of gloves from the drawer and stuffed them into her pocket. If she did happen to slip over at least she would have some dry gloves to put on.

The dogs sensed they were going out and began to weave themselves around their legs prior to having their leads fastened to their collars.

'Do you think they'll be warm enough?' asked Saffron.

'Of course. They have their fur coats and they'll be running around. It will be a new experience for them.'

'You won't throw snowballs at me or put snow down my neck, will you?' She remembered the miserable experience she had suffered when still at school and the boys had thought it great fun to torment the girls.

Vasi looked at her reproachfully. 'Of course not. Are you ready?'

Saffron nodded, she was still unsure that she wanted to leave the warmth of their apartment and go out, but she had to admit that the dogs needed a walk each day regardless of the weather.

Having driven up the main road and down to the pedestrian

area of the salt flats Vasi parked the car close to where there was a narrow track leading off through the bushes.

'That looks like a pedestrian area so we should be able to leave the car here without causing a problem for anyone.'

Vasi opened the door and both dogs jumped out immediately and began to nose around. They did not seem to notice the weather. Juni went over to the track to investigate and her reaction surprised Vasi. Her ears went down and she let out a howl before racing back to his side, shivering violently.

'Come on, Juni. It's not that cold.'

He and Saffron walked down towards the paved pedestrian area that led to the Causeway.Saffron shivered as an icy blast of sleet blew in from the sea and hit her in the face. Even the dogs stopped walking every so often and looked back at them reproachfully before running off to investigate where the sleet had gathered in a small white heap.

It was even colder and windier as they began to walk along the Causeway and Saffron finally stopped. 'I can't go any further, Vasi. I'm frozen. I can't feel my feet and I'll probably end up with chilblains on my toes.'

Vasi gave a puzzled frown. 'Why would you have chillies on your toes?'

'Not chillies, chilblains.'

'Oh,' Vasi smiled. 'I thought you said chillies. I know what you mean by chilblains. Are you really that cold?'

Saffron nodded miserably. 'It's the dampness. It seems to go right through me.'

Vasi placed his arm around her. 'We'll turn back. The dogs have had a run and I don't want you to become ill.'

'Don't you feel cold?' asked Saffron.

'Yes, but I probably have more body fat than you so I don't feel it as badly.' Vasi whistled to the dogs and Seni ran towards him, whilst Juni continuing to nose around at something she found interesting.

'Come here, Juni. Come.' The pup took no notice of him and Seni ran back and gave her a push with her nose and then another until Juni reluctantly began to trot back to where Vasi and Saffron were waiting.

'I'll have to start some serious dog training with that young puppy. She needs to come when I call her name.'

Saffron nodded. 'Maybe we should have named them differently, Senior and Junior means nothing to them.' She just wanted to return to the car and drive back to their warm apartment.

'Nor would any other name,' remarked John. 'Seni obeys when I call her. Juni just needs some time. I don't know what frightened her when we first arrived.'

Luke copied the papers he had found relating to when the family entered Australia and emailed them to John.

'I don't know if these will be of any help to you, but when you have time to visit the churches they could at least give you an idea of the dates that would be relevant to a search. You must also let me know how much I owe you for your time.'

John grinned. 'My time can be given freely, but do you think I can send him a bill for the whisky and the meals we've spent money on?'

'That sounds reasonable. It will only come to about seventy Euros. If he asks for the bills I'm sure we can ask Kyriakos for a some blank bill heads and fill them in as appropriate.'

'There is also the petrol you have used and we'll probably have to give the churches a donation if they give us access to their records.'

John shrugged. 'I'll not send him a bill until I can work out a final reasonable amount. I hope we won't have to reimburse Mum for baby sitting.'

John printed off the certificates and showed them to Nicola. 'We can work backwards from Eirini's date of birth to see if she was baptised and then back from there for her mother and aunts.'

'Do you think those records will still be held at Fourni?'

'I don't know. They may have been sent away to a central storage depot after a number of years.'

'Well before we go up there why don't we go and ask Father Emmanuel if he knows if old records are sent away? He could probably tell us where the repository is.'

'Probably Athens,' remarked John gloomily. 'Good idea of yours, though. It could save us a wasted journey.'

'We could drive in tomorrow and ask him. We can say how much we enjoyed the church services and even allowed the girls to stay up late so they could come with us.'

Father Emmanuel was delighted to see them and hear that the family had enjoyed the services he had held.

'It is always so gratifying to see the parents bringing their children. It gives them a good grounding and respect for the church as they grow older.'

'Quite right,' agreed John. 'Of course, when we are busy during the season we are not always able to attend services. Unfortunately the needs of the tourists have to come first.'

Father Emmanuel nodded. This explained why he saw them irregularly during the year. 'You are always welcome just to walk in, light a candle, say a quick prayer and kiss an icon.'

'We tend to do that at Plaka as we are so much nearer to the church there. We were married there, and the children were baptised there,' answered John.

Father Emmanuel gave him a dubious look. He would have to check how frequently the priest in Plaka saw members of the family.

'We also wanted to ask you something about baptisms,' continued John. 'A friend of ours lives in Australia although he was born here in Elounda. He knows so little about his mother's family that he asked if we could find out any details for him. It would mean going back over a hundred years and we wanted to

167

ask if the parish registers would still be in the churches or if they have been sent to a repository elsewhere.'

'That would depend. If the church has subsequently closed down for whatever reason then the records would have been sent to the Archive Offices or the Town Hall. If the church is still functional they probably have their records. I have those for Elounda here in my safe keeping.'

'We are actually looking in the village of Fourni as that was where the family lived originally.'

'In that case I cannot help you. I can only suggest that you go to Fourni and ask the priest there. If he does not have them he should be able to tell you where they have been deposited.'

'Thank you for your help.' John took a ten Euro note from his pocket and placed it in the donation box.

'I really gave him far too much,' said John as he and Nicola left the church, 'But I felt I should be generous.'

'Add it on to Luke's bill,' grinned Nicola. 'You'll probably have to give even more if the priest at Fourni allows us to see the records and make some notes.'

'At least we know the records should be there. I would hate to tell Luke they were in Athens and expect him to pay for me to go over there to look at them.'

'If that turned out to be the case you'd do better to tell him that they are too old to be available.'

John shook his head. 'I wouldn't want to do that. I'd like to know more about the family. Do you think there would be any records at the church at Schisma?'

'It's unlikely. They don't have a regular priest in attendance. The church is left open for visitors to go inside and look around, but I'm sure they wouldn't leave anything of any value in there. Unfortunately tourists have a bad habit of helping themselves to souvenirs.'

'We should have asked Father Emmanuel. We should also have asked him the name of the priest in Fourni,' sighed John.

'I'm sure Despina at the Fourni taverna can tell us his name and if the church is open all the time. We can call in at the taverna for a drink and then go across to the church. If it is closed part of the day I'm sure Despina will know when the priest would be available. He probably goes over to the taverna for his evening meal if he lives alone.'

John shrugged. 'We can't do anything until this weather has cleared through and we know the roads are open. I wouldn't want to get stranded up there for the night.'

'I'm sure Despina would be willing to provide us with a bed, but I'd far rather be back here in Elounda. I have a feeling their living quarters at the taverna could leave something to be desired.'

'We could throw ourselves on the mercy of the priest,' suggested John and Nicola looked at him scathingly.

'I don't think they believe in comfort. Being cold and sleeping on a hard bed is all part of being a priest.'

'I'm sure Father Emmanuel has a lovely warm house and considers that is his due.'

'I'll take your word for it. I found it really cold in the church,' Nicola shivered. 'Have you noticed how fat the priests begin to look in the winter? They probably have so many layers of clothes on that the cold can't get through.'

January 2017
Week Three

'Well, that spell of bad weather did not last long,' observed John. 'The girls were disappointed that we didn't find enough snow to build a snowman, but they enjoyed throwing snowballs for Skele to chase after.'

'We might get some more later on. Shall I phone Ronnie and see if the road to Kastelli is clear?'

'Good idea. She will probably know if Fourni is accessible also. Then we could go up and visit the taverna and the priest at the church.'

'I'm so pleased that we were able to visit Vasilis and Cathy for their New Year drinks evening. I wish we could have stayed longer but I felt obliged to get home at a reasonable time so you could take Lena home. Did you talk to Vasi at all? '

'I have to admit that I hardly had time to talk to anyone except Monika and Ackers. Monika says her mother is concerned that she will have to move from her apartment next season and find some other work. I'm not sure if she was hoping we could offer Litsa some work at the apartments. Ackers was telling me how his mother is progressing and the fact that she and Ronnie are on better terms. It was fortunate that it was Marianne's mother who helped her initially so that she was able to get to know other members of the family and realise that Americans are decent people.'

'I'm pleased some good has come out of her accident. Vasi told me a strange story about taking his dogs for a walk. Apparently they parked where the track leads down to the cottage at Schisma and the young dog freaked out.'

'Really? I'll have to ask him more about that.'

'What more is there? We know there is something horrible about that area. We felt it and Panayiotis had a really bad experience when he went and opened the cottage door.'

'At least we know it was not a figment of our imagination. I did think we could have been influenced by the knowledge we had of the old lady who had lived down there.'

'Panayiotis would not have been influenced by that. He's a policeman,' replied Nicola sceptically. 'Something certainly disturbed Skele when we walked along there.'

'It's possible that the smell is coming off the salt pans, algae or some dead fish that has accumulated locally. We may find the next time we go down to that area the smell has gone.'

Nicola shook her head. 'Smell or no smell I am not walking along that lane to the house again. It's not just a smell, it's like an aura coming from it that feels evil.'

'Are you scared that the old lady is still around and will put a spell on you?' Before Nicola could reply John grinned at her. 'I'm only teasing. Let's concentrate on finding out more about the family in Fourni.'

John and Nicola drove up to where the Lassithi Plain began, noticing that the higher they went the more snow there was accumulated in the ditches and beside the bushes.

'I should have brought the girls up here. Looks as if they would have had plenty of snow to build a snowman.'

'That would not have been sensible. Suppose you were stuck up here? It would be a long way for the girls to walk home in the cold.'

'I would have phoned you and asked you to drive up as far as possible to meet us. Now, let's see what it is like driving down to Fourni.'

The road was clear and they were able to draw up outside the taverna. 'It looks deserted,' said Nicola.

'They're probably all inside keeping warm. I'll knock the door and see if anyone comes.'

The door opened to John's touch and he and Nicola walked inside. The whole family were gathered around the somba and looked at them in surprise.

Despina stood up. 'We weren't expecting any customers.'

'We will be quite happy just to have a warm drink,' smiled John. 'We were here a few weeks ago and you were very helpful to us.' John removed his hat and unwound his scarf from his neck.

Despina peered at him. 'Oh, it's you. I remember now. I thought you looked familiar.'

'We all look different when we're dressed for cold weather. I'm pleased that you are so nice and warm in here.'

'I have very little food. We're waiting for supplies to be delivered now the road is clear again.'

'We wouldn't dream of troubling you for a meal. As I said, a warm drink would be appreciated, but nothing more.'

One of the aunts left her place close to the somba and moved into the kitchen area, calling back as she went. 'That's my chair. I'll be back in a few minutes and expect to sit down there again.'

The two other ladies took no notice, each one moving the chair out of the way so they could be closer to the heat.

'We did wonder if you would be able to help us again,' began John and Despina shook her head.

'I've told you all I know about the Tsantakis family.'

'You were certainly very helpful,' agreed John. 'This time I would like to ask you about the priest at the church. Is he there all day or only when he has to take a service?'

'He's always there unless he's been called out to give comfort to a sick person. He has a small house at the back of the church.'

'In that case I hope we will be able to find him at home.'

'I doubt that he will know anything more about the family than I have told you.'

'We actually want to ask him about some old records that could be in the church for safe keeping. They may not be there, of course, but he should be able to tell us their whereabouts.'

Despina seemed to lose interest and as soon as coffee was placed on the table before Nicola and John she returned to the somba, ensuring that the chairs were moved back to their original positions.

Having paid for their drinks John and Nicola crossed the road to the church. They tried the door and it was locked.

'Round the back, then to see if he is in his house.'

Nicola followed John and as they approached the small house they saw the curtains twitch and by the time they reached the door it was being opened.

'Good morning. How can I help you?'

'May we come in, please. Despina at the taverna said you were probably keeping warm in your house.'

The priest opened the door wider. 'Visitors are always welcome.'

John and Nicola followed him into the small room where his chair was drawn up in front of the somba.

'Please have a seat.'

Apart from the armchair that obviously belonged to the priest along with a small wooden table beside it there were only two wooden chairs pushed beneath the table. John turned them round so they could face the priest whilst they talked to him.

'This is rather a long story and before we tell you we would like to ask if you have the old registers for the church here. We are interested in marriages and baptisms from over a hundred years ago.'

'I do have them, but I will need to get them from the repository. I am Father Christos. You are?'

John introduced them and shook hands with Father Christos.

'A friend of ours, whose mother was born in this village, has asked us if we can trace her family and find some information about her grandparents and also her aunts.'

Father Christos raised his eyebrows. 'So why does this friend not come with you and ask for this information?'

'He lives in Australia,' replied John. 'I can tell you the whole story if you have the time to spare. We have the date of birth for our friend's mother and we are hoping there will be an entry in the old registers of her parents' marriage and the baptism of their three daughters.'

The priest considered for a moment. 'I doubt that the reason behind your friend's interest has any relevance to me. If you will come with me to the Church I will open the repository. The record books are heavy so I would appreciate your help in carrying them back here.'

'Of course.' John stood up and refastened his coat. 'Will you need my wife to help carry them?'

'No, she may stay here.' Father Christos took a heavy cloak that hung behind the door and wrapped it around himself before taking a heavy key from the hook above the handle.

Nicola smiled thankfully. She did not relish having to go into a cold church and wait around whilst the priest found the relevant record books. Once John and Father Christos had left Nicola took the opportunity to look around the living room. The furnishings were sparse, but adequate. On one wall there was a dresser with a glass cupboard at the top that held plates and glasses on two shelves. By the designs on them she thought they had probably belonged to his grandparents and were considered family heirlooms and never used. She guessed that the drawers beneath held cutlery but she was not ill mannered enough to open them and look. Old photographs were mounted on the walls and she assumed that the men and women shown in them were his parents, grandparents and possibly great grandparents judging by their clothes. She hoped the opportunity might arise whereby John could ask the priest about them.

The far wall held a single bed with a woven cover of intricate pattern and the pattern was repeated in the curtain hanging across an alcove that she assumed led to the kitchen area. The thing that surprised her most was seeing the title of the book the priest had laid on the table beside his chair. It was a modern novel by Patricia Wilson set in Crete that she had read and enjoyed. Somehow she had never imagined that priests read anything except religious literature.

Nicola sat there patiently waiting for John and the priest to return. She hoped Father Christos would not be too long before bringing the registers back to his house; although having removed her coat, enveloped in the warmth of the somba, she was beginning to feel incredibly sleepy.

The sound of the door opening and heavy items being placed on the table jerked her awake. John removed his coat whilst Father Christos hung his cloak up and placed the heavy key back on the hook.

'I hope these cover the years you are interested in and when you have finished I'll ask you to help me carry them back.'

'Of course,' John answered immediately. 'May I sit at the table and could you direct me to the years that I want? I don't want to damage the pages with my cold fingers.'

Father Christos opened the first large ledger at random and looked at the heading before turning back a number of pages and scanning the heading again. 'This ledger begins in nineteen twenty.'

'The date of birth we have been given for Eirini Ionnides is seventeenth of August 1922. Would that have been recorded or only the date when she was baptised?'

'We'll start from there and work forwards.'

The writing was cramped and small, some of it so faint that John could hardly read it, but Father Christos did not appear to have any difficulty. He ran his finger down each line, finally stopping at a date in mid September.

'I think this is what you are looking for.'

John took out his notebook and handed it to Nicola. 'Can you take notes for me, please?' He turned back to Father Christos.

'Could we look back and find out when her mother was born? We are hoping there will be a record of her marriage and then we can try to trace her two sisters. I believe there may have been a gap of some years between each of them.'

Father Christos sighed. 'They would be in the earlier ledger and the only way to look for them is by the father's name. Do you have that?'

'Yiorgo Koronakis. He was married to a lady named Maria.'

Father Christos frowned. He closed the ledger and placed it to one side. 'I think we need to start looking in nineteen hundred.'

John shook his head. 'No, that's too late. The oldest of them must have been born about eighteen eighty or shortly after.'

'In that case we will have to examine the earlier records.' He placed the two large ledgers to the far end of the table and opened the third. 'This one begins in eighteen fifty. There were quite a number of people living in Fourni at that time.'

'Not too many named Koronakis I hope.'

It took far longer to go through the earlier ledger, but finally the priest squinted at the page. 'There is a record of a baptism to a girl child in January eighteen eighty three, born to a father named Yiorgo Koronakis.'

John gave Nicola a delighted look. 'That could be the oldest child. Do you have her name?'

'She was baptised Andrula. Do you need me to look further?'

'Yes please. She had two younger sisters and the youngest girl married Dimitris Ionnides. Her name was Doretta.'

'There appears to have been another child, a boy, born in eighteen eighty four. Sadly he died within a few weeks of his birth.' Father Christos looked rapidly down the next two pages.

'The next entry of a child born to Yiorgo Koronakis is another girl who was baptised in the summer of eighteen eighty five. She was called Soula.'

'Please continue,' urged John. 'This is exactly the information our friend is hoping we can find.'

Father Christos stopped three more times, relaying the fact that a boy child had been born in eighteen eighty six and subsequently died a year later, and then another in 1888 who had met the same fate a few months afterwards. Finally Father Christos's finger pointed to an entry for eighteen ninety.

'This is an entry for the baptism of Doretta Koronakis in September eighteen ninety.'

'Wonderful,' remarked John. 'We now know the names of the three sisters and the years they were born. Sad that none of their boys survived, but that accounts for the age gaps between the girls.'

Father Christos sighed. 'Many women gave birth each year to another child. They were still nursing the previous one and often working out on the land until the child arrived. It is hardly surprising that there were so many fatalities.'

'Maybe that was why Doretta did not marry earlier. She may have been worried about child birth. At least marrying the local school teacher she knew he would have been better educated and not expected her to have one child after another or work out on the land.'

'Do you wish to delve further into the archives?' asked Father Christos.

John shook his head. 'Certainly not at the moment. You have been very generous with your time and so helpful. If we have any further queries may we come back to you again?' John took a twenty Euro note from his pocket and pressed it into the priest's hand. 'For your collection box.'

Father Christos pushed the note into his own pocket. 'Your donation is much appreciated. Now, if you will just help me to take these ledgers back to the repository.'

John replaced his coat and waited whilst the priest wrapped himself back up in his cloak and took the key from the hook and Nicola shrugged herself into her coat and wound her scarf around her neck. She hoped John and Father Christos would not be very long as she did not relish waiting outside in the cold.

'Yes,' said John and punched the air. 'That was a very worthwhile visit. When we get home we'll sit down and sort out everything we learnt. I imagine we could have delved even further back into the family but it seemed a bit pointless. We had the information we were looking for. I can then email Luke and it will be up to him how he wishes to proceed.'

'I wish we could have asked the priest about the photographs on his wall. They looked old by the style of their clothes. The china in the dresser looked as if that was from about the same age.'

John raised his eyebrows. 'So what else did you find out whilst I was looking for heavy ledgers in a cold room?'

'Something that I would never have guessed. Did you see the book that Father Christos had beside his chair?'

John shook his head. 'Tell me.'

'A modern novel. It's one that I've read, but I would never have expected a priest to read it.'

'What's wrong with it? The language or is it full of sex scenes?'

'Neither,' replied Nicola. 'I don't read books like that. It is set in Crete and describes how the author found a field gun buried in her garden. She talked to the local people and heard about the events in the village when it was under occupation during the war.'

'So is it history or a novel?'

'Both, I suppose. It is historically correct but the author has been clever enough to make it into a novel. You should try reading something other than photographic magazines.'

'Does the author still live in Crete?'

Nicola shook her head. 'Not now. She's moved to another island.'

'Shame. She may have been interested in Luke's family history.'

January 2017
Week Four

Saffron spent a long time looking on the internet for tiles that she felt would be suitable for the bathrooms up at the big house. It was difficult to ascertain the quality by looking at photographs and many looked exactly the same although varying considerably in price.

'The price could be different because of the dimensions of the tile,' commented Vasi.

'According to the description they are all the same size on this page.'

'I think we should go up to the house and ask one of the Palamakis men to measure up each bathroom properly so that we know exactly how many we will need. They have to allow a certain amount for cutting round the fitments and we don't want to find that we are one or two short and they have no more that match.'

'Maybe we should look at the fitments first and make sure we don't need to renew any of them, Have the showers in the spare bathrooms been tested? We only ever used the one in our bedroom.' Saffron felt frustrated and exited the web site.

'That would probably be a better idea. If you want to make any changes to the fitments now is the time to do so.'

'What about the floor? We need tiles that are not slippery if they get wet.'

'The ones I have in the bathrooms at the hotel are not slippery.'

'Then we need some like those, but I'm not sure that the colour is right. If we are having white tiles on the walls I don't think they will go well with fawn tiles on the floor and some of those that are there at the moment need to be replaced.'

Vasi sighed. Saffron had been looking at ceramic tiles for days and still not found anything that she considered satisfactory.

'Leave it for today. We can drive up to the house tomorrow and discuss the fitments. We have to make sure that we do not choose any items that are too large. People need a certain amount of space to be able to towel themselves dry.'

Saffron shrugged. 'We should have looked into the costing more carefully before we started. With four rooms, even if we are fully booked throughout the season, we will only cover our overheads and not be recouping our expenses. There are the utility bills, laundry and cleaning that has to be taken into account.'

'I'm not expecting to make a profit in our first few seasons. We will need to become known and recommended by those who have stayed there.'

'We'll also need a gardener and someone to maintain the swimming pool,' continued Saffron. 'I begin to wish we had never thought of this idea and just asked your father if you could sell it.'

'Attention would still have been needed if we expected to receive a decent price for the property. It will all work itself out in time. I'm not short of money and the more I tell the tax man I have spent on the house the less he'll be able to charge me for making a profit at the hotel. Are you coming with me to take the dogs for a walk?'

'That's another thing, how are we going to cope with them when we are both working during the season?'

'Saffie, stop worrying. You are making problems where there aren't any. I'm sure I'll be able to find someone who is willing to take the dogs out for a while each day. Get your coat on and let's go and blow your doubts away.'

John sat down with Nicola and selected a sheet of paper. 'Bring your notebook, Nick, and let me see if I can work out the relationship Luke has with Eirini's family.

'It's not that difficult. Andrula, the one who had the house at Schisma, was his great aunt.'

'I need to see it written down so that I'm certain. I don't want to send Luke misleading information. Let's start with Eirini's grandparents and work down from there.'

John headed up the paper.

EIRINI'S FAMILY

Yiorgo & Maria Koronakis (grandparents)

CHILDREN

Andrula born 1883 (went to Turkey 1898, returned to Crete 1903)

Soula born 1885 (married salt pans worker)

Doretta born 1890 (married Dimitris Ionnides – school teacher)

Boys born between the girls but none survived.

Dimitris & Doretta Ionnides one daughter

EIRINI

Born 17th August 1922

Son – Lucas Tsantakis

Son – Dimitris Tsantakis

'Does that look clear enough?' asked John.

'It does to me,' said Nicola. 'Andrula was Eirini's aunt which makes her Luke's great aunt. I can only see one problem. If Luke is interested in claiming the cottage at Schisma is he the rightful owner? Wouldn't the two boys that Andrula had by the Turk be classed as closer relations?'

'It's very unlikely that Andrula and the Turk were ever legally married. We don't know his name so we can't try to trace him. The boys were young when they were taken to Turkey. They'll be old men now if they are still alive. It's doubtful that they would have any memory of living on Spinalonga or their birth mother. It's better that Luke considers himself her closest surviving relative. As it is it could take years before Luke has any reply confirming that he is the owner of the property. If we start adding in the possibility of Turkish descendants it will probably take for ever. I'll send Luke the details we have worked out about his mother's family and after that it is up to him.'

Although Vasi had spoken so confidently to Saffron he was also concerned how they would be able to cope once the season started. Saffron would be busy at Plaka with her gift shop and could not be expected to return to take the dogs for a walk during the day. He would be able to take them out first thing in the morning and again in the evening, but during the day he was usually busy at the hotel. It might be possible to leave the back door of their apartment open so the dogs could go out onto the patio if necessary.

That did not solve the problem of meeting any guests when they arrived at the new apartments and settling them in. They could arrive and depart at various different hours and he would need to be there to give them the keys, show them around and answer any questions they might have. He also needed to be there when they left. Their initial payment would include a deposit that would only be returned to them after he had checked to ensure no damage had occurred during their stay. He decided to speak to his father and see if he would be willing to manage the hotel on the days when he would be needed up at the apartments.

Vasilis listened to Vasi and shook his head. 'I have retired, remember. I do not want to have to spend my time sitting in a hotel foyer again or being called upon to sort out problems with the guests or staff. An odd day in an emergency I would agree to, but I do not want to be there on a regular basis.'

'Maybe I could ask Lambros to open up the apartments. He was always very reliable when he looked after the dogs. I could leave keys with him and he should be able to answer any questions they have. I could go up after the guests have left and check out the premises.'

Vasilis nodded. 'That might be possible, but remember you have to allow time for a cleaner to go in. If people left at mid-day you could have more arriving in the early hours of the following morning.'

Vasi shook his head in despair. 'I wish we had never thought about this idea. It would have been easier to leave the house closed up and put it up for sale.'

'You could still do that once Mr Palamakis's has finished all the decorating.'

'Once the rooms have been painted there are the bathrooms that need to be tiled. The current ones look very old, some are stained and one or two have a chip in the corner. No one would want to buy a house that still needed so much work on it. Saffron has spent hours looking on the internet and cannot find any tiles she thinks will be suitable.'

'So why doesn't she contact Pietro? I'm sure John or Giovanni would help her compose a letter to him in Italian setting out her exact requirements.'

'Now that is a good idea. I'll talk to Saffie about that when I get home. I left her looking at towels and bedding. In the meantime I can drive up and see if Lambros is available.'

Vasi drove up to the house and was pleased to see that Mr Palamakis's men were working up there. He could call in and see what progress had been made and also ask them to check that all the taps and showers were working efficiently. If he needed to renew anything it was unlikely to be of the same dimensions as the current appliance. He would also ask them to give him the exact dimensions of the wall area that needed to be tiled and a separate measurement for the floor. Saffron would need to know this to work out the quantity and price of tiles whether they purchased them from Pietro or bought locally.

He stopped outside Lambros's house. He wished he had brought the dogs up with him. They could have had a run around in the garden of the house provided he shut the gate and asked the workmen not to let them out. He could see someone sitting in the window and he waved before he knocked on the door.

To his surprise Lambros's son answered him. 'What can I do for you?'

'I was hoping to speak to your father. Is he available?'

'Not really. He has dementia. My mother is no longer able to cope with him. I have sold my grocery shop in Heraklion and my wife and I have moved up here to look after them.'

Vasi's face fell. 'I'm very sorry to hear that. I had come to ask him if he would be able to help look after the big house when the conversion is completed. It is going to be let out as self catering lets during the season.'

Stelios shook his head. 'He could not possibly do that I'm afraid.'

'Then I will have to think again. If you hear of anyone who might be suitable please could you contact me.' Vasi handed over his card with the details of his mobile phone.

Stelios looked at it and then placed it in his pocket. 'What exactly do you want someone to do?'

Vasi explained that someone needed to be on hand to let the guests in and out and deal with any problems that might arise.

'What about the cleaning? Would they be expected to do that as well?'

'No, I'd employ someone else for that.'

Stelios nodded. 'Well I'll let you know if I hear of anyone.'

Vasi drove over to the house and parked behind the workmen's vans. He was sorry to hear about Lambros, but that did not help his immediate problem. At least he could go inside and ask for the bathrooms to be measured accurately before he approached John or Giovanni and asked one of them to write a letter to Pietro on Saffron's behalf.

Stelios went back into the house. His father was sitting in his chair by the window mumbling to himself whilst his mother sat opposite looking down at her hands. Not for the first time Stelios thought that his mother was also showing the first signs of dementia. She had little interest in anything and when he or his wife talked to her she seemed unable to comprehend the most simple requests.

Christalia was in the kitchen where she seemed to spend most of her time preparing suitable meals for her in-laws along with her and Stelios.

'Who was that?' she asked.

'The man who has the big house where all the work is taking place. He told me he planned to ask my father if he could help with dealing with the guests during the season. I told him it was impossible.'

Christalia nodded. 'What exactly did he want him to do?'

'I didn't go into details as Pappa can't help. He did say he would not expect him to do the cleaning.'

'I could probably do the cleaning,' frowned Christalia.

'You?'

'Why not? Your mother is still capable of looking after her personal requirements. I only cook the meals and do the necessary cleaning in the house. It would help financially.'

'I suppose so,' Stelios nodded. 'Maybe I should have asked him to come in and explain exactly what the other work entailed. I might be able to do that.'

'Is he up at the house now? You could speak to him there.'

'I have a phone number for him.'

'Then call him. If he really is looking for someone to do the work he should be willing to at least talk to you and tell you what was expected of you.' Christalia looked at her husband challengingly. 'Call him now before he asks anyone else. Ask him to come back down to the house. I can have a quick tidy up before he arrives.'

Vasi was surprised when Stelios called him so quickly after his visit. 'I'll certainly come back and talk with you and your wife. Give me about half an hour as I'm with the workmen at the moment sorting out some details.'

Vasi looked at Lambros sadly. The old man obviously had no idea who he was and just asked if it was time for lunch. Vasi shook his head and approached Lambros's wife. She looked at him and Vasi realised that she did not recognise him.

'Lambros used to walk my dogs when I was living in Heraklion.'

She nodded. 'Two big dogs. Guard dogs.'

'That's right. They were very gentle with people they knew.'

'Big dogs. Where are they?' She looked around the room. 'Not here.'

'I haven't brought them with me today.' Vasi saw no need to explain that his original dogs had died years ago. 'I'll bring them to see you another day.'

She nodded, obviously content with that and looked back down at her hands.

Stelios indicated that Vasi should sit down at the table and Christalia brought coffee from the kitchen and a plate of biscuits. She gave Lambros a child's plastic cup that would not spill if he dropped it and placed his hands on the handles. To his wife she gave a china cup and a biscuit.

'That should keep them both occupied for a short while,' she said as she sat down with the two men. 'Stelios tells me that you need to employ people to help at the big house in the season. Tell us exactly what it is that you require.'

Vasi explained that guests could arrive at all hours during the day, possibly in the early hours of the morning and might also leave at inconvenient times. That someone needed to be there to meet them and see them in and also see them out when they left. 'Would you be able to manage that?'

'Is that all?' asked Stelios. 'I used to be busy in my grocer's shop all day.'

Vasi nodded. 'We would expect most visitors to stay for at least a week so you would only need to go up twice unless there was an emergency. I'd obviously show you exactly where everything is and how it works. If there was a real problem you could call me and I would come up. When they check out I would need you to go through the house and ensure there was no damage anywhere. Again, if it was something serious you could ask me to come to look.'

Stelios nodded. It sounded very easy work.

'And the cleaning?' asked Christalia. 'Is Stelios expected to do that as well?'

'Only the swimming pool. The maintenance company will have visited and it should only need any debris that has blown in removed and ensuring that the steps and hand rails are not slippery. I can employ a gardener to come once a month to keep the garden looking decent. The cleaning of the house only needs to be done twice in a week whilst people are staying; making sure the kitchen and bathrooms are clean, changing the towels and sheets, nothing much until they leave and then it will need to be cleaned throughout.'

'What about the washing?' asked Christalia.

'There is a washing machine in the house, but if you found it too much I could always collect it and take it back to the hotel. I could send it off with the washing from there.'

Stelios and Christalia looked at each other. 'We could do that. One of us can always be here to look after the parents.'

'How much to you propose to pay us?' asked Stelios.

'I would pay each of you seventy Euros a week whilst there are guests. That should also be adequate to cover any extras that you have to do.'

'Suppose you do not have anyone staying for a number of weeks?'

Vasi smiled. 'Then you will not have any work during that time, but I will pay you a retainer of thirty Euros each a week during the season. Does that sound fair?'

Both Stelios and Christalia nodded. At present they were living on the proceeds of the sale of the grocery store, but that money was not going to last for ever. It was more than fair; it was more than they had expected to be paid.

Vasi gave a sigh of relief. That was one problem solved.

'And in the winter months?'

'We can discuss that in more detail later. I won't know what needs to be done on a regular basis until then.'

Lambros dropped his cup and Christalia hurried over to pick it up before any coffee dribbled down his clothes. 'Lunch?' he said.

'Very soon,' Christalia assured him.

Vasi stood up. 'Thank you. I appreciate that you are willing to accept my offer. Should anything happen to make you reconsider please phone me. As soon as the house is completed I will be in touch and give both of you a conducted tour. Now I will leave you in peace. Lambros obviously would like his lunch.'

Christalia nodded. 'I always give him his first as I have to feed him, although that isn't always easy and he often needs a change of jumper afterwards.'

'You obviously have a good deal of patience.'

Christalia shrugged. 'It's necessary, Stelios will see you out.'

Vasi returned to Elounda feeling he had accomplished a good deal that morning. Despite his father's refusal to help him he had employed Stelios and Christalia and also received the accurate measurements for each bathroom. Whilst he and Saffie had their lunch he would tell her and whilst she sat and worded a letter to Pietro with her requests he would take the dogs for a walk. At that thought he frowned. There was still the problem of walking the dogs each day.

John received an email from Luke, thanking him yet again for all the trouble he had taken to find the information about his family. Towards the end he reiterated his intention of approaching the government to see if he could claim the Schisma property.

'I do have one big problem. I can still speak Greek, but I am certainly not capable of writing a letter to the Greek government. If I stated my case in English would you be able to translate it for me? I could then copy your letter and ask them to send me an email reply and also one to you. If they sent me a reply in Greek I doubt I would understand what they were saying or answer any further questions that they might have.'

John smiled at the request. 'I'll have to add on being an interpreter to Luke's final bill.'

That evening Vasi telephoned John. 'I have a big favour to ask of you.'

'You can ask; I can always refuse.'

Vasi explained that Saffron wanted to contact Pietro and ask him for some details about floor and wall tiles for their bathrooms.

'The rooms have all been measured up accurately and Saffie knows what she would like. She's spent hours looking on the internet and not found anything to her satisfaction. I mentioned this to my father this morning and he suggested she contacted Pietro. We should have thought about that earlier. The problem is neither of us can speak Italian. If Saffie sends the details over to you would you be willing to compose a letter and sent it to Pietro?'

John laughed. 'This is my second request today to act as an interpreter. Luke wants me to write a letter to the Greek government for him and now you want me to write to Pietro. Of course I'll do it. Send me all the details and I'll make a start on it tomorrow.'

February 2017
Week One

Saffron looked at the photos of the tiles that Pietro had sent through to her. She did not like the patterned ones at all; they were far too fussy. Mr Palamakis had confirmed that two showers needed to be renewed as they had seized up where they had not been used for so long and the basin taps also needed to be renewed where the washers had perished. It was a nuisance that the taps had then dribbled into the basins and left a residue of lime scale. He thought he might be able to remove this, but otherwise the basins would need to be replaced.

Saffron gave a sigh of relief. She was beginning to feel guilty about the way the costs were adding up, despite Vasi's assurance that there was plenty of money available. She looked at Ronnie's paintings of the bathrooms and decided that her suggestions were not practical. If she chose grey tiles for the bathroom floors and walls and then brought in colour with the towels they would look far more elegant.

'What do you think Vasi?'

'I'll agree to whatever you think is suitable.'

Saffron shook her head. 'No, I want your opinion. If you walked into a bedroom that had blue curtains and bedding would you find it acceptable that the bathroom also had blue towels?'

'Perfectly.'

'What about the tiles being grey?'

'No problem. Grey will accept any colour that is put with it.'

Saffron bent back over the measurements for the bathrooms. 'I'd like to check with Mr Palamakis before I make a final decision and order them. They are going to be expensive so I don't want to make a mistake.'

'If we are ordering a quantity Pietro may well offer us a discount.'

'We'll still have to pay for transport over here.'

'You can't order the same item from a stockist in Heraklion or Athens?'

'They're not the same quality if we buy locally. We don't want to find that they are slippery when they have been laid or crack within a year so we have to buy more and have to pay to have the damaged ones replaced. The new showers, taps and basins we can buy from Heraklion as I've decided they can be basic items.'

'If you have decided I'll call Mr Palamakis and ask if we can visit him at the house and he can give us his expert advice. On the current measurements you have can you work out the cost of the purchase? Mr Palamakis will obviously charge for cutting and laying them. We don't want to find his price works out more than the cost of the tiles.'

'If you take the dogs out I can sit and do that whilst you're gone. I have looked into the price of good quality towels and bedding and decided to buy really good quality. It can be cheaper to buy them in bulk and have them shipped over from England.'

Vasi shook his head. 'That could be an unnecessary expense. Visitors won't respect them and we may find we have to renew them regularly so it will be more practical if we buy everything here. If Mr Palamakis is available we can drive up to the house this afternoon and then on to Aghios. If they have nothing suitable we can always go up to Heraklion tomorrow.'

'I think you may have been better qualified to work all this out than me,' smiled Saffron.

'Not at all. At the hotel all the tiles, bedding and towels are the same everywhere. I couldn't cope with working out different colour schemes. I'll leave you to it and we can phone Mr Palamakis when I return and make our plans accordingly.'

Saffron looked at the lists she had made. Vasi was correct when he said that good quality towels were an unnecessary expense. He knew the way some of the visitors to the hotel treated them; leaving them covered in makeup or sun oils or even mopping up a spillage on the floor. The tiles from Pietro were going to be expensive so it made sense to economise elsewhere.

Saffron greeted Vasi with a smile when he returned. 'Have we time to sit and talk before we phone Mr Palamakis?'

'Of course. It is not essential that we see him today or go into Aghios later.'

'I've decided on a slight change of colour scheme. I had worked on having four sets of bedding for each room but it would be more practical if all the bedding was white. We'd be unlikely to find a bed cover that matched the curtains unless we had both made up from the same bale of material. I've seen on the internet that a piece of material, like a sash, placed across the bed cover, is ideal to pick up the colour of the curtains and bathroom towels and it would not matter if it did not match the curtains or towels exactly. Once people moved in they would remove it from the bed anyway and probably never put it back on.'

Vasi nodded. 'That sounds practical. We can always buy new white bed covers if necessary. If, for any reason, we should suddenly be short of sheets, I could always bring some up from the hotel. In the unlikely event of a pair of curtains getting damaged we can always buy a replacement pair from Aghios and we can certainly buy the nets there. It's rare that the curtains at the hotel are damaged, just an occasional broken hook or a rip in the net.'

'I still need to check the kitchen equipment and see what needs to be renewed. I'm going to take your advice and not go for the most expensive items on offer.'

'We need to ensure that everything we order is already in stock or will arrive soon. Ideally we need to be ready to have our first lets at Easter.'

'We still need to have photos taken and a web site for advertising.'

'I'm sure John will be willing to take the photos and putting them on a web site is no problem. If we are not ready by Easter we say that the property will be available to rent from a certain date. Provided we begin to have customers by June this year I will be happy and if we have sufficient bookings we should cover most of this year's expenditure. Next year we should make enough to cover Mr Palamakis's costs and make a small profit. If we find we are making a loss overall we can always put the house on the market.'

Saffron looked at Vasi dubiously. Many Russians had bought land or property in and around Elounda. It was doubtful that there were an unlimited number who wanted property in the area and had sufficient finance.

Pietro was delighted to receive the email John had composed on Saffron's behalf asking for further details of tiles and replied to her immediately. He offered to send her tile samples and asked her to let him know which size would be most suitable. Once she had confirmed her choice he would need the exact quantity and provided that amount were in stock he would despatch them immediately.

John translated the letter into English and sent her a copy.

'I finally feel we are making progress,' said Saffron. 'Once the new showers, basins and taps have been fitted we can ask Mr Palamakis to measure up for the walls and floors. I'm pleased I took your advice and we went to Aghios for the bedding, nets and curtains as these tiles are going to be expensive. As soon as each bathroom area has been completed we can make up the room.'

Vasi shook his head. 'Better to leave everything packed up until Mr Palamakis has completely finished. We can then ask Christalia to help you organise the rooms. That will give me the opportunity to show Stelios where the electrical controls are for the house and the pool and explain anything he does not fully understand.'

Saffron was delighted with the tile sample that Pietro sent to her. She covered it with water and then ran her hand across to see if it felt slippery. It was difficult to tell for certain on such a small area, but according to Pietro the tiles were guaranteed to be non slip. Provided Vasi agreed and Mr Palamakis approved, she would order the largest tiles. They would be ideal for the floor even if Mr Palamakis said they were impractical for the walls due to the amount of cutting that would be necessary around the fitments.

John read through the letter that Luke had sent and asked him to translate into Greek. It was far too long and rambling, explaining how his mother had left Crete for Australia with no knowledge of her aunt or the house at Schisma.

'I can't send the government a letter like this. They'll not have the patience to read through Luke's family history.'

'Then compose the salient facts in English and send a copy to Luke. If he approves then you can translate it into Greek for him,' replied Nicola.

'Can you help me with it this evening? My written English is not as good as yours and I don't want to make any spelling mistakes.'

'You make a start on it whilst I take the children out and once they have gone to bed we can look at it together.'

'So how does this sound?' asked John and began to read the letter he had composed on Luke's behalf.

"My name is Lucas Anstruther. I was born in Elounda, Crete. (copy of my birth certificate enclosed)

My mother was Eirini Koronakis and my father was Lucas Tsantakis.

My parents were not allowed to marry as Lucas Tsantakis had been diagnosed with leprosy and lived on Spinalonga. My mother insisted I was given the surname Tsantakis and she also used that name.

My mother, along with her parents and myself, left Crete and entered Australia when I was a small child.

I enclose copies of our official entrance papers and our Citizenship papers that we were granted at a later date.

Ten years after our arrival my mother remarried and I was legally adopted by my stepfather and took his surname (Anstruther).

Having researched into my Cretan relatives I have discovered that I had a great aunt who owned a house at Schisma. She died during the war.

Despite further enquiries I have been unable to find any other descendants of the Koronakis or Tsantakis family who are still alive.

I believe I am now the legal owner of the property at Schisma.

Please can you confirm this for me as I understand the property is derelict, needs to be demolished and the land cleared to enable the area to be sold. "

'Have I left anything relevant or important out?' John asked Nicola.

Nicola shook her head. 'I can't see anything wrong, but it might be helpful if you sent through a copy of his family tree so they can see how he claims Andrula as a relative. You could also add that the information was found in the old church registers at Fourni. If they doubt his word they could check with Father Christos.'

'I hadn't thought of either of those things. I'll add them now.'

John sat back at his computer and typed rapidly whilst Nicola watched.

'I'll check it through for any spelling errors and then you can send it to Luke. If he approves you can then translate a copy of the letter into Greek and ask him to forward that to the Greek Government. I wonder if he will ever have a reply from them?'

'I hope so, but he may have to be patient. If he has heard nothing in six months time I will offer to write another letter on his behalf and hope they will take notice of that.'

The meeting Saffron and Vasi had with Mr Palamakis was encouraging. He agreed that the large tiles would be ideal for the floors in the bathroom, but it would be better to have the smaller ones for the walls.

'I will need to cut round the fitments and to use a large tile for that and have about half of it left over would be a terrible waste of money.'

'How long do you estimate the tiling will take?' asked Vasi.

'If I put one man to each bathroom we should have them completed within a week. Chopping off the old tiles and ensuring that the wall beneath them is smooth and sound will be the major work. We'll be careful, of course, but if the fixative pulls off plaster we'll have to spend a day repairing the damage. Can't lay tiles on a bumpy wall.'

'I'll let you know when Pietro has confirmed a date to send them over.'

Marianne was pleased to receive the photos from her mother of the new property she was buying.

'It has taken some time for all the paperwork to be completed, but all being well I can now move in whenever it suits me. I want to have the kitchen and bathroom completed, then I can think about new carpets being laid along with new curtains for every room. I will send you some more photos when this has been done.'

No sooner had Marianne finished looking at the photos than Helena phoned her.

'At last,' she announced. 'Mother has finally made up her mind and bought somewhere else to live. She won't give us a definite date for when we can move in to her old house, but we have placed ours back on the market and hope we will have a sale very soon. We will need the money as there is redecoration needed everywhere and the bathroom is hideous. I cannot live with an avocado basin and toilet. It may have been fashionable originally but certainly not now. She really has neglected the current house.'

Marianne waited for her sister to draw breath. 'I'm very happy that Mamma has found somewhere suitable. She has sent me through photos and I think when she has done the refurbishment that is needed it will be ideal.'

'She has sent you photos? We have not even been told the address so we can see it from outside.'

Marianne smiled to herself. No doubt this had been deliberate on the part of her mother. Helena would have managed to find fault and put doubts into her mother's mind regarding suitability.

'I'm sure she is waiting until she has everywhere looking just as she wants before showing you.'

'Greg and I feel we should look at it. It could be in a poor, rundown area with unsuitable neighbours, quite unsafe for an elderly lady.'

'I understand that Mamma has friends who live there. There is also a perimeter fence with a security gate so no one unauthorised can enter. Mamma should be quite safe.'

Helena snorted. 'I hope so as she has finally made up her mind. I hope she will take all the furniture she has everywhere with her or we will have to dispose of it. That's another job we could do without.'

'Before you start to throw away anything you need to check with Mamma. She may have overlooked something that has sentimental value to her.'

'Then she should have taken it with her. She has refused all the help I have offered over recent years. She can't expect me to start running around after her now. Send me through the photos she has sent to you and I'll be able to see for myself if she has made the right decision.'

'I'm not sure if I can send them on to you and it's too late anyway. Mamma has signed the purchase agreement.'

'She should certainly not have done that without consulting us.'

'Helena, you have been badgering Mamma for some years to sell the house to you. Be grateful that you finally have what you want. Mamma is quite capable of making up her own mind. She is not senile.'

'I'm not so sure, but then you have always sided with her in any dispute.'

'When she was staying with us she was mentally competent and no problem. Just leave her to arrange whatever she wants to do and I'm sure you will be able to move into the house and begin to make any alterations you want. I really have to go now. I'm looking after Yiannis. He's very quiet and I need to see what he is up to.'

Marianne replaced the phone and shook her head. Helena was never satisfied.

Panayiotis kept thinking about the strange reaction he had experienced at the house at Schisma. It had to be imagination. The hospital had confirmed that there was nothing physically wrong with him, but his blood pressure had been a little high. Maybe that had caused his nausea and shortness of breath? He decided he would pay another visit to the house and ask Vasi to go with him and take his dogs.

Vasi listened to his request. 'Saffie and I went up there a while ago. We planned to take the dogs up to the windmills and parked close to the entrance of the salt flats as it was rather cold and windy. Juni ran across to the grass and immediately ran back shivering and shaking. We thought she had just been thoroughly chilled when she first left the car, but when we walked back neither dog would go anywhere near the grass on that side of the road. We can go again and see if they have a similar reaction.'

'I'd be grateful,' said Panayiotis. 'I'd like to make sure there was someone there to help me if I should have another strange turn. I know the hospital gave me a clean bill of health, but mistakes can happen.'

'I'll ask Saffie if she wants to come with us, then get my coat.'

Saffron considered. 'I'm willing to come with you, but I think I should stay by the car. That pathway looks so overgrown that a mobile might not be able to receive a signal up there,' she replied finally.

'I'll have my police whistle,' Panayiotis assured her. 'I will blow that if we encounter a problem.'

'You really think that there is something up there that is affecting you?' asked Saffron incredulously.

'I don't know. If your dogs show no reaction this time I'll know it was a one off occurrence. If there really is something dangerous up there then it needs to be dealt with.'

'What kind of dangerous?'

Panayiotis shrugged. 'I don't know. I can only think of a chemical that has leaked from a canister that has been stored somewhere close by and that makes people feel ill. In that case it needs to be investigated and if it is found to be hazardous waste it must be professionally removed.'

Saffron nodded. She though Panayiotis was over reacting, but none the less she placed a light scarf in her pocket and handed one to Vasi. 'If it is something you are breathing in this might help,' she said as she handed it to him. 'Do you want one, Panayiotis?'

Panayiotis hesitated. 'I might as well. It will do no harm to cover our nose and mouth.' He pushed it into his pocket. He would have to remove it if he needed to blow his whistle to let Saffron know that they had encountered a problem.

Vasi clipped the dogs' leads to their harnesses. 'I think it would be best if we kept them on their leads until we see if they are happy to go near the grass. If they are still worried we can leave them in the car with Saffie. Is your mobile fully charged?'

Saffron checked and nodded, whilst Vasi did the same with his. She was not entirely happy with their proposed visit to Schisma.

Vasi parked in virtually the same place as previously. He and Panayiotis climbed out and he took the dogs' leads. He allowed them to sniff around for a short while beside the car and then began to walk over towards the grass. At first the dogs walked happily beside him, then as they reached the path Juni let out a howl and tried to escape back to the car. The hair on Seni's back was standing up and she was growling deep down in her throat.

Vasi looked at Panayiotis. 'I can't force them to go any closer. Something definitely disturbs them. I'll put them back in the car with Saffie.'

Panayiotis waited until Vasi rejoined him. He took his gun from the holster.

'Is that necessary?' asked Vasi looking at the gun.

'I hope not, but better to be prepared. If there is someone sleeping rough up there he could be violent. It's even possible that I was hit over the head and that was why I felt so ill and breathless. I was longer up there than I had realised so it's even possible I blacked out temporarily. If someone did attack me they can only attack one person at a time so look out for anyone lurking in the bushes.'

Cautiously and slowly the two men made their way up the overgrown pathway. Vasi became conscious of the smell that seemed to be enveloping them as they neared the house and placed the scarf Saffron had given him over his nose and mouth. He tapped Panayiotis's arm and indicated that he should do the same. On reaching the house he parted the bushes so the house came into view and stepped through, holding them back for Vasi to follow.

They stood there and looked around, both of them scanning the bushes for any sign of movement or a person hiding amongst them. Satisfied that there was no person or animal lurking up there they walked forward to the cottage. The smell seemed to become even stronger as they approached.

'I'm going to push the door open,' said Panayiotis quietly. 'There could be someone hiding behind it as that was when I felt so nauseous and breathless. If it happens again please drag me back to the path and keep blowing my whistle to alert Saffron that there could be a problem and then phone for an ambulance.'

Vasi nodded, hoping he would not have to carry out Panayiotis's instructions.

Saffron stood outside the car to ensure that she would hear Panayiotis's whistle if it was necessary for him to blow it. She scanned the area continually for anyone who might appear, ignoring the dogs who did not understand why they should be shut inside the car and were whining and scratching to be released.

Panayiotis covered his mouth and nose with the scarf Saffron had given him. He looked back at Vasi to check he had done the same. Vasi was bending over and retching violently, holding his chest. Immediately Panayiotis pulled down the scarf and began to blow his whistle. He placed his hands beneath Vasi's arms and began to drag him back to the gap in the bushes. Saffron stiffened. This was surely the signal that the men had encountered a problem.

She pulled out her mobile phone and dialled the emergency number, first asking for the police and then for an ambulance. She had difficulty in describing her exact location and had no way of telling either service the exact problem. She just hoped they would believe that she needed help.

Back on the path Vasi appeared to recover to a certain extent. He was able to sit up unaided and tried to take deep breaths, despite the obnoxious smell.

'Can you stand up and walk?' asked Panayiotis. 'We need to get back to the car.'

Vasi nodded weakly and with Panayiotis's help he regained his feet. Clutching at the policeman's arm he managed to stagger back along the pathway, both of them beginning to breathe more easily as they arrived closer to the road.

As they emerged from the bushes Saffron ran towards them. 'What happened? I've called for the police and an ambulance.' She opened the car door and pushed Vasi into the passenger seat.

'What happened, Panayiotis?' she asked anxiously.

'I'm not sure. All was well until I tried to push open the door. I turned to speak to Vasi and he had collapsed on the ground.'

'Thank goodness you were with him.'

'We'll wait for the emergency services to turn up. It won't hurt to have Vasi checked out and I can have a word with the police and ask them to talk to the fire service about coming here to investigate. They should be able to find out if there is a toxic chemical in the air and know how to deal with it.'

February 2017
Week Two

The paramedics had been unable to find a cause for Vasi's unexpected collapse and he refused to go to the hospital, saying that there really was no need now he had recovered.

'I bent down to remove a creeper that had twisted round my ankle. I'd pulled the scarf down so I could see what I was doing and the smell must have affected me.'

Saffron insisted that Vasi stayed at home and rested despite him assuring her that he was feeling perfectly well. When she had been practising as a doctor, despite bones being her speciality, she had never heard of anyone being affected so badly by a smell that they collapsed unless they were asthmatic or had an allergy.

Panayiotis had spoken to the police regarding the incident and also with the fire service. The fire brigade had been somewhat sceptical, saying that if there was a chemical spillage of some kind it would probably have affected a wider area and it was more likely to be an infestation of caterpillars or beetles that was causing the smell. Panayiotis was insistent that for everyone's health the bushes should be sprayed with an insecticide as the problem could spread to other areas and affect people.

Reluctantly the fire chief, Lefteris, agreed and Panayiotis accompanied them to ensure they were dealing with the correct area and also anxious to find out if they had been successful in removing the smell. As they reached the area where the house was situated Lefteris stopped and began to walk back to where Panayiotis had parked his car.

'It's certainly pretty nasty, but I can't put a name to the cause. My men will put on breathing apparatus as a precaution and start to spray from the road in to where you say this house is situated. I suggest you stay here in your car with the windows closed until we return.'

Panayiotis agreed. He had no wish to go along to the house and watched with interest as a large canister was placed on a wheeled trolley and a spray was attached. Their breathing masks in place the firemen began to move forward. Without disobeying their instructions and getting out of his car Panayiotis could not watch their progress. He switched on his radio, but whichever station he tried to tune into he received nothing but atmospheric crackling. He wished he had brought one of his fishing magazines to read.

Lefteris returned with his men following and dragging the empty canister behind them and thankful to remove their breathing apparatus.

'We'll wait an hour before we go back and assess the situation. You can go home if you want or stay here in your car with the windows up. We don't want to take any chances until we're sure the area is clear. I'm sending my men down to the salt pans to check if there's a smell coming from there. Algae can often give off a smell that makes people cough. It could be blowing in land and then unable to disperse due to all the greenery.'

Panayiotis nodded. 'I'd rather stay. We don't want to alarm any of the people who live round about, but if the cause is due to an insect infestation or algae on the salt pans it could very likely spread and begin to affect them.'

Panayiotis waited patiently until the men returned from the salt pans. He had the impression that the fire brigade thought he had wasted their time and resources.

'Nothing down there,' declared Lefteris. 'Very little algae, although the water looks somewhat stagnant. We could do with a storm to freshen the area up. We'll take a walk along the path and make sure the smell has gone.'

The men hung their breathing masks around their neck and began to walk down the overgrown pathway whilst Panayiotis waited. It was no more than twenty minutes later when he heard them rushing back to the road. Two of the men were being helped along and they had all placed their breathing apparatus back in place. Panayiotis looked at them in consternation.

Having ascertained that the two men had recovered sufficiently Lefteris approached Panayiotis's car.

'What happened? he asked anxiously as he rolled down his window.

'The smell seemed to have gone or at least lessened until we reached the house. Once through the bushes it came back as strongly as ever. We decided it must be coming from the house and two of my men went in to investigate. Even wearing their masks they began to feel ill and we brought them back as quickly as possible. They are being taken back to the fire station where they can be checked out although they say they are feeling perfectly well again now.'

Panayiotis gave a sigh of relief, pleased that the men were uninjured and also that Lefteris now believed him that the problem was something more than an insect infestation in the bushes.

'We're going to return tomorrow and spray again. This time we'll go further through and spray the house. It must be a due to insects in the rotten timbers.'

'I'd like to come down again and wait to hear the result.'

'If you're happy to spend a boring hour sitting in your car I can't stop you.'

'I'll make sure I have a magazine with me to read whilst you're working. What time should I get here?'

'Provided we are not called out for an emergency we should be here by nine.'

207

Panayiotis knocked on Vasi's door. 'Is it convenient to come and tell you about the fire service?'

'Of course. Saffron has finally decided that I am not an invalid although she insisted that she took the dogs for a walk.'

'Which way did she go?' asked Panayiotis as he took a seat.

'Along into the town and then she planned to go up the hill towards the house.'

'Could be a good idea to continue to avoid the salt pans. All the bushes were sprayed and that seemed to clear the smell. The men went down and checked the salt pans and declared the smell was not emanating from them. They went back along the path, but they said as soon as they went through the bushes to the house the smell returned. Two of the men went inside and were immediately taken ill, not seriously as they were wearing breathing apparatus. They are going back up tomorrow and will spray around the house. They think it could be something in the old rotten timbers. I'm going up again so I can give you an update when they have done that.'

'Can I go up with you?'

Panayiotis shook his head. 'I don't think Saffron would be very happy to hear you had gone back up there and there's nothing you can do except wait until the men have completed their job.'

'I suppose there isn't a blocked drain under the house?'

'It's possible. I'm sure they'll investigate, although it's not likely. After a while drains stop to smell if they are not used. The house has been uninhabited for so long that any waste down there would probably have disintegrated years ago.'

Vasi's query about a blocked drain gave Panayiotis food for thought. Due to the age of the house it was unlikely that there was a drainpipe in situ that could have become blocked. If the waste had just been allowed to run away into the ground outside it could have penetrated quite a wide area encouraging the insects and worms to feed there and spread the waste even further afield. If that was the case it did not explain the lack of wildlife in the area who would surely have taken advantage of the food source that was available to them.

Saffron returned with the dogs and was relieved to see Vasi was still sitting in front of his computer.

'Good walk?' he asked. 'I've made a start on an advertising brochure. Come and have a look and tell me what you think.'

Saffron made sure the dogs had a large bowl of water and hung up her coat. 'It was quite windy when I started to walk up the hill. I should probably have gone along the causeway.'

'Panayiotis has said to avoid that area for a while. Apparently the fire brigade sprayed all the bushes and the smell went until they reached the house. They actually went inside and then the smell was as bad as ever and made two of his men feel unwell. They're going to go back up tomorrow to spray the house. They think it's coming from rotting timbers.'

Saffron wrinkled her nose. 'It didn't smell like rotting timber. I can't exactly put a name to the smell except to say that it was similar to the smell there is in the forensic department when they do an autopsy.'

'Really?'

'Yes, it's pretty horrible. Certainly not a job that I would like to do. Anyway, let me see what you have written so far.'

Vasi turned his computer round for Saffron to read.

"Luxury self catering house.
Four double bedrooms with bathroom en suite.
Private swimming pool.
Fantastic views.
Ideal location for artists or hikers.
Own transport needed to visit
local village or outlying areas.
View on website for details and
availability."

Saffron nodded. 'That's fine so far, but I think you should mention that there are shops and tavernas in the village along with access to the beach.'

'I'll add that in after local village - how about - *"to visit local village where there are plenty of shops and tavernas"*.'

'Yes, but I think you should also add in the various places that can be visited. You don't want people to think that it is only suitable for walkers and artists.'

Vasi sighed. 'I thought this was going to be so easy.'

'Why don't you copy some of the wording from the web site you have for the hotel?'

'Do you think Ronnie could draw a map? We could add the mileage to each place of interest and if there is an entrance fee to a museum etc.'

'I think you're over complicating things. I'm sure Ronnie could draw a map and the information could be there about the mileage and entrance fees, but not everyone would be interested. We could have the details in a plastic folder at the house so customers could look at it as they pleased and decide where they wanted to go.'

Vasi closed his computer down. 'I can't concentrate on this any more today. I should have gone out with you to walk the dogs and blow my cobwebs away.'

Saffron looked at him anxiously. Was he still suffering from the effects of the previous day?

Panayiotis had been quite surprised that none of the local residents had come to see what was happening in the area the previous day, but as he had driven home he had seen the notice saying it was forbidden to travel down the road and he guessed that a similar notice had been placed down by the salt pans. Now he sat in his car, waiting for the firemen to arrive. After half an hour he began to wonder if they were already down at the site and was on the point of walking down to find out when he saw them arrive. He pulled his car over to one side so their vehicle could get through and then followed them down.

He climbed out of his car and sniffed the air. There was still a smell of insecticide around, but nothing more.

'I suggest you stay in your car again with the windows closed.' said Lefteris. 'We're going to spray the bushes again and then we'll go down and spray the house. Hopefully it will then be safe enough for my men to go inside and see if they can ascertain the cause of the smell. I'll let you know when we have finished.'

Panayiotis moved his seat back as far as possible, placed a pillow behind his neck and took up a fishing magazine. It would probably take two or more hours for the men to do the work and he might make himself as comfortable as possible. He had three magazines with him along with a flask of coffee and a bottle of water. He watched the men put on yellow oilskins over their uniforms and then their breathing apparatus. They were obviously not taking any chances today.

He turned his attention back to his magazine but every so often he looked out of the car windows to see if they were returning. He began to lose interest in the magazine and felt his eyes closing. It would not hurt to have a nap for a while.

The next thing he was conscious of was Lefteris tapping on his window. He blinked himself awake and sat up straighter.

'All done?' he asked.

The chief shook his head. 'We sprayed the house thoroughly with an even stronger solution of insecticide. After that all we could smell was the chemicals. Two of my men went inside, two more followed and I made sure they would be able to help each other out if necessary. Once inside the smell was as strong as ever. They sprayed again and we waited outside. The smell was back. I can only think that there is a problem under the floor.'

'So what will you do now?'

'The house needs to be pulled down and the rubbish carted away. Then we can investigate the ground beneath it. I can only conclude that there is a sewer under there that is leaking.'

'That did occur to me, but unless the same drain serves many of the other houses in this area I would not expect it to smell so strongly and it doesn't really smell like sewerage.'

Lefteris shrugged. 'Do you know who owns the building?'

'I'm not sure. Give me a day or so to make enquiries.'

'In the meantime I will be approaching the government and requesting an urgent demolition contract given to a firm who specialises in hazardous situations. We can't expect an ordinary builder to do the work just in case there is a canister somewhere leaking its contents.'

'I'll let you know if I can find out the name of the owner. If you have an official demolition order from the government will the owner be able to stop you from going ahead?'

'The house doesn't belong to you?'

'Certainly not,' declared Panayiotis vehemently. 'What gave you that idea?'

'You seem to be very interested in the outcome.'

'I am. I would be failing in my duty as a police officer if I ignored the problem. It could be necessary to evacuate the whole area if the contamination began to affect other properties.'

'In the meantime the area is going to stay cordoned off. That also includes access to you,' said Lefteris firmly.

'I have no reason to come down here except to ask you about progress. I will be happy to contact you at the fire station if you prefer.'

'That could be better.' With a curt nod Lefteris walked back to his men and Panayiotis backed and turned his car; he felt he had been summarily dismissed.

Panayiotis drove back to his house and then knocked on Vasi's door. 'Do you want to hear the latest news?'

'Definitely,' said Vasi. 'Come on in.'

'Well, the bushes were sprayed again and also the house.

When the firemen entered the house the smell was as bad as ever. The chief thinks it can only be a sewer that is running under the property and discharging or a canister containing a chemical of some sort. He is getting an urgent demolition order from the government. The building looks ready to collapse anyway. He asked if I knew who owned the place. Do you happen to know?'

Vasi shook his head. 'I've no idea. I can ask my father and also other acquaintances but I've never heard anyone mention that the property belonged to them. I can only think it belongs to someone who went to America years ago. They may have forgotten about it or just not be interested.'

'I'll leave you to make some enquiries. It's possible the government have details of the owner even if they do live abroad. Let me know if you have any luck.'

Vasi asked his father who shook his head. 'I had no idea there was a house along there. If Cathy and I go to the tavernas out on the headlands we always go by car. I'd have no reason to walk along that way. Ronnie was making enquiries some time back about Elounda as it was fifty or so years ago. She may know something.'

'Worth asking her.'

'You could also ask John. He's done a lot of delving into the history of the area. He found the Italian soldiers' graves, remember.'

'That's another good idea.'

'Sorry I couldn't be more helpful to you, but why do you need to know? Are you thinking of building another hotel along there?'

'I couldn't possibly consider that at the moment. We need to get the big house up and running before we could consider another investment of any kind. It's a bit of a strange story, but I'm willing to tell you what I know. Panayiotis may be able to tell you more details.'

'You tell me and when I ask Panayiotis I'll see if your stories agree.'

213

Vasi returned to Saffron and told her that his father had suggested he asked Ronnie if she knew the owner of the house.

'I don't see how she would know,' remonstrated Saffron. 'She's only lived here for a few years.'

'She could ask Kyriakos and he could ask his mother. She might have some information.'

'That's possible, I suppose. Call Ronnie and explain what it is that you want.'

'Why don't we arrange to meet her for lunch in Kastelli? I'll be on the phone for hours otherwise explaining everything.'

'That's a better idea. We can ask her about doing the map for the house at the same time. I'll make a list of the local places of interest and ask her to make sure to include those.'

Ronnie agreed to meet Vasi and Saffron for lunch. 'Much as I love Kastelli it is no more exciting during the winter than anywhere else. Provided the light is good I can get a lot of paintings prepared and I'm also visiting Kyriakos's mother regularly. Now we are on better terms I want to keep the relationship going. Kyriakos is bringing me down tomorrow morning to visit her whilst he is up at the taverna redecorating. Why don't I meet you in Elounda? I'm sure there will be a few tavernas open where we can have a meal.'

'I'll phone round and book a table for us and let you know the time and the place,.' promised Vasi. 'That's good,' he said to Saffron. 'Ronnie is coming down to Elounda tomorrow so she can meet us here.'

'Why don't you ask Kyriakos to join us? That way he'll be able to take her back to Kastelli and you can also ask if his mother would have any information about the house. I'll make a start on the list of interesting places. You can check later to see if I've left off anywhere important.'

As Vasi explained to Ronnie about the house at Schisma she seemed to have a job controlling her laughter.

'It was not a funny experience,' said Vasi feeling offended.

'That is not what I'm laughing about. John told us about a weird experience he had when he and Nicola went and looked at the house. The old lady who lived there was regarded locally as a witch who placed curses on people.'

Vasi automatically crossed himself.

'John said that Kyriakos and I should not go down there as the smell was unhealthy and could make us ill.'

'I can certainly confirm that,' said Vasi.

'Anyway,' continued Ronnie, 'I believe that the house belongs to a man in Australia. I did some paintings of Spinalonga for his mother as she had lived on the island for a while.'

'I remember,' said Saffron. 'He and his wife came to the shop and wanted souvenirs to take back to Australia with them.'

'He sent me his mother's memoirs after she died and I became very intrigued. I asked John for help, of course, and he and Nicola have traced his family back as far as possible. The woman who was considered to be a witch was his great aunt. He is the only living relative and he is planning to write to the Greek government to claim the property.'

Vasi sat back and shook his head. 'It's unbelievable. Are you quite sure?'

'Positive. You can ask John.'

Vasi pulled out his mobile phone. 'I must tell Panayiotis. He needs to inform the fire service as they are planning to get a demolition order so the house can be pulled down.'

'Luke is waiting to get confirmation that he is the rightful owner and then he plans to have the house demolished and the land cleared so he can put it up for sale. He will probably be delighted if that has been done for him by an order from the government.'

'He'll probably be charged by the fire service and whoever removes all the rubbish.'

'No different from having to pay local contractors.'

'I'll have to tell Panayiotis. I hope it won't stop the work going ahead.'

Ronnie shrugged. 'I don't see what difference it will make. Speak to John. I'm sure he can explain what is happening to Luke far better than I can. Now, you said there was something else you wanted to ask me about a map.'

February 2017
Week Three

Panayiotis was delighted when Vasi phoned to say he knew who owned the derelict house.

'I'll phone Lefteris and let him know. Under the circumstances the government do not need the owner's permission for the work, but it would be a courtesy to let him know that demolition will be undertaken place by a specialist company and no doubt he will be billed for their services. Where can he be contacted?'

Vasi chuckled. 'Australia. More than that I do not know. I've gained this information from Ronnie Vandersham. She has an email address for him, but she suggested that you speak to John Pirenzi and asked him to explain the situation fully to Luke. John was the person who discovered the house and its history in the first place.'

John was surprised when Panayiotis arrived at the house. 'Who have you come to arrest? he asked.

'Does anyone have a guilty conscience?' Panayiotis smiled. 'It's actually you I have come to visit.'

'I can assure you I'm innocent.'

'That's what every criminal says but there's nothing for you to be concerned about. Miss Vandersham tells me you have been in contact with an Australian and due to the research you have undertaken on his behalf he is probably the owner of a derelict house at Schisma.'

John nodded. 'Nick and I looked into the old church records and it appears he is the only family relative still alive. I've sent him a letter to send on to the Greek Government stating his case. Do you want to see it? I have a copy.'

Panayiotis shook his head. 'Vasi told me about the reaction from his dogs when he went to the area. I then went up to have a look for myself and felt very ill whilst I was there.'

'Probably due to the smell. Nick and I noticed it when we went up. It's really strong when you get close to the house. We only had a quick look through the windows and came away.'

'Very wise. Anyway, to cut a long story short, I went up again with Vasi and he was also taken ill. I then decided to speak to Lefteris, the chief fire officer. His men went up and sprayed around thinking it was an insect infestation. It didn't seem to do much good and he is concerned that there is a canister somewhere that is leaking hazardous chemicals. As the house is in somewhat of a dangerous state and could collapse he has contacted the government and asked for an emergency demolition order to be completed by a specialist company.'

'I doubt that Luke will mind. He had planned to demolish it and have the land cleared so he could sell the plot to a developer.'

Panayiotis nodded. 'His permission for the work is not needed, but he should be made aware that it is going to happen and he will be billed for the work.'

John grinned. 'So who would have paid for the demolition if no owner could have been found?'

'The government, I presume, and then they would have claimed the land and sold it to cover their costs.'

'So what do you want me to do?'

'Miss Vandersham thought you would be able to explain the situation more clearly than she could.'

'I only have an email address for him.'

'That would be sufficient to apprise him of the current situation. Would you be able to ask him for a phone number where he can be contacted? The government will probably drag their heels regarding his request to be declared the rightful owner but if they know he is accepting responsibility for the work they will probably move quickly if they can speak to him directly.'

John nodded. 'I can certainly ask him. What he then does will be up to him.'

Luke replied to John's email the following day. He confirmed that he would be willing to pay all the demolition and clearing costs and it would save him from having to organise the work himself.

"Have you any idea how long the work will take? Hope the old witch won't put a curse on them that holds them up. It will be much more convenient for the government to phone me. I could spend hours sitting on the phone otherwise waiting to be put through to the correct department."

John phoned Panayiotis who in turn phoned Lefteris.

'Thanks to the information from your friends the work should be able to start fairly soon. I'll let you know how the men progress and also when the site has been completely cleared.'

John waited anxiously to hear from Panayiotis and when the news came it was disconcerting.

'The demolition crew took every precaution. They cut down all the bushes that bordered the path and gradually cleared the garden of debris. They found a number of dead animals and birds as they did so.'

'How horrible. I imagine that was where the smell was coming from.'

'Partly, no doubt. I'm no scientist, but I'm told that carbon dioxide is heavier than oxygen and once in the air it stays close to the ground. Dead foliage and animals create carbon dioxide. That accounts for the dead birds and animals that were found when the bushes were cleared. They would have gone to the area to feed and been overcome immediately by the poisonous air. That also accounts for the reaction that some of us have had.'

'It didn't affect Nick or me,' remonstrated John.

'That was because you didn't bend down and breathe the gas in. It doesn't take very long for it to affect a human. I was fortunate to get away from the area in time. Even after clearing the area as much as possible the smell was still there. They then began to demolish the house and cart the debris away. They have found no sign of a canister with hazardous chemicals leaking, thank goodness.'

'So the smell has gone and the area is safe?'

'Not exactly. There was a small room at the back. It was obviously the toilet originally. It was the old Turkish style where the waste went down between some stones and then dispersed into the ground.'

'I know, like the ones on Spinalonga. They were quite efficient.'

'They may have been there as the waste may have gradually gone down to the sea, but when they investigated further they found there was an earthen cellar beneath the house. It was not only full of human waste, but also the remains of animals.'

'What?' John was horrified.

'It can only be assumed that the old lady caught whatever she could for food and disposed of the fur, bones, feet and claws, anything that was inedible, down there. It has become a festering mass over the years creating methane gas and carbon dioxide.'

'What does that mean? Can the gasses be burnt off?'

'If they tried to do that they would probably cause an explosion. Methane is highly flammable. The demolition experts say they can deal with it, but it will take a while before they are able to declare the area completely safe. They have to clear that awful cellar area first.'

John shuddered. 'What a disgusting job.'

'They have a machine that will suck up the debris. They use it to clear blocked drains. The debris will then be placed in containers that can be sealed and taken to a safe site for disposal. Once that has been done the earth down there will need to be removed and probably some of the surrounding area.'

'Does Luke know about this?' asked John.

'I thought it could be better if you explained the situation to him. The government are only likely to send him the bill but not a detailed account of the necessary work.'

'Leaving me to do their dirty work.'

'Be thankful that you and Nicola were not affected and that you are not one of the men clearing out the cellar.'

John sat and thought about the information that Panayiotis had given him. His knowledge of science was scanty but this was now giving him cause for concern. If the house at Schisma had a cellar full of methane gas and carbon dioxide did Spinalonga have similar areas where the gasses had been trapped between the rocks? Visitors were told not to smoke on the island to prevent a fire, but if that directive was ignored and someone threw away a lighted cigarette end could that cause an explosion? He dreaded to think how many people would be killed or maimed in such an event during the height of the tourist season.

Nicola found him sitting in front of his computer with a worried frown.

'What's wrong?'

'I've had a phone call from Panayiotis. That house at Schisma is far more dangerous than we thought.' John proceeded to tell his wife about the methane gas and carbon dioxide that had been found.

Nicola shrugged. 'I'm glad that the professionals are dealing with it. Suppose we had asked Mr Palamakis and his men to knock down the house and remove the debris? His sons and grandsons smoke outside wherever they are working. It could have been a disaster.'

'I'm worried about Spinalonga. The toilets over there were the Turkish design. Suppose there are pockets of methane gas in between the rocks?'

'Is that possible?' asked Nicola 'Wouldn't it have dispersed once the island was no longer inhabited?'

'I don't know. I've been sitting here looking up facts about the gasses, but not being of a scientific turn of mind I'm not finding the information terribly useful.'

'Then leave it. Find out exactly who is doing the clearance work at Schisma and ask their opinion.'

'They'll probably think me pretty stupid.'

'Better to be thought stupid than blame yourself for ever if an accident occurred on Spinalonga.'

John nodded. 'You're right. I'll phone Panayiotis and ask if he knows of a phone number where I can speak to the contractors and ask their expert opinion. He also wants me to write to Luke and explain to him exactly what is taking place.'

'Phone Panayiotis first. Australia is about seven hours ahead of us so Luke is likely to be in bed and asleep. You can write an email this afternoon and send it first thing tomorrow morning. There's no urgency for Luke to know at the moment.'

'I don't think he will be very happy with the bill he receives for the work.'

'Probably not, but he would have had to pay unless he was willing to give the land to the government.'

'That area of land should be worth more than the cost involved in clearing it. When it is declared safe I'd like to go along and see just how much he has inherited. Someone will want to build there, probably a hotel complex as it's close to the sea and not far from Elounda. It could be worth a small fortune.'

'Good luck to whoever does buy it. Knowing the history I would not want to stay in any hotel or house that is finally built there.'

'You think Old Andrula will haunt them?'

Nicola gave John a withering glance. 'No, but if any contamination is left in the ground the same problems could reoccur.'

John phoned Panayiotis and asked for information about the specialist contractors.

'I don't know any details. I'll have to phone Lefteris. What's your concern?'

John explained that he was worried about methane gas being present on Spinalonga.

'It's possible, I suppose. I'm sure the contractors have some marvellous appliance that they can put into crevices to detect harmful gas. I've seen them use it when divers have been exploring caves, particularly if they have to send more divers in to rescue any that are trapped.'

'I don't think there are any caves under Spinalonga. I dived around there for years and never came across any.'

'Then your concerns could be unwarranted. The government certainly would not want the island shut down. Think of the income they would lose along with the local businesses. Once they've been alerted to the possibility I'm sure they'll investigate quickly.'

With that John had to be content and he turned his attention to composing an email to Luke.

February 2017
Week 4

'They look superb', commented Saffron as she looked at the tiles that had been laid on the bathroom floor. 'I wish we'd had all the old tiles pulled up and replaced with these.'

Vasi smiled. 'If we were going to live here you could have whatever you wanted, but we're letting it out. People will look at the tiles once when they arrive and if you ask them what colour they were by the time they leave they will have forgotten.'

'I know. I wish the towels had arrived and then we could put one in here to see how it looks.'

'The workmen would probably think we had placed it there for them to wipe their hands on. We don't want to unpack anything that could be spoiled before everywhere has been completed and cleaned through.'

Saffron appreciated that Vasi was being practical. She would just have to be patient.

'Shall we take the list of places that we want Ronnie to put on the map up to her?'

'Have you completed it?'

'I think so. You check it and see if I have missed anything.'

'What kind of distance are you planning to cover?'

'I've split the list into two parts. An area that can be covered by walking and other places that you need transport to access. I thought the map could be on one side and the list on the other.

We'll need some copies to replace it if visitors decide to take it out with them and ruin it.'

'We can do that this afternoon after we've taken the dogs out for their walk.'

John contacted the specialist contractors and explained his concern about pockets of methane gas being amongst the rocks on Spinalonga.

'I think it unlikely,' said Andreas. 'Before the island was officially opened to tourists a safety check was carried out.'

'I know,' persisted John, 'But that was of the buildings to ensure that any in a dangerous state of imminent collapse were removed. Any area that was found to be disintegrating due to the weather and age was cordoned off, some of it still is until they have carried out the necessary repairs, but as far as I am aware no one has ever checked for lethal gasses on the island.'

'Have you noticed any smell when you have visited the island?'

John automatically shook his head, although the man at the end of the telephone would not be able to see him. 'It would not have occurred to me until after the house at Schisma had a methane and carbon dioxide build up under the ground.'

Grudgingly the contractor agreed to go to the island and take measurements.

'Are you paying for this?' he asked.

'The island does not belong to me. It has a preservation order on it and is listed as a National Heritage site so I imagine the government is responsible for paying for any work carried out over there.'

The man sighed. 'I'll have to speak to the appropriate authorities before we can agree to carry out any work over there. It will probably take some time.'

'I appreciate that,' replied John. 'I think you should impress upon them that the survey should be completed before the start of the tourist season. If anything is found it would mean closing the island and a tremendous loss of revenue. I'm sure they would want to avoid that.'

'Leave it with me.' Andreas replaced the receiver and rubbed his forehead.

'Crank call?' asked his colleague.

'Not sure. A man wants us to carry out chemical checks on Spinalonga. He's concerned that there could be pockets of methane gas over there.'

'The island was declared safe long ago.'

'I know, but were any checks made for hazardous waste or gas?'

'No idea. You'd have to look up the records.'

Andreas sighed. He dared not ignore the call, but nor did he relish the thought of spending the afternoon looking through the old records of the various places they had attended.

'Even if we decide we need to go over there it will have to wait until that site at Schisma has been finally cleared and declared safe. The diggers are going in next week to remove all the top soil. Then we'll have to run the tests again. Good job local builders were not asked to do the clearance. They could have pulled the house down and then set fire to the debris to save them having to cart it away. Could have been a very nasty accident.'

'The owner of that property is not going to like the bill we'll be sending him. He'll probably say he can't pay until he's sold the land.'

'Can't he be given a time clause saying that the money has to be paid by a certain date otherwise the government will claim the area?' asked Andreas.

'That would probably have been a better proposition for him in the first place.' Yiorgo cleared his desk. 'I'm off. Let me know if you find anything in the records.'

Having commenced looking through the old records Andreas worked far later than he had intended. He skimmed over anywhere out of the immediate area and found only two references to the services having been called out. One was to defuse a bomb that had been washed up on the far side of Kolokitha and the other was to remove a land mine that was left from the war years up in the hills beyond Pines. He then asked for details of any tests or clearance that had been carried out on Spinalonga. There was nothing listed.

He tapped his fingers on his desk. There had to be a record somewhere of the work that had taken place on the island. With a sigh he closed his computer. It was possible that when the paper records were digitalised the record was missed off. It would not be the first time that had happened. He would think about the problem overnight and hope he would find a solution. It would take days to go back through the paper records that were stored in the basement of the building.

Vasi and Saffron sat together checking the list of places that they felt should be included on the map.

'We also need to say what there is there to see,' frowned Saffron. 'If we say go to Mavrikiano people will want to know why we are recommending it.'

'There is a superb taverna up there,' said Vasi.

'I know, and we could probably mention that and the view but we can't list every taverna in the area. If we left some out the owners would be offended and it would also make everything far too long. I suggest we list everywhere alphabetically, the approximate distance from the house and add something like "archaeological site" or "traditional village". Just enough to let people know if there is something there to interest them.'

'What about the churches?' asked Vasi. 'Many people like to visit churches.'

Saffron sighed in exasperation. 'That would be as difficult as listing all the tavernas. I'm sure a covering sentence could say that the churches in every village and passed en route can be worth a visit.'

Luke read through the email from John with the details of the work carried out at Schisma. It was certainly going to cost him a lot of money, but had he tried to organise the work himself it would probably have cost a good deal more.

He would arrange to go over to Crete later in the year and look at the site for himself. In the meantime he would ask John to send him some photographs so he could get an idea of the size and location. He hoped John would be able to recommend a trustworthy agent to supervise the sale of the land on his behalf.

'What do you think, Nick? Shall we go along to Schisma? We can take Skele with us, there shouldn't be a problem now.'

'I'm still not sure I want to go anywhere near that house again.'

'It should be fine now the contractors have cleared everything. Better than me sitting here waiting to hear if they have investigated Spinalonga.'

Nicola hesitated. 'I'll come with you, but if I smell anything or feel uneasy about being there I want to leave immediately.'

'You think Old Andrula will still be there haunting the place?'

'I don't believe in ghosts,' said Nicola firmly, 'But there was certainly something spooky about that house.'

'Then let's go along and make sure that all the spooks have gone.'

John parked where the path leading down to the house started. Skele jumped out of the car and followed them as they looked around and then began to walk along. Nicola continued to look around them. She still did not feel comfortable in the area. As the path narrowed it was obvious that the contractors had removed the bushes to enable them to get their equipment through the foliage.

'That certainly looks better without all that overhanging greenery,' remarked John. 'If they have cleared to the boundary of the site there is far more land than I realised. Luke will be pleased. I'll take some photos from here and then we'll go further down.'

Skele stood behind them. Usually he would run off to explore a new area, but he had dropped his ears and his tail was down between his legs.

'Come on, Skele,' called John, but his dog did not obey him. He stood on the edge of the cleared area and watched John and Nicola begin to walk over to where the house had been demolished. A wide area had been dug away until the bedrock below had been reached.

'Well, if Luke fancies putting in a swimming pool half the work has been done for him,' grinned John. 'I'll take some more photos then we'll go back. There's really nothing to see here now.'

'Be quick, John. I want to go. I still don't like being down here and Skele won't come onto the land.'

'Skele, come here, boy.'

The dog let out a whine and made no move to obey John's command.

'Something is worrying him, John. Let's go now.'

'Just a few more photos.'

John took shots of all the area and then he and Nicola walked back to where Skele was waiting. Once they were back on the main path Skele appeared pleased to see them and trotted off ahead towards the car.

'We'll take him up to the windmills and he can have a good run up there. Do you want to drive up or walk?' asked John.

'Drive,' replied Nicola without hesitation. 'Luke is welcome to this land. It still gives me the creeps. I still didn't hear any birds or a sound of animals in the undergrowth.'

'You're as bad as Skele,' laughed John as he opened the car door and the dog jumped in. 'The machinery the contractors would have used will have scared all the wildlife away. I hope these photos have all come out well otherwise we'll have to make another visit to take some more.'

John took Skele back to Dimitris for the night and then transferred the photos from his mobile onto his computer and looked at them critically. All except one seemed perfectly ordinary, just the green of the bushes.

'Nick, come and look at this.'

'I can't come now, I'm bathing Yiannis. I thought you were going to read the girls a story?'

'I'll make sure I read them a story before they go to bed. They're playing happily at the moment.'

John looked through the photos again. When Nicola came and looked at them he wanted to know if she saw the same as he did or were his eyes playing tricks. He pressed his forehead as he had done when he first had a problem with his sight, but it made no difference. He waited impatiently for Nicola to join him.

'Sit there, and look at each photo in turn.'

'They all look good to me,' said Nicola as she looked at the gallery before her.

John shook his head. 'You're looking at all of them at once. I want you to look at each one individually.'

Dutifully Nicola concentrated on examining each photo and then moving on to the next. She was half way through when she caught her breath.

'I don't believe it. That must be a trick of the light.'

'It might well be, but the photos before and after were not affected in any way. Now you've seen it I want to enlarge it and see if we can pick out any more detail.'

John clicked on the controls and the photo filled the screen.

Nicola's hand flew to her mouth. 'That looks like a person standing there. It can't be. There was no one around except us. It has to be a trick of the light or a shadow. Have you got a smudge on your lens?'

'Of course not. I always make sure the lens is clean. Why didn't it show up in any of the others?'

'I don't know.' Nicola shook her head. 'You're the one who knows about photography.'

'This has nothing to do with photography. Did your Mum ever tell you the story about her camera when she left it on Spinalonga?'

'Something about Marianne going over in the teeth of a storm to retrieve it.'

John nodded. 'And when Dad took the film to be developed what did they find? Old Uncle Yannis's daughter, Anna.'

'No, John, I don't believe it.'

'Ask Mum. She'll tell you that is true.'

'I'm not doubting that photo, but this is just not possible.'

'I'm going back tomorrow to take photos of that area again. If nothing shows up then we'll forget about it and delete the photo.'

'I'll come with you.'

'You don't have to. I know you don't like being up there.'

'I need to know you're safe. Maybe you should ask Panayiotis to go up so that he has his gun with him.'

'I don't think you can shoot ghosts.'

'If it's someone playing a trick then a bullet at their feet would soon drive them away. Ask Panayiotis. I'll feel much safer if he's around.'

'He'll probably think I'm crazy.'

'Crazy or not, it's better to be safe.'

Panayiotis was surprised by John's request. 'The area is no longer restricted. You can go up there as you please.'

'Nick and I went up yesterday to take some photos to send to Luke. We think there may have been someone around trying to scare us away.'

'I doubt they'll still be around today.'

'Probably not, but I'd be happier if you were there with your gun. I'll send you through a copy of the photo we took.'

Reluctantly Panayiotis agreed to drive up, but admitted that the photo John had sent through to him did look as if there was a figure standing there, half hidden by some bushes. He frowned. The contractors must have left the boundary bushes in place, but if so they had certainly not trimmed them back.

'I was standing about here,' explained John. 'I took photos of the bushes down that side and the area where the house used to stand and where all the top soil has been removed. I then started to take photos of the side bushes. They have been left quite tall, but thinned out. I imagine that is the boundary of Luke's land. I'm going to take the same series of photos again and Nick is going to take the same ones on her mobile. When we've finished we'll compare photos and see if the strange phenomenon shows up again.'

Panayiotis stood patiently whilst John and Nicola took photographs of the area. They held their phones side by side and Panayiotis compared one photo with the other. They were nearly identical. Finally John stopped scrolling through and looked at Nicola's mobile.

'It's the same,' she whispered, hardly daring to speak.

'This is the one we are interested in.'

Panayiotis looked at both the photos and had to agree that it did look as if there was someone standing in the shadow of the bushes at the side of the property.

'I'll go and investigate,' he said and pulled his gun from the holster.

Nicola clutched John's arm as the policeman moved forward.

'If there is someone hiding there come out now. I am a policeman and prepared to shoot if necessary,' Panayiotis shouted.

There was no movement at all. When Panayiotis reached the bushes he pushed them apart. There was no sign of anybody. He moved up and down, parting the foliage and trying to see if anyone was hiding further back. Finally he shook his head, holstered his gun and walked back to where John and Nicola were waiting.

'Nothing there,' he said. 'Take a photo again of that area and see if it looks the same as the previous ones.'

Nicola had to stop her hand from shaking as she lifted her mobile phone and tried to focus on the same area again, whilst John happily took a number of different shots panning all the way down the bushes.

Once again they compared photos and the image was still there.

'I want to go,' said Nicola. 'There's something or someone here.'

Panayiotis shook his head. 'There's definitely no one hiding in those bushes to give you a fright.'

'What is it then?' asked John.

Panayiotis was not a particularly religious man but he crossed himself fervently. 'I think you should consult a priest and ask him to come and perform an exorcism.'

'Really?' Both John and Nicola stared at him in amazement.

'That's the only advice I can give you.'

Father Emmanuel listened to John and Nicola's account of the house at Schisma and looked at the photos. He seemed perplexed. 'Why are you showing me?'

'Would you be willing to perform an exorcism?'

'I've never had a request like that before. I can try, but I'm not sure how successful I will be. You may need someone higher up in the church than I am or someone who specialises in such things as the paranormal.'

'Would you be willing to visit the area tomorrow and at least try to remove any evil that is up there?'

'No, I would need to ask some of my colleagues to be with me. If there really is something malignant up there and it is not just your imagination it would be sensible to have four of us. That way we could cover all sides of the area. Nothing would escape us.'

'How long will that take?' asked John.

'Two or three days. I'll contact you when we can arrange a date. I'll need you to be there to show me the exact area.'

March 2017
Weeks One and Two

John decided it would be a good idea to go to church in Elounda that Sunday. He would make sure Father Emmanuel saw him and wait until after the service to ask if a day had been arranged for an exorcism of the land at Schisma.

Father Emmanuel did not look best pleased when John accosted him. 'We are busy people. We do not only hold a church service we have to visit the sick and dying along with the pleasant events of weddings and baptisms.'

'I appreciate how beneficial your services are to everyone. Very soon we will be having visitors arriving and many of them walk in that area. I'm sure you would not want a gathering of tourists watching you as if you were performing a spectacle on their behalf rather than a religious ceremony.'

'I'll see what can be arranged.'

'Thank you, Father. Please let me know when you and your colleagues will be visiting the Schisma site. My wife and I would like to be there to receive a blessing from you.'

Father Emmanuel nodded and walked further down the line of parishioners who were waiting for his attention.

'Do you think he will let you know?' asked Nicola when John told her he had confronted the priest.

'He should do. He's a man of the cloth and as such should keep his word.'

Two days later John received a message from Andreas to confirm that a survey of Spinalonga had taken place and no pockets of methane gas or any other form of gas had been found to be present on the island.

'Well, that's a relief. If they had found something the island could have been closed down all season. No one would have been very happy about that. Some of our visitors come to the area primarily to visit the island.'

'Any word from Father Emmanuel?'

John shook his head. 'Not yet. I'll go to church again on Sunday and give him a reminder.'

Saffron looked up from her computer with a delighted smile. 'We have a booking. Two weeks over Easter. Four adults and two children.'

Vasi smiled back at her. 'It's a start. If they are willing to put a good review on our website we should get more enquiries.'

'I hope we'll be ready for them. We still need to finish buying some china and cutlery.'

'Of course we'll be ready. You can order anything else that you think we need this evening. We'll go up tomorrow and ask Stelios and Christalia to join us in unpacking everything and making sure all is in order.'

'What about the dogs?'

'We can take them with us and shut the gates so they can't go wandering off.'

'No,' Saffron shook her head. 'How are you going to manage walking them once I am back at the shop and you have guests at the hotel?'

'We'll leave the door open so they can go out onto the patio if it becomes necessary. I can probably say I am having a lunch hour and take them for a short walk most days. I'll just have to get up a bit earlier and then I can take them out again before you come home.'

'I wouldn't want them to feel neglected and become miserable.'

'I assure you I would not let that happen.'

Elena phoned Marianne. 'I've finally moved into my new home. I'll send you some photos tomorrow.'

'Have you told Helena that you have moved now and given her your new address?'

'That's another job for tomorrow. I don't want her rushing round here today. Once I've called her she and Greg can move into the house as soon as it suits them and that should keep her occupied for a while. I've been invited to my friends this evening for a meal. Once I'm properly settled in I'll invite Helena and Greg over for a meal and they can meet my neighbours. I also thought I'd ask Andreas if he would like to come and stay when he's next in the area.'

'I'm so pleased for you, Mamma. You'll probably find that Helena is easier to get on with now she has what she wants.'

'I doubt that somehow. She'll probably complain that house prices have dropped recently and if I'd given the house to them earlier they would have made more on their property.'

'Just remind her that she is lucky to have the house. You could have sold it to someone else and she would still be in her original home.'

'I may have made a mistake. She'll probably tell me that there is so much wrong with it that they are having to spend a fortune.'

'Then take no notice. You know there was nothing wrong with the house. It may need redecorating to her taste but that's her problem. If she becomes a nuisance to you let me know and I'll have a word with her.'

Father Emmanuel saw John waiting for him and held up his hand. 'Before you ask I have arranged for a number of my fellow priests to visit Schisma on Wednesday. If you and your wife wish to be there to witness the event you must stand well back and not interfere in any way with our actions or prayers.'

'I wouldn't dream of it,' John assured him. 'May I ask Panayiotis, our local policeman to join us? He has been involved in our investigations on behalf of the owner.'

'I suppose so. No one else. We don't want a gawping crowd whilst something so serious takes place.'

'Of course. I understand. What time should we be there?'

'Arriving at ten in the morning should have given all of us sufficient time to conclude our early morning prayers.'

'Thank you, Father.' John was not sure if the priest had been hinting that he should also say a prayer before visiting the site.

Five priests solemnly processed briskly along the path with John, Nicola and Panayiotis following them at a distance.

'What do you think is going to happen, John?' asked Nicola.

'Probably nothing. I'm not expecting to see a witch fly off on her broomstick or rain down curses upon us,' John squeezed Nicola's hand. 'Don't worry.'

Upon arriving at the cleared land Father Emmanuel stopped and intoned a prayer. John looked surprised. Was that all there was to conducting an exorcism?

Before John had time to move or say anything four of the priests walked onto the land, standing one at each corner. Father Emmanuel strode into the centre and once again began to intone prayers whilst the other priests walked slowly up and down the boundaries, sprinkling holy water as they went and waving their incense burners backwards and forwards. Finally all five met in the centre and Father Emmanuel raised his voice.

'In the name of the Father and Holy Spirit we are asking any evil entities in this area to leave. This is now hallowed ground and they are not welcome.'

John felt a shiver go down his spine and Nicola clutched his arm. The bushes on the far side of the site shook violently although there was no wind. The priests fell on their knees and began to direct prayers in that direction until the shaking subsided.

Father Emmanuel rose and brushed off his cassock. He looked pale and was trembling as he walked towards them.

'I trust we have been successful. Exorcism is an exhausting experience.'

'Thank you, Father. We appreciate that you took our concerns seriously. Please can you also give us a blessing? We found the ceremony very moving, but also quite draining.'

Each priest blessed John, Nicola and Panayiotis before they began to walk back down the path. The priests did not speak and were moving slowly like old men.

John waited until they had driven away in their car and turned to Nicola. 'I don't think I would want to witness that ceremony again. Something very strange happened. Why did those bushes start moving when all the others were still?'

'Please can we go, John?' asked Nicola. 'I still don't like being up here. I'd like to go into the church on our way home. I feel I need to be cleansed somehow, even though we received a blessing.'

Panayiotis nodded. 'I'd like to join you. I feel like you, Nicola.'

During the rest of the week John thought about the ceremony that had been performed at Schisma.

'I want to go up to Schisma tomorrow and take some photos,' he said to Nicola. 'I know I've sent all the original ones to Luke, apart from the one with the strange shadow, but I want to make quite sure that shadow has gone. Then I'll send both photos to Luke and tell him the story.'

'Why don't you leave well alone, John? An exorcism has taken place. Surely that is sufficient?'

'You don't have to come with me. I'll take Skele. If he has a bad reaction we'll know the exorcism ceremony wasn't effective.'

Nicola shook her head. 'I'm not happy with you going up there alone, even if you have Skele with you.'

'I'll only take a couple of photos.'

John and Nicola walked up the path to where the house had once stood. Skele followed them happily, investigating various scents and smells on the way. He appeared to have no problem standing there with them as they scanned the area.

'You take some photos on your mobile,' said John 'And I'll use my camera. Then we can compare shots again. Start from where the house originally stood and take photos all the way up the remaining bushes.'

Standing side by side they took the photographs. As they finished a sparrow flew down and plucked something from the ground before flying back with it in its beak.

'That's a good sign,' remarked John. 'No bad reaction from Skele and a bird in the area. We'll take the children up to the playground at Plaka before I take Skele back to Dimitris. We can look at the photos when the children have gone to bed.'

Despite John's obvious nonchalance Nicola still did not feel comfortable in the area and was only too pleased to follow her husband back to the car and drive home.

Once the children had been settled into bed John and Nicola examined the photos. There was not a sign of a shadowy figure amongst the bushes. Nicola gave a sigh of relief.

'I was worried that these photos would show the same as the earlier ones.'

'I'll be able to send the evil spirit ones to Luke and tell him the story. It seems that Old Andrula has finally been released from the site. I can't help but feel sorry for the poor old lady. She had been disowned by her family, the man she had trusted and loved abandoned her and took their children back to Turkey with him.'

'What about the curses people accused her of placing on them?' asked Nicola.

'She may have been shouting abuse at them in Turkish. When someone fell ill from a natural cause they blamed her. People were very superstitious and ignorant in those days.'

'It must have been difficult for her to survive before the war; and then to be accused of cannibalism and bayoneted to death.' Nicola shuddered.

John put his arm around Nicola. 'She certainly did not deserve such a barbaric end to her life.'